BIG STAR OTTO

WRITTEN BY BILL SLAVIN
WITH ESPERANÇA MELO
ART BY BILL SLAVIN

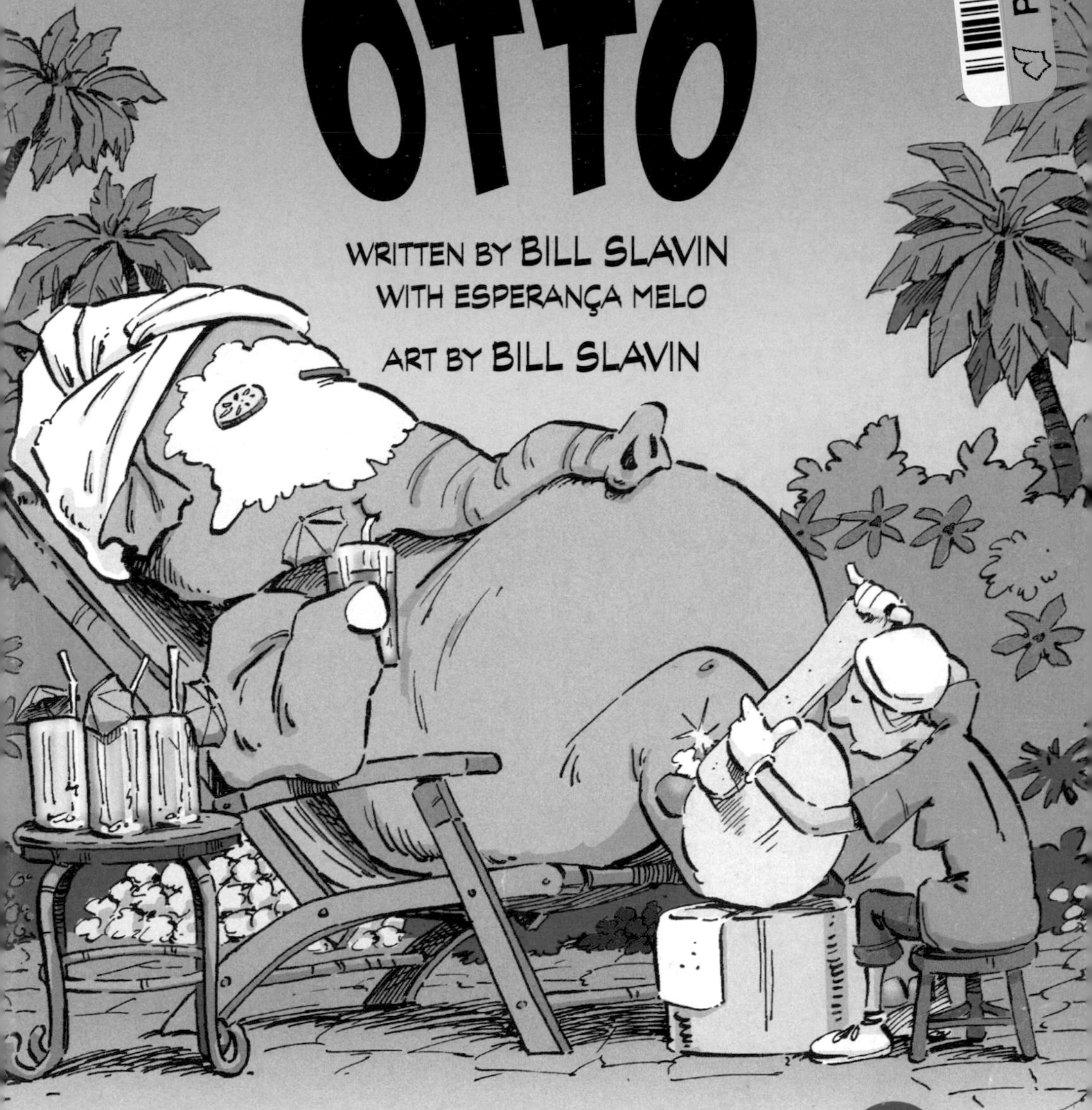

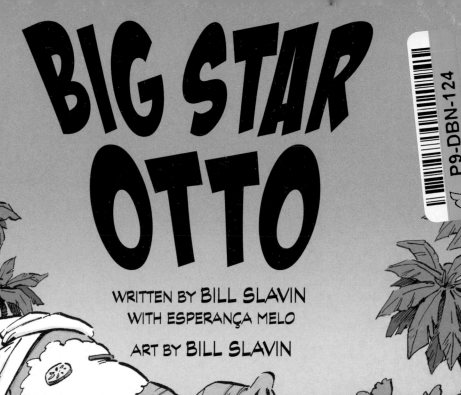

ELEPHANTS NEVER FORGET 3

KIDS CAN PRESS

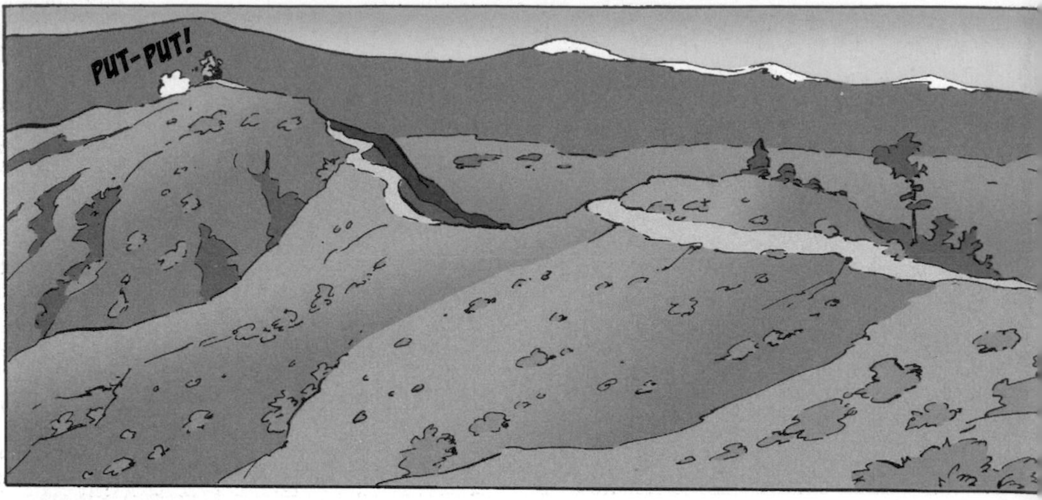
PUT-PUT!

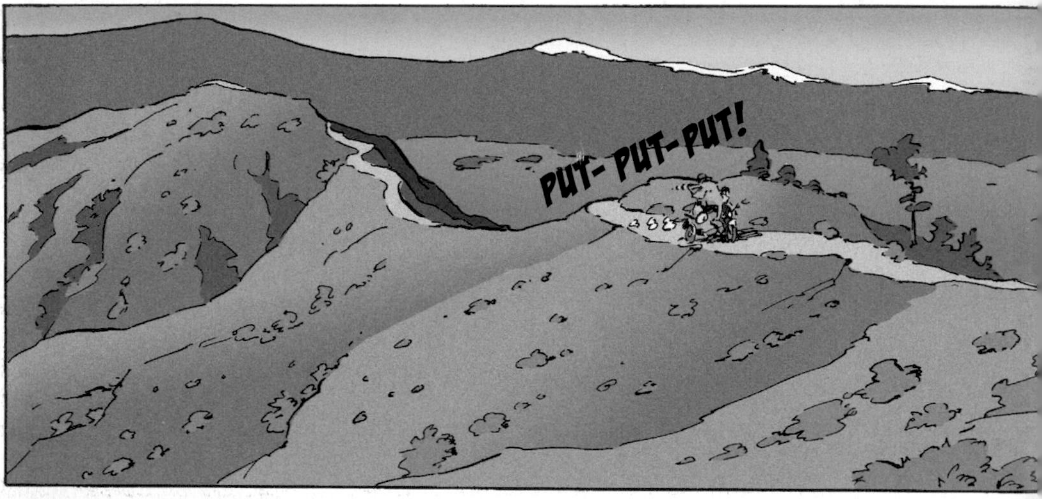
PUT- PUT-PUT!

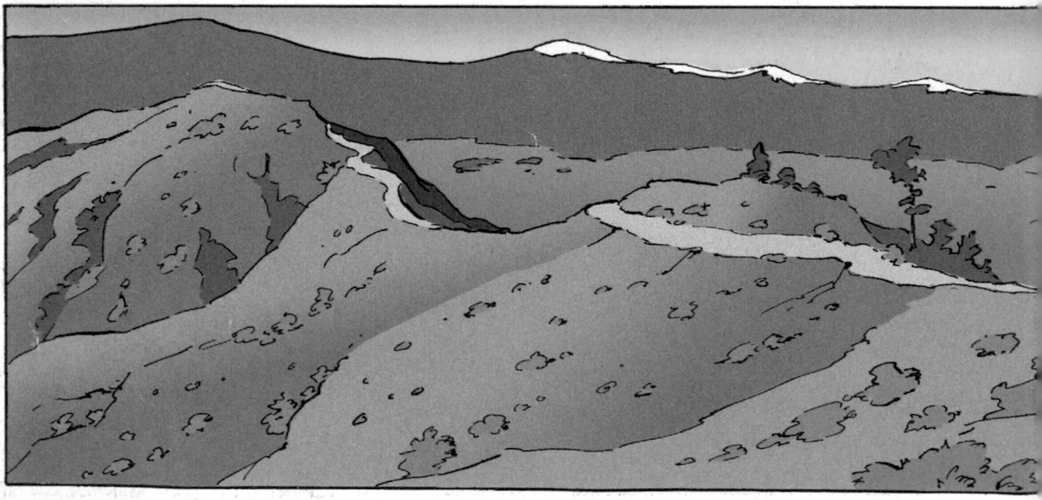

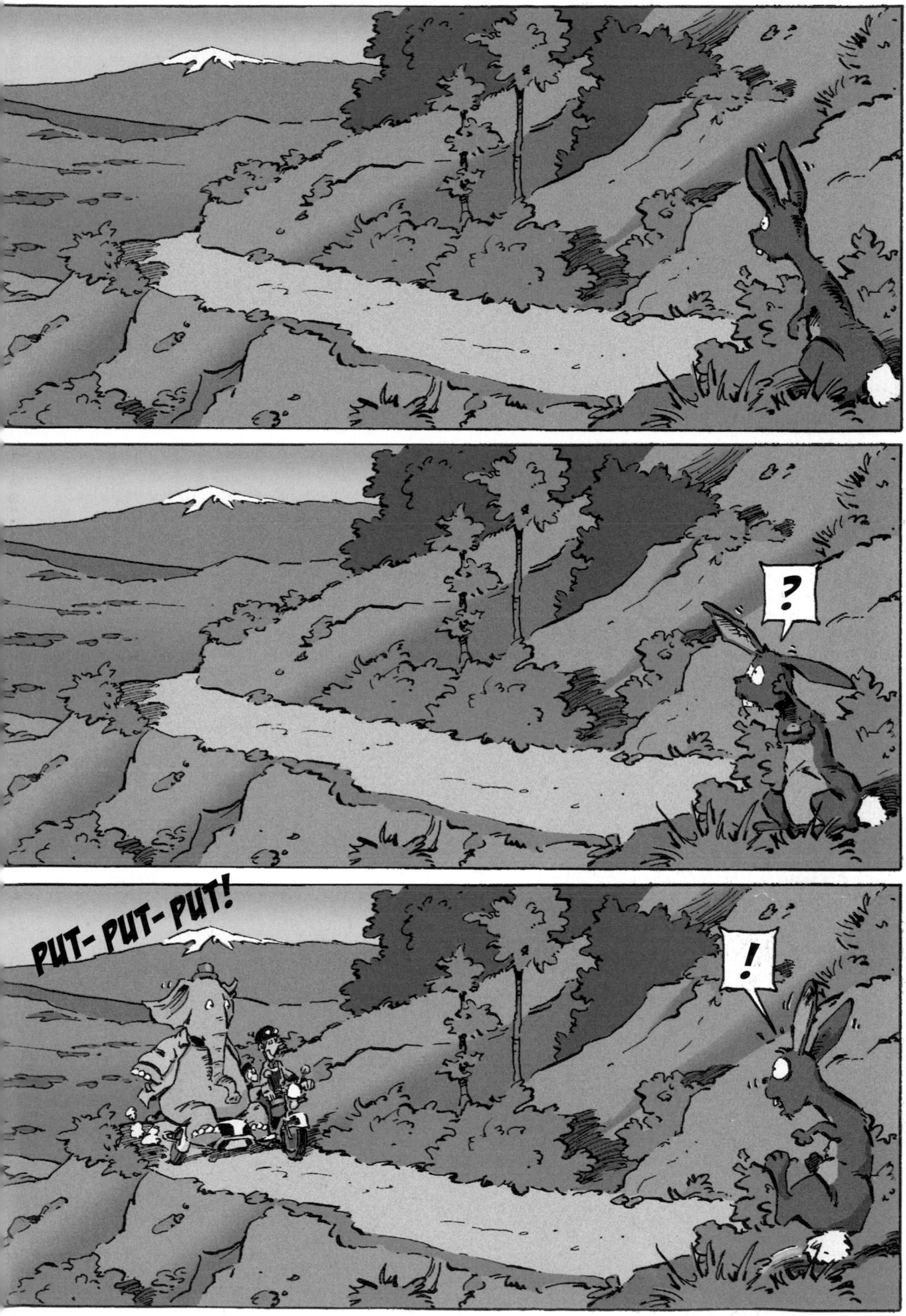
?
PUT- PUT- PUT!
!

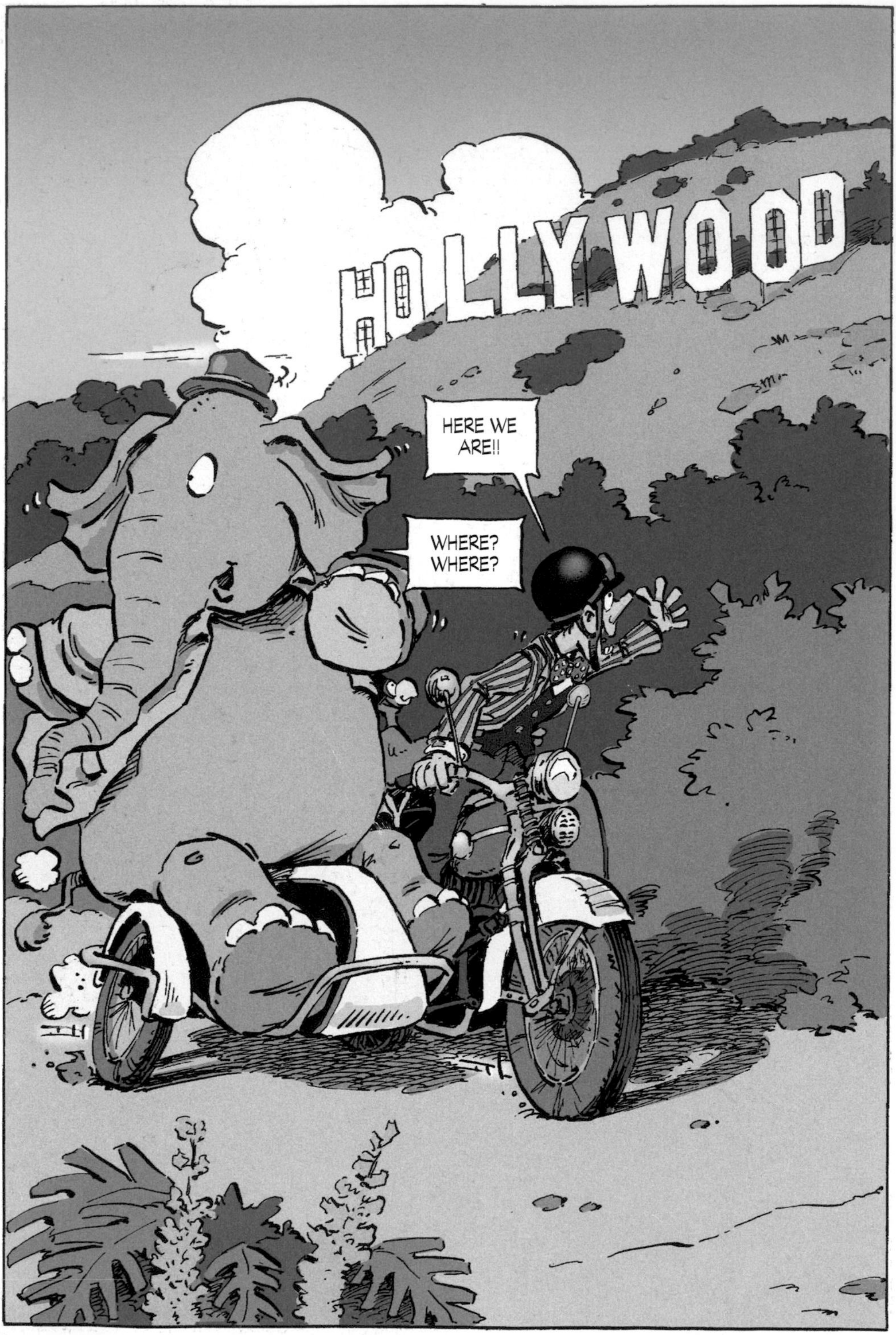
HOLLYWOOD
HERE WE ARE!!
WHERE? WHERE?

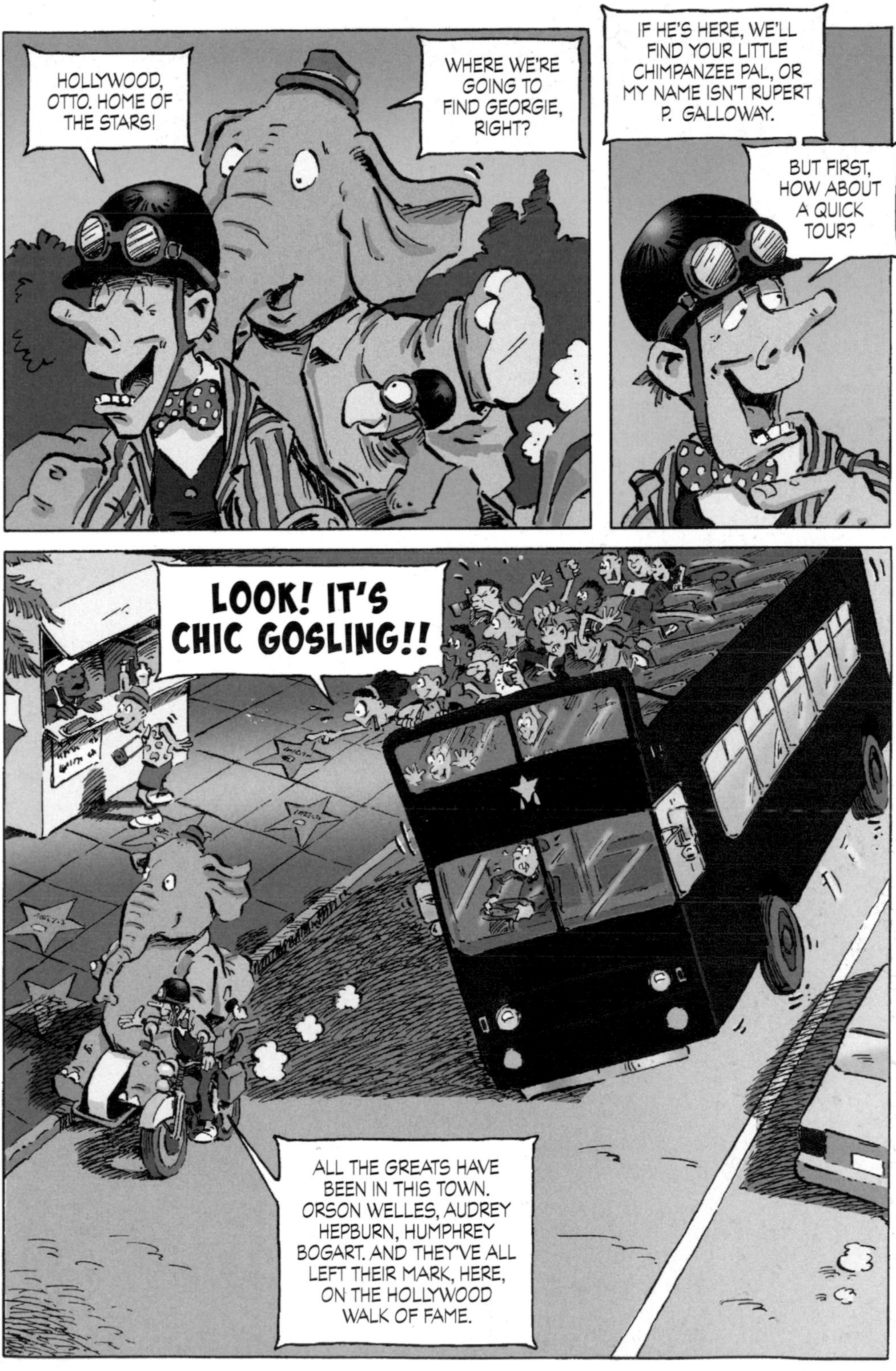
HOLLYWOOD, OTTO. HOME OF THE STARS!
WHERE WE'RE GOING TO FIND GEORGIE, RIGHT?
IF HE'S HERE, WE'LL FIND YOUR LITTLE CHIMPANZEE PAL, OR MY NAME ISN'T RUPERT P. GALLOWAY.
BUT FIRST, HOW ABOUT A QUICK TOUR?
LOOK! IT'S CHIC GOSLING!!
ALL THE GREATS HAVE BEEN IN THIS TOWN. ORSON WELLES, AUDREY HEPBURN, HUMPHREY BOGART. AND THEY'VE ALL LEFT THEIR MARK, HERE, ON THE HOLLYWOOD WALK OF FAME.

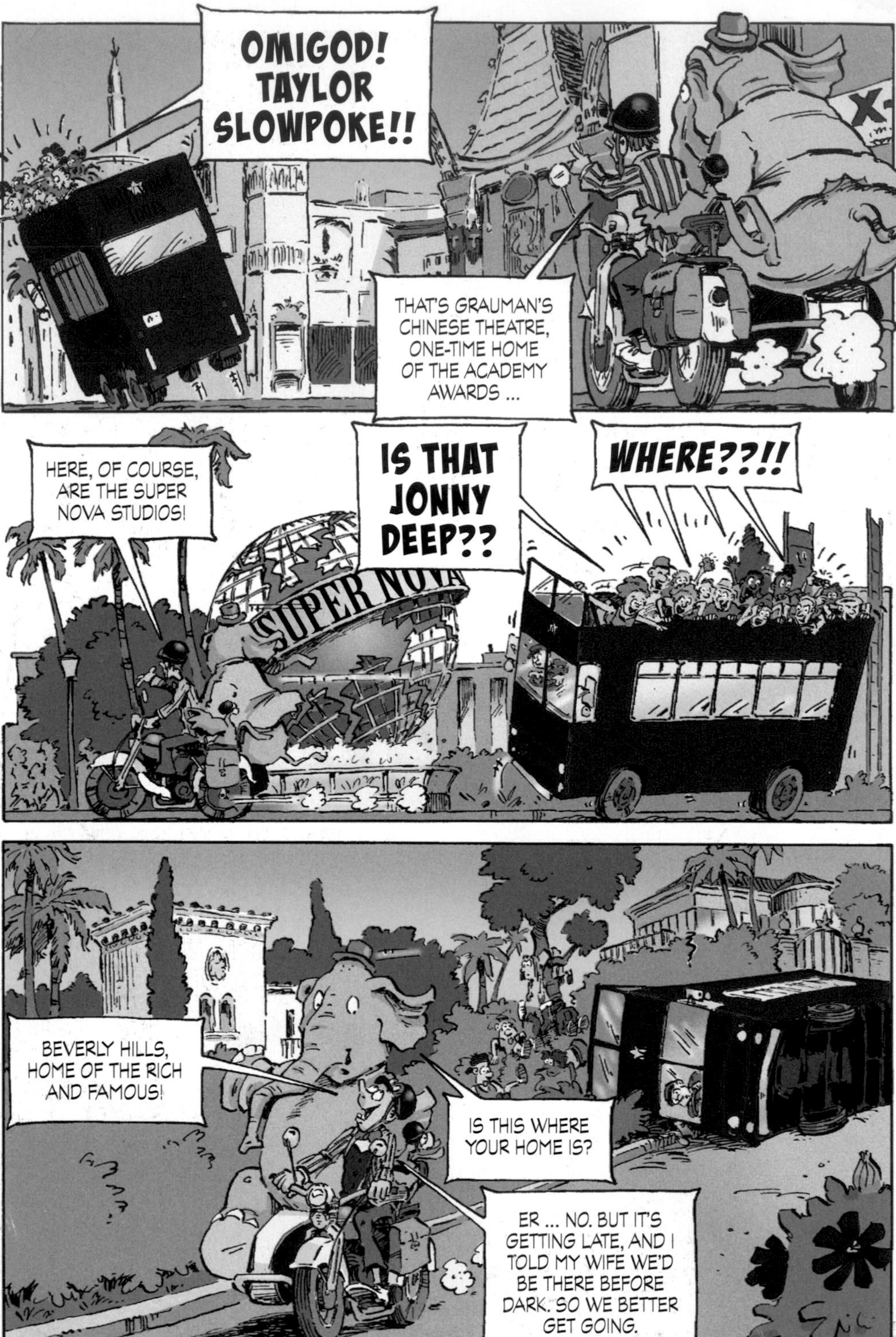
OMIGOD! TAYLOR SLOWPOKE!!
THAT'S GRAUMAN'S CHINESE THEATRE, ONE-TIME HOME OF THE ACADEMY AWARDS ...
HERE, OF COURSE, ARE THE SUPER NOVA STUDIOS!
SUPER NOVA
IS THAT JONNY DEEP??
WHERE??!!
BEVERLY HILLS, HOME OF THE RICH AND FAMOUS!
IS THIS WHERE YOUR HOME IS?
ER ... NO. BUT IT'S GETTING LATE, AND I TOLD MY WIFE WE'D BE THERE BEFORE DARK. SO WE BETTER GET GOING.

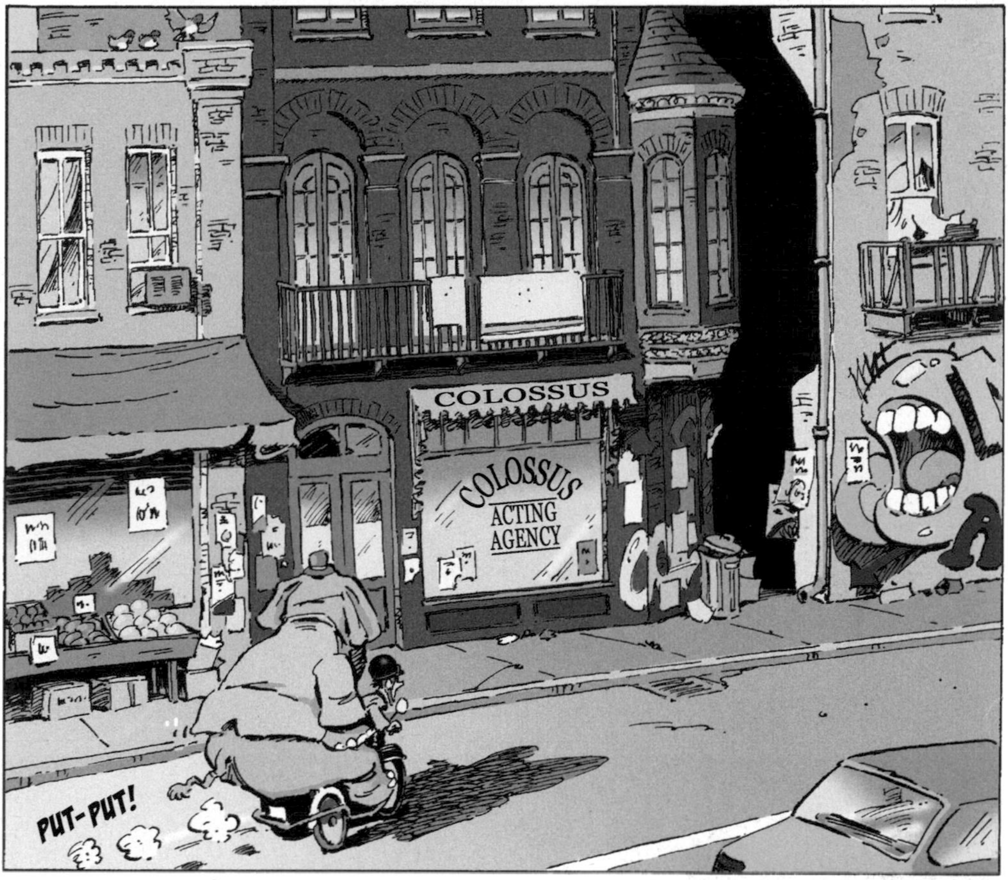
COLOSSUS
COLOSSUS
ACTING
AGENCY
PUT-PUT!

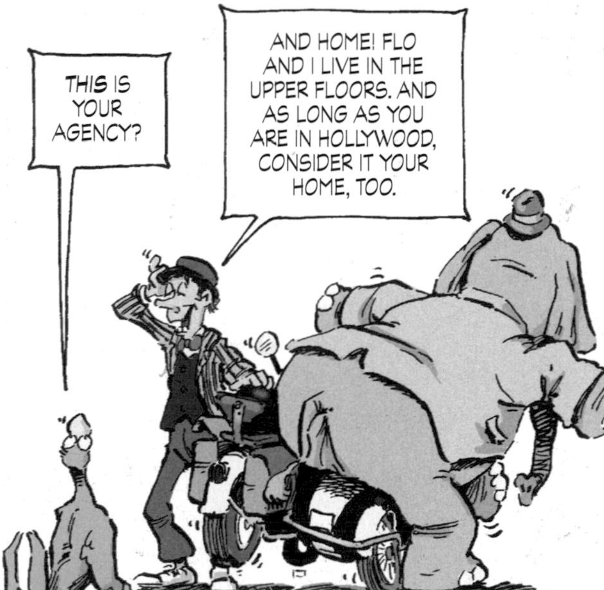
THIS IS YOUR AGENCY?
AND HOME! FLO AND I LIVE IN THE UPPER FLOORS. AND AS LONG AS YOU ARE IN HOLLYWOOD, CONSIDER IT YOUR HOME, TOO.

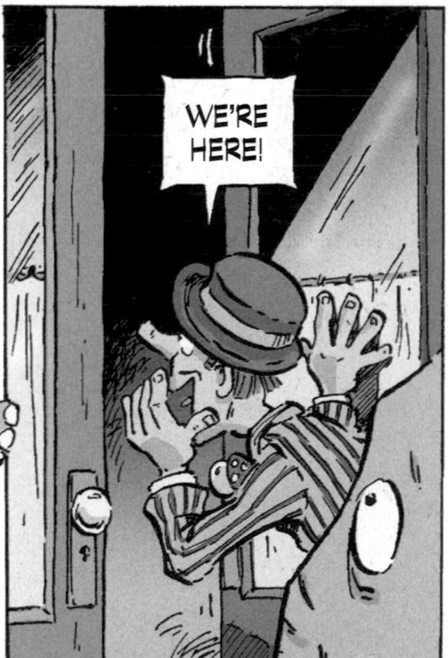
WE'RE HERE!

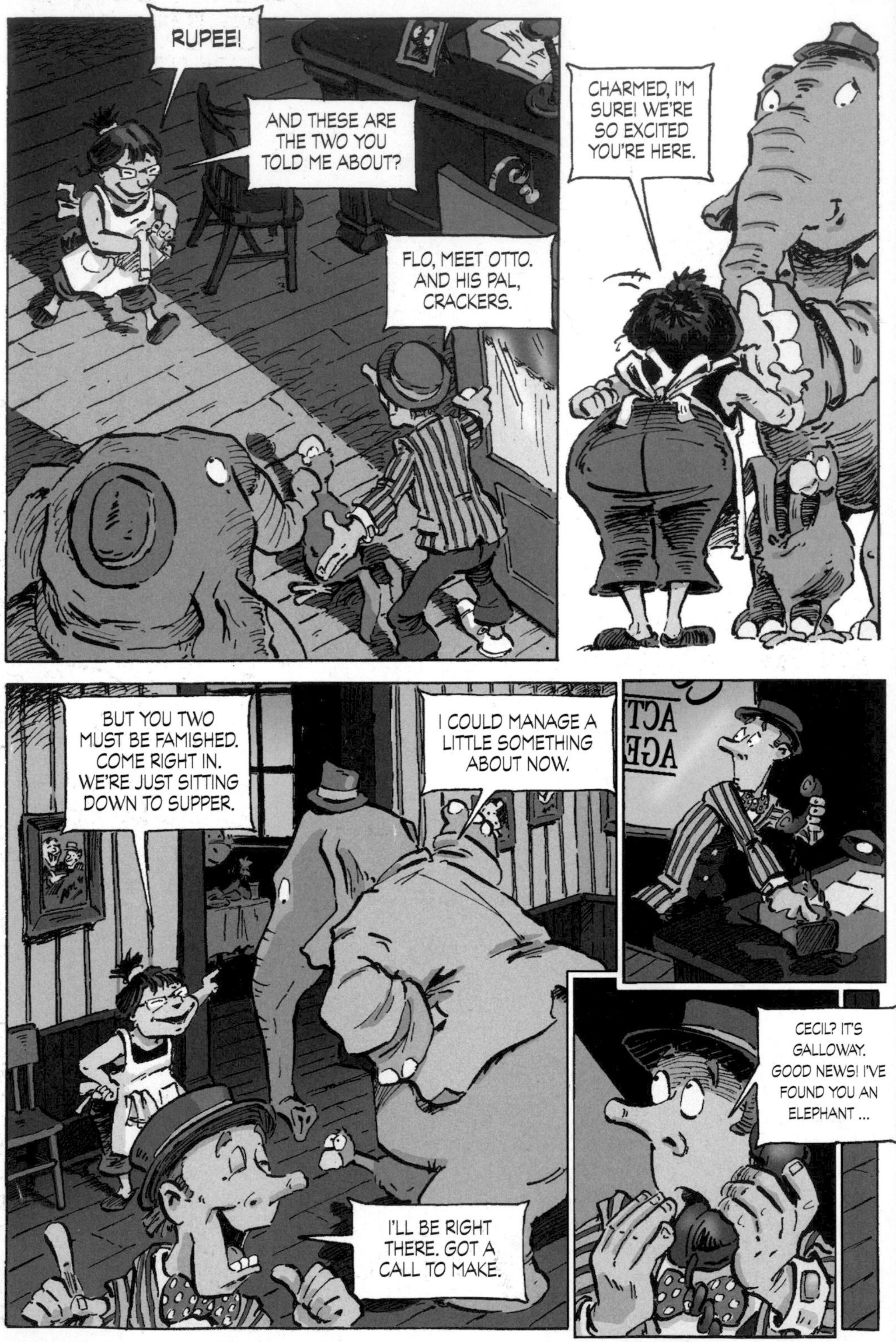
RUPEE!
AND THESE ARE THE TWO YOU TOLD ME ABOUT?
FLO, MEET OTTO. AND HIS PAL, CRACKERS.
CHARMED, I'M SURE! WE'RE SO EXCITED YOU'RE HERE.
BUT YOU TWO MUST BE FAMISHED. COME RIGHT IN. WE'RE JUST SITTING DOWN TO SUPPER.
I COULD MANAGE A LITTLE SOMETHING ABOUT NOW.
I'LL BE RIGHT THERE. GOT A CALL TO MAKE.
CECIL? IT'S GALLOWAY. GOOD NEWS! I'VE FOUND YOU AN ELEPHANT ...

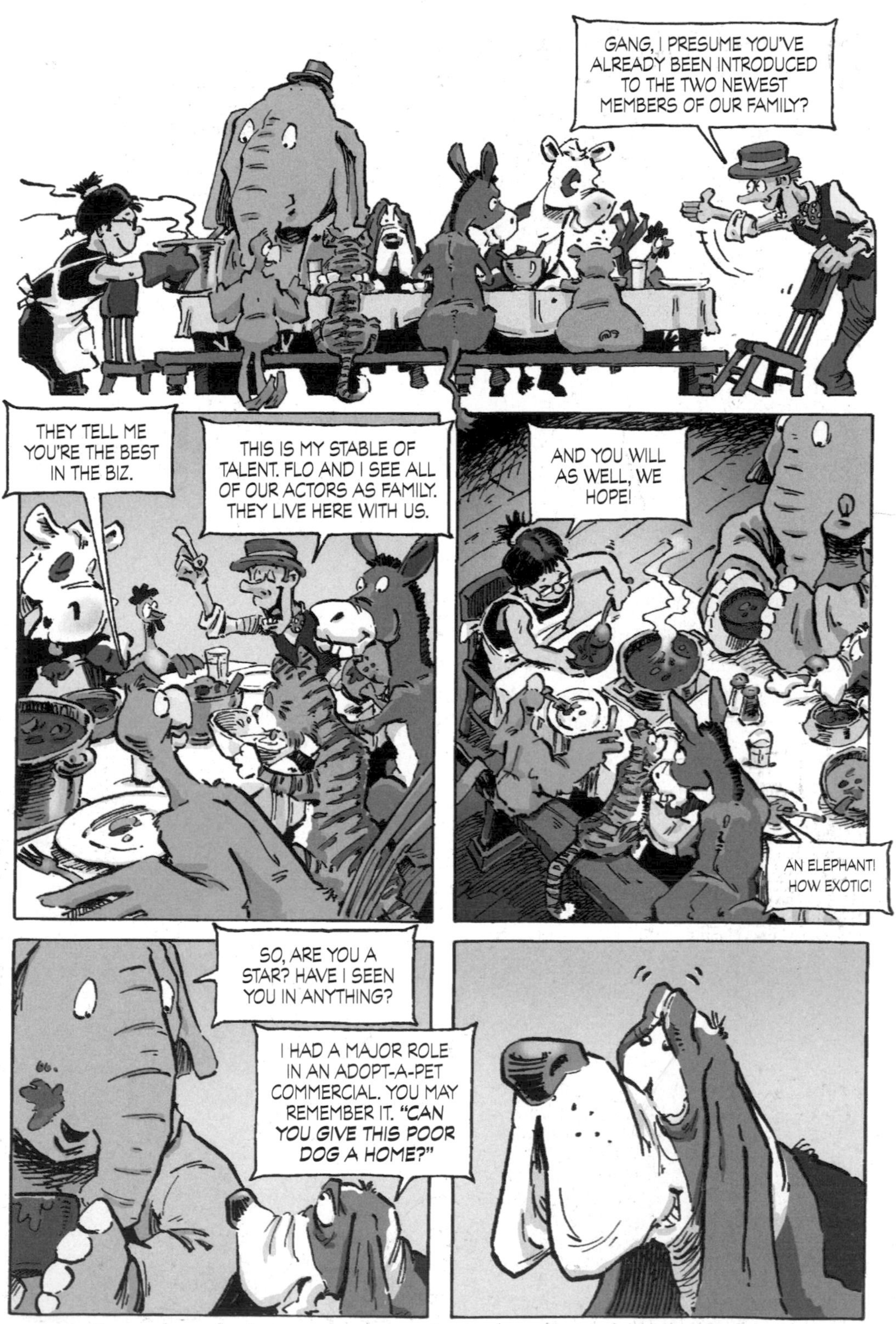
GANG, I PRESUME YOU'VE ALREADY BEEN INTRODUCED TO THE TWO NEWEST MEMBERS OF OUR FAMILY?
THEY TELL ME YOU'RE THE BEST IN THE BIZ.
THIS IS MY STABLE OF TALENT. FLO AND I SEE ALL OF OUR ACTORS AS FAMILY. THEY LIVE HERE WITH US.
AND YOU WILL AS WELL, WE HOPE!
AN ELEPHANT! HOW EXOTIC!
SO, ARE YOU A STAR? HAVE I SEEN YOU IN ANYTHING?
I HAD A MAJOR ROLE IN AN ADOPT-A-PET COMMERCIAL. YOU MAY REMEMBER IT. *"CAN YOU GIVE THIS POOR DOG A HOME?"*

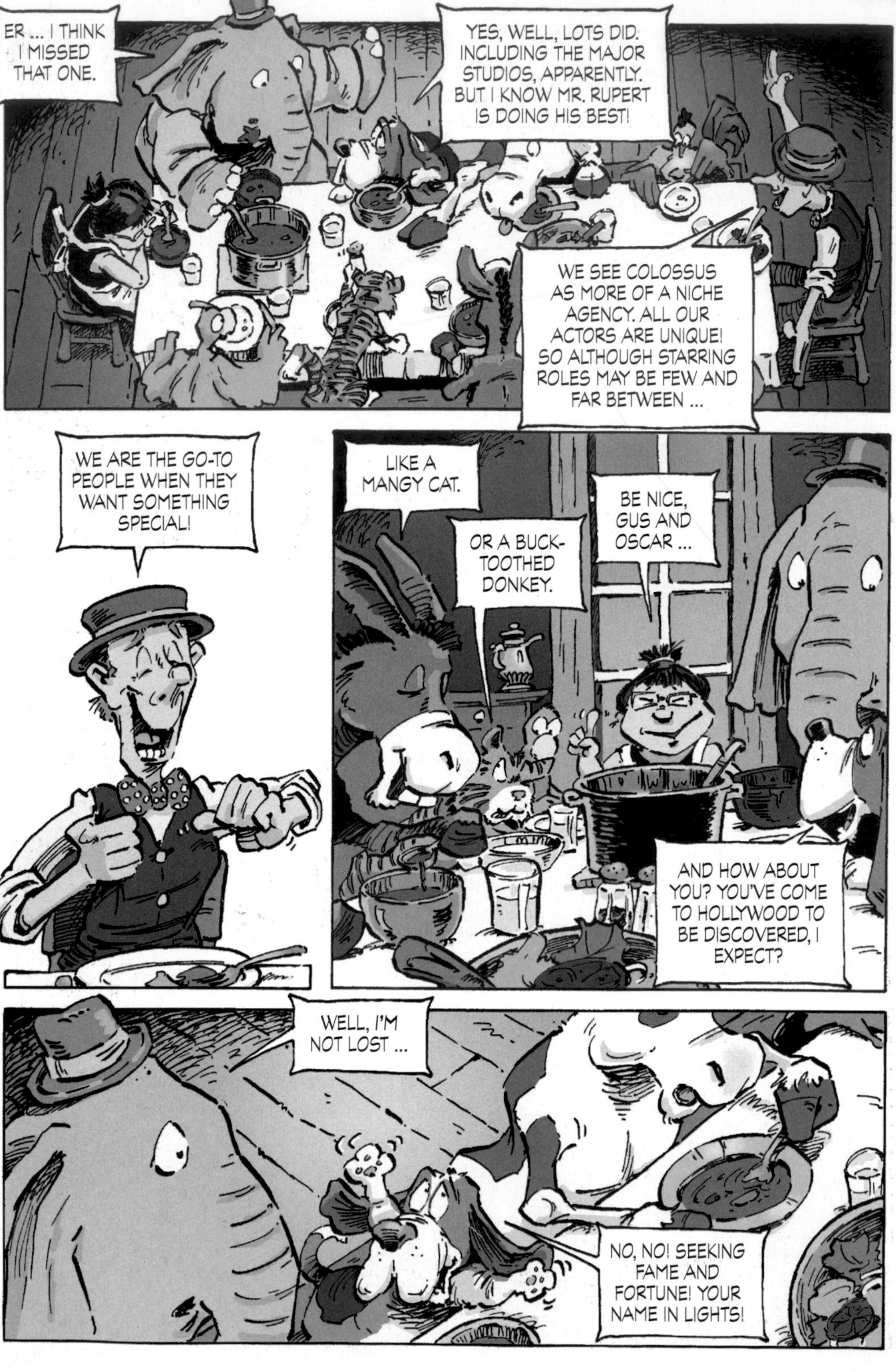
ER ... I THINK I MISSED THAT ONE.
YES, WELL, LOTS DID. INCLUDING THE MAJOR STUDIOS, APPARENTLY. BUT I KNOW MR. RUPERT IS DOING HIS BEST!
WE SEE COLOSSUS AS MORE OF A NICHE AGENCY. ALL OUR ACTORS ARE UNIQUE! SO ALTHOUGH STARRING ROLES MAY BE FEW AND FAR BETWEEN ...
WE ARE THE GO-TO PEOPLE WHEN THEY WANT SOMETHING SPECIAL!
LIKE A MANGY CAT.
OR A BUCK-TOOTHED DONKEY.
BE NICE, GUS AND OSCAR ...
AND HOW ABOUT YOU? YOU'VE COME TO HOLLYWOOD TO BE DISCOVERED, I EXPECT?
WELL, I'M NOT LOST ...
NO, NO! SEEKING FAME AND FORTUNE! YOUR NAME IN LIGHTS!

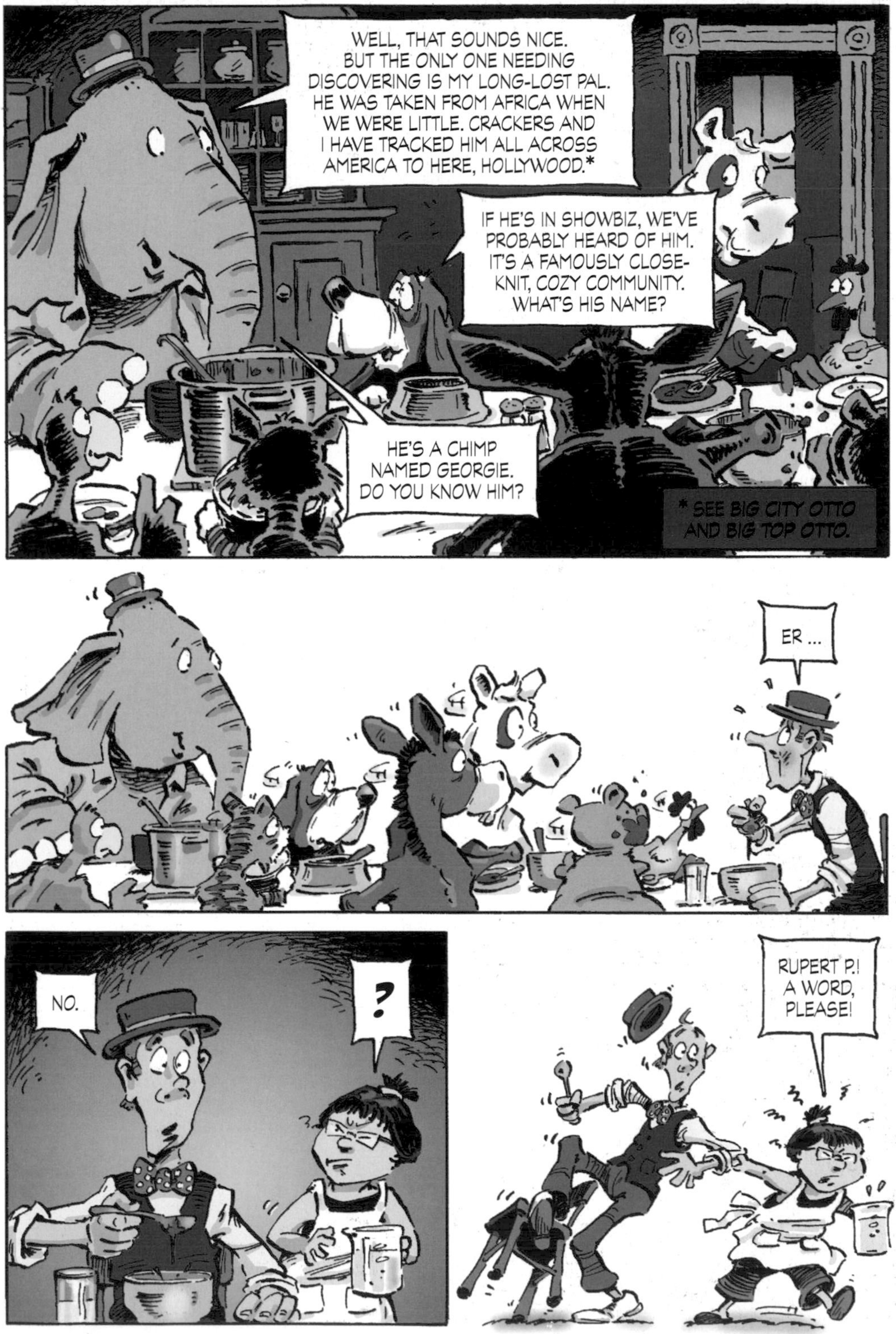

WELL, THAT SOUNDS NICE. BUT THE ONLY ONE NEEDING DISCOVERING IS MY LONG-LOST PAL. HE WAS TAKEN FROM AFRICA WHEN WE WERE LITTLE. CRACKERS AND I HAVE TRACKED HIM ALL ACROSS AMERICA TO HERE, HOLLYWOOD.*
IF HE'S IN SHOWBIZ, WE'VE PROBABLY HEARD OF HIM. IT'S A FAMOUSLY CLOSE-KNIT, COZY COMMUNITY. WHAT'S HIS NAME?
HE'S A CHIMP NAMED GEORGIE. DO YOU KNOW HIM?
* SEE BIG CITY OTTO AND BIG TOP OTTO.
ER ...
NO.
?
RUPERT P.! A WORD, PLEASE!

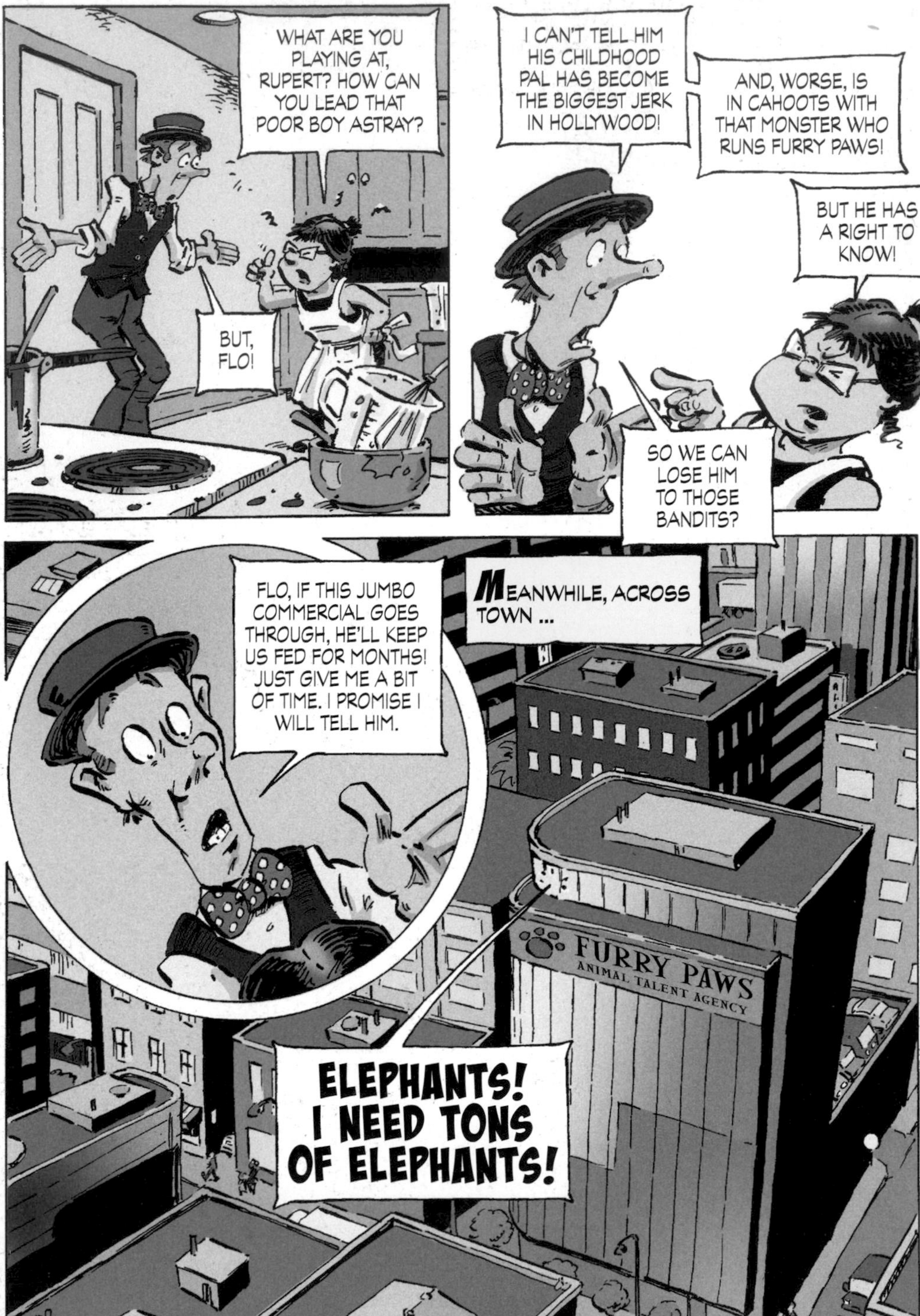
WHAT ARE YOU PLAYING AT, RUPERT? HOW CAN YOU LEAD THAT POOR BOY ASTRAY?
BUT, FLO!
I CAN'T TELL HIM HIS CHILDHOOD PAL HAS BECOME THE BIGGEST JERK IN HOLLYWOOD!
AND, WORSE, IS IN CAHOOTS WITH THAT MONSTER WHO RUNS FURRY PAWS!
BUT HE HAS A RIGHT TO KNOW!
SO WE CAN LOSE HIM TO THOSE BANDITS?
FLO, IF THIS JUMBO COMMERCIAL GOES THROUGH, HE'LL KEEP US FED FOR MONTHS! JUST GIVE ME A BIT OF TIME. I PROMISE I WILL TELL HIM.
MEANWHILE, ACROSS TOWN ...
FURRY PAWS
ANIMAL TALENT AGENCY
ELEPHANTS! I NEED TONS OF ELEPHANTS!

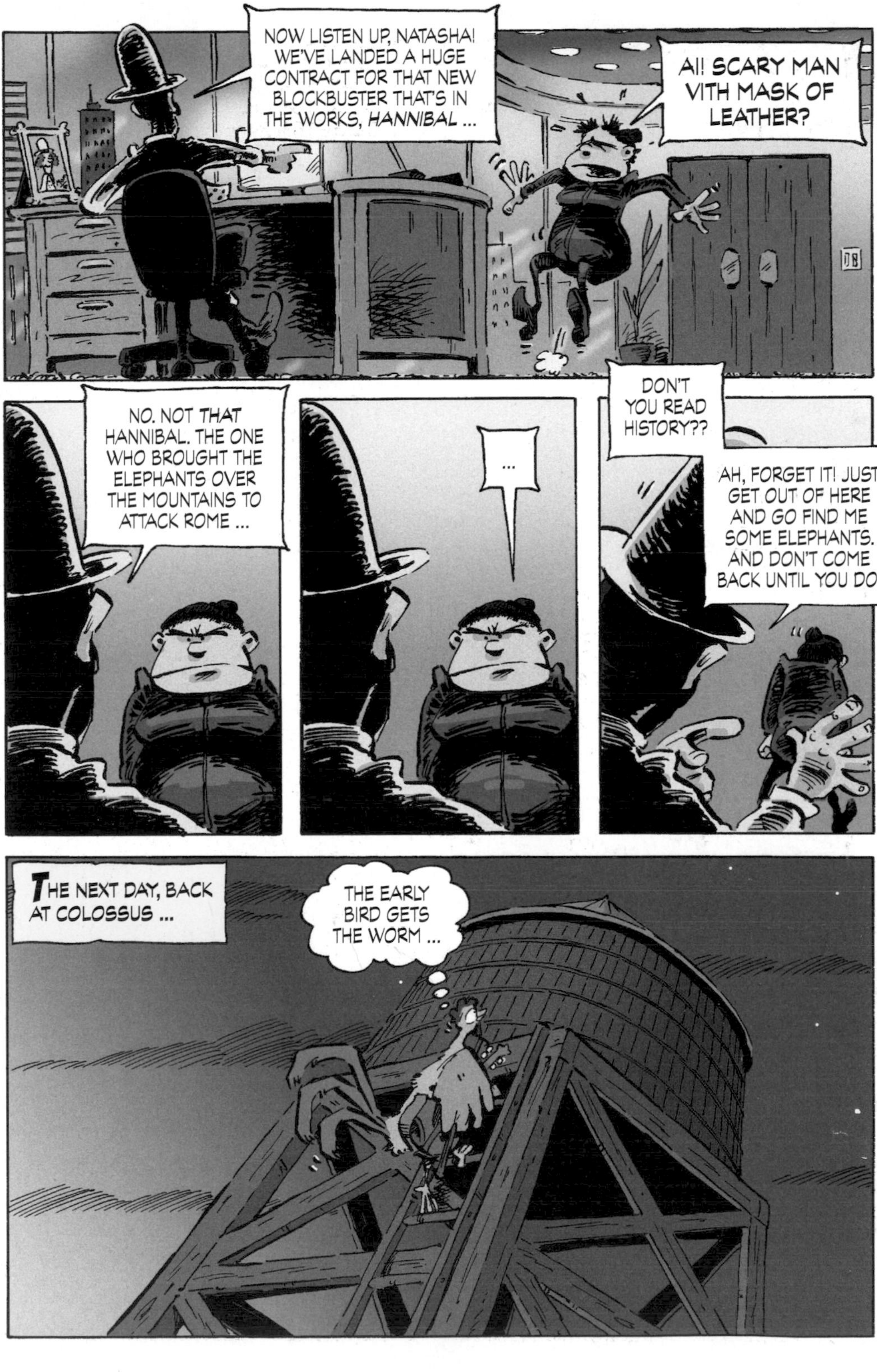
NOW LISTEN UP, NATASHA! WE'VE LANDED A HUGE CONTRACT FOR THAT NEW BLOCKBUSTER THAT'S IN THE WORKS, *HANNIBAL* ...
AI! **SCARY MAN VITH MASK OF LEATHER?**
NO. NOT *THAT* HANNIBAL. THE ONE WHO BROUGHT THE ELEPHANTS OVER THE MOUNTAINS TO ATTACK ROME ...
...
DON'T YOU READ HISTORY??
AH, FORGET IT! JUST GET OUT OF HERE AND GO FIND ME SOME ELEPHANTS. AND DON'T COME BACK UNTIL YOU DO!
THE NEXT DAY, BACK AT COLOSSUS ...
THE EARLY BIRD GETS THE WORM ...

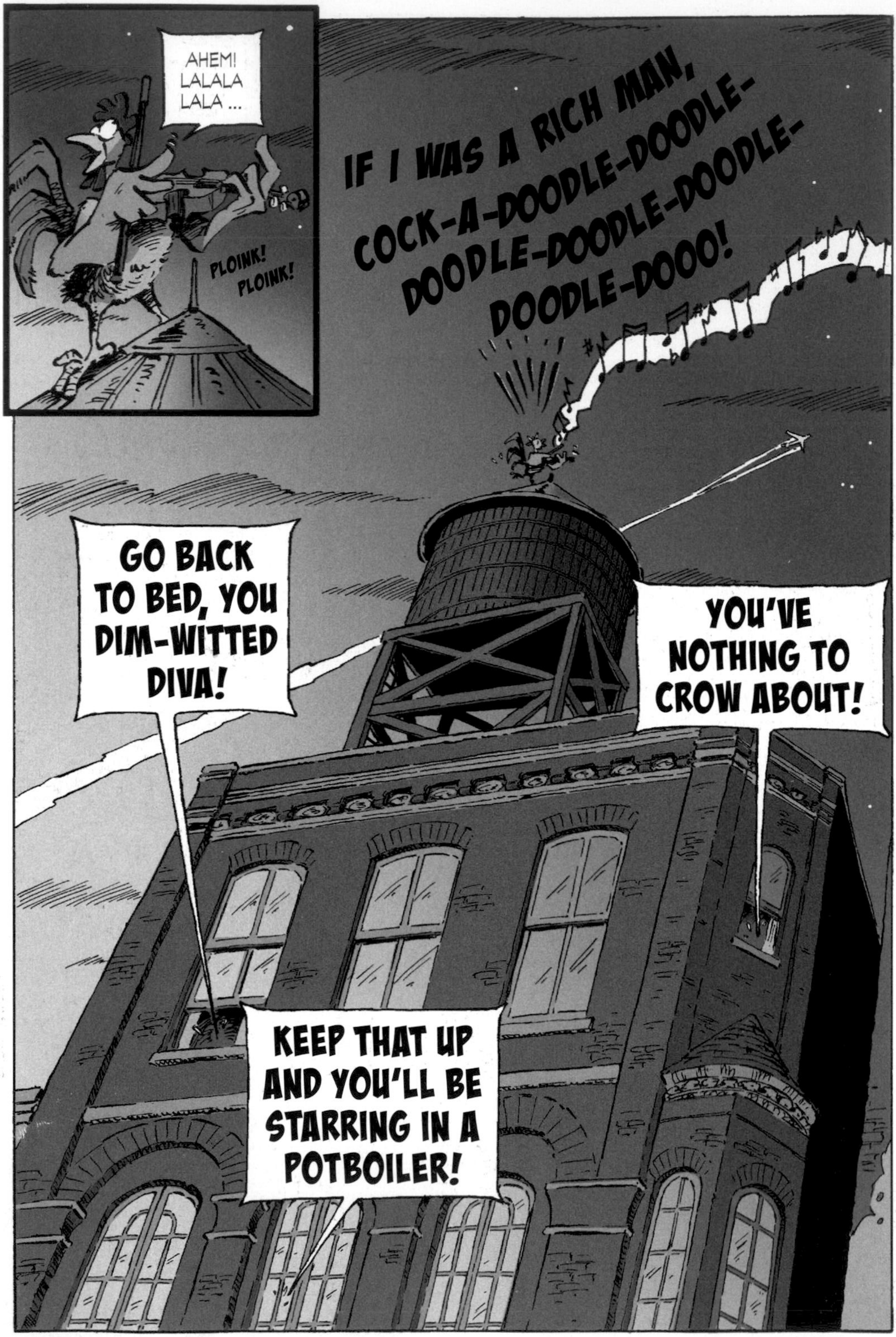
AHEM! LALALA LALA ...
PLOINK! PLOINK!
IF I WAS A RICH MAN, COCK-A-DOODLE-DOODLE-DOODLE-DOODLE-DOODLE-DOODLE-DOODLE-DOODLE-DOOO!
GO BACK TO BED, YOU DIM-WITTED DIVA!
YOU'VE NOTHING TO CROW ABOUT!
KEEP THAT UP AND YOU'LL BE STARRING IN A POTBOILER!

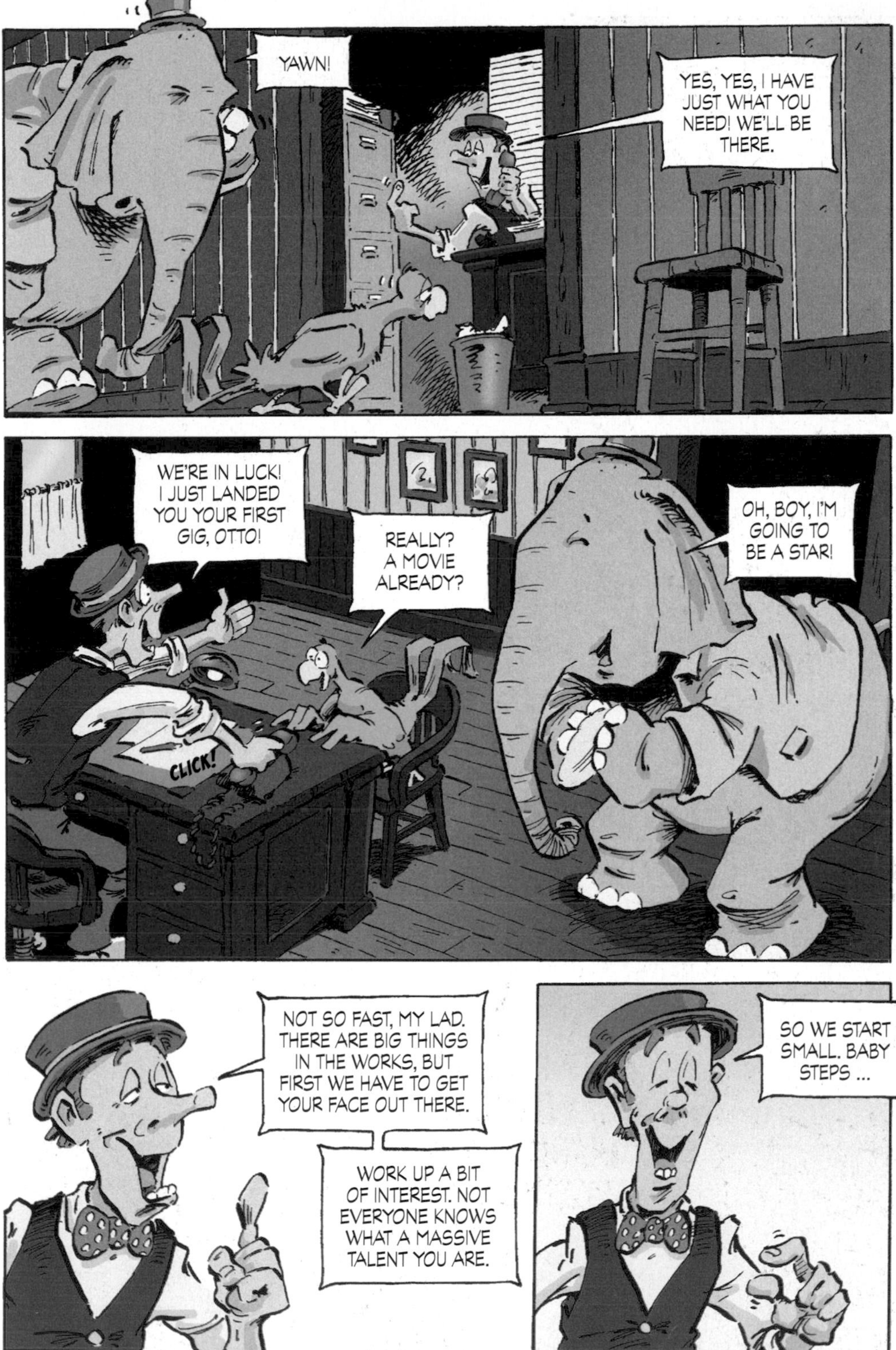
YAWN!
YES, YES, I HAVE JUST WHAT YOU NEED! WE'LL BE THERE.
WE'RE IN LUCK! I JUST LANDED YOU YOUR FIRST GIG, OTTO!
CLICK!
REALLY? A MOVIE ALREADY?
OH, BOY, I'M GOING TO BE A STAR!
NOT SO FAST, MY LAD. THERE ARE BIG THINGS IN THE WORKS, BUT FIRST WE HAVE TO GET YOUR FACE OUT THERE.
WORK UP A BIT OF INTEREST. NOT EVERYONE KNOWS WHAT A MASSIVE TALENT YOU ARE.
SO WE START SMALL. BABY STEPS ...

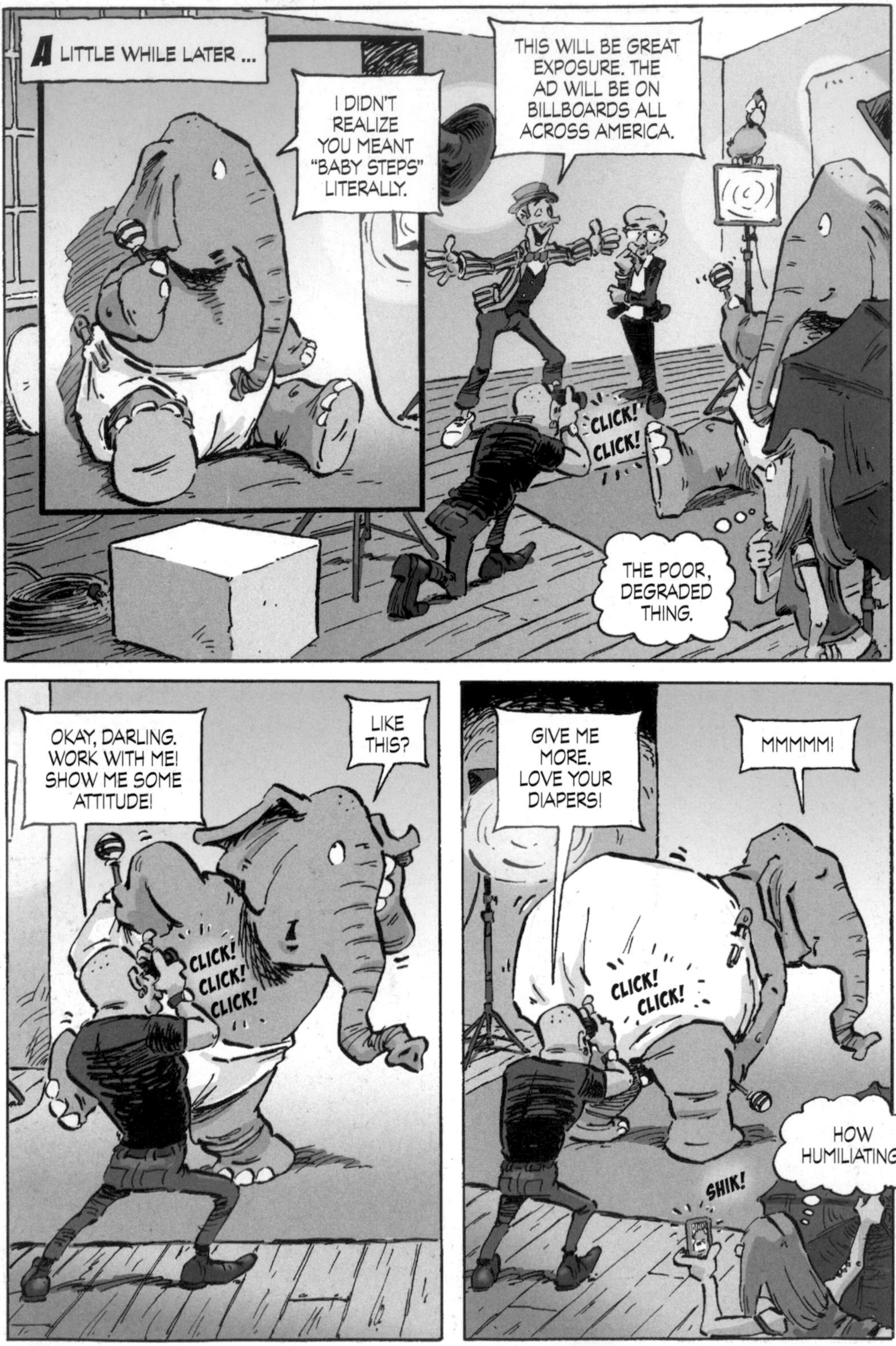
A LITTLE WHILE LATER ...
I DIDN'T REALIZE YOU MEANT "BABY STEPS" LITERALLY.
THIS WILL BE GREAT EXPOSURE. THE AD WILL BE ON BILLBOARDS ALL ACROSS AMERICA.
CLICK! CLICK!
THE POOR, DEGRADED THING.
OKAY, DARLING. WORK WITH ME! SHOW ME SOME ATTITUDE!
LIKE THIS?
CLICK! CLICK! CLICK!
GIVE ME MORE. LOVE YOUR DIAPERS!
MMMMM!
CLICK! CLICK!
HOW HUMILIATING!
SHIK!

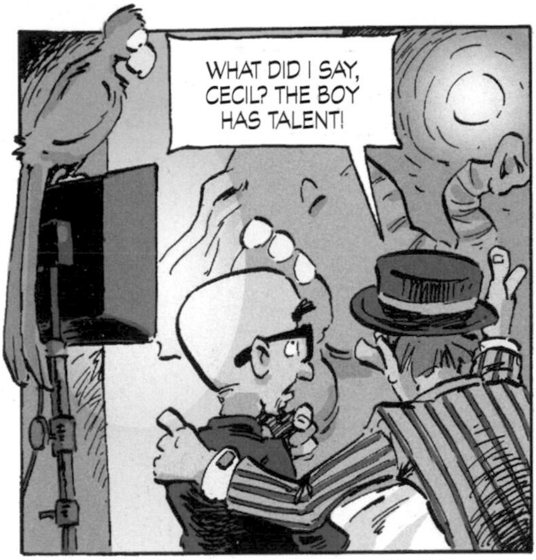
WHAT DID I SAY, CECIL? THE BOY HAS TALENT!

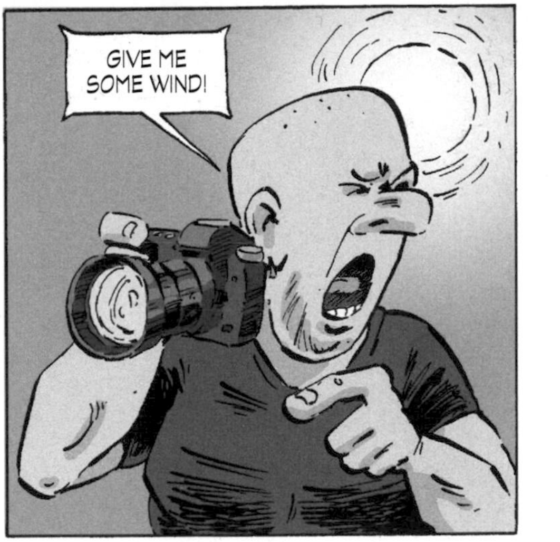
GIVE ME SOME WIND!

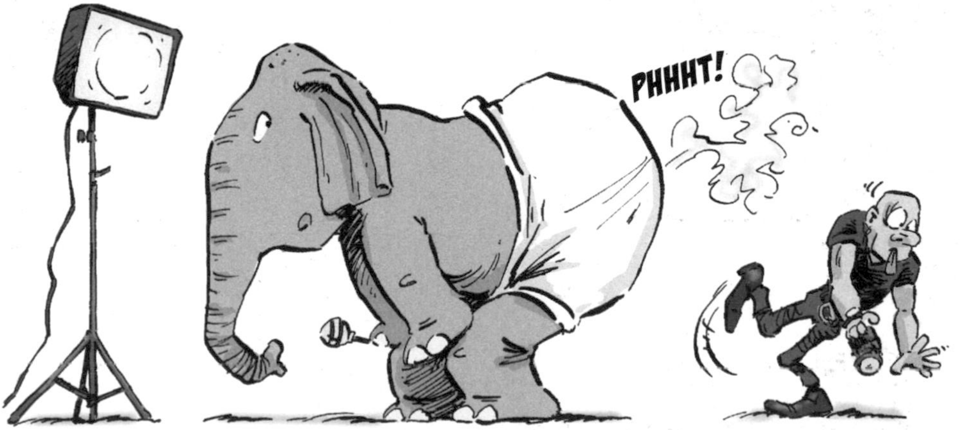
PHHHT!

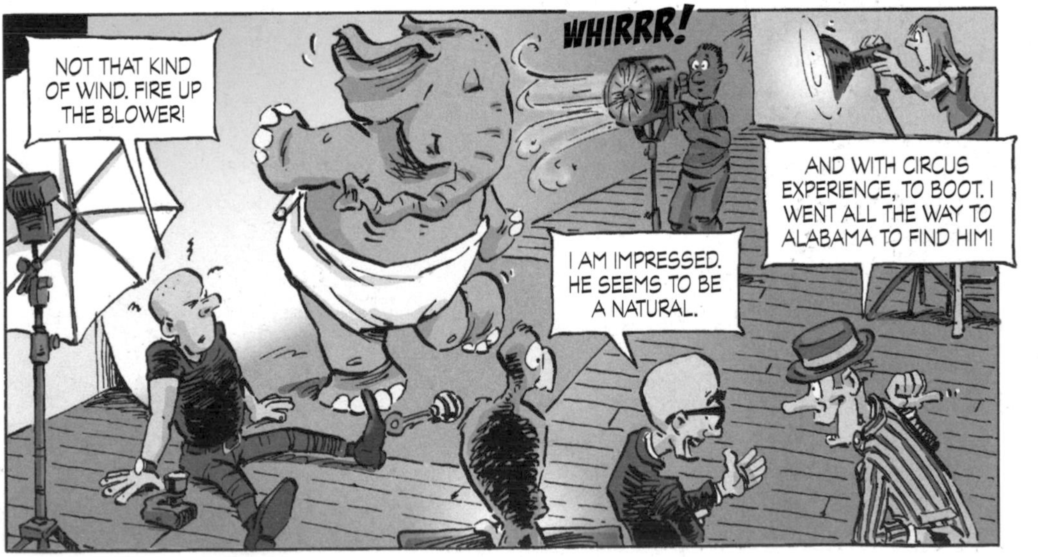
WHIRRR!
NOT THAT KIND OF WIND. FIRE UP THE BLOWER!
I AM IMPRESSED. HE SEEMS TO BE A NATURAL.
AND WITH CIRCUS EXPERIENCE, TO BOOT. I WENT ALL THE WAY TO ALABAMA TO FIND HIM!

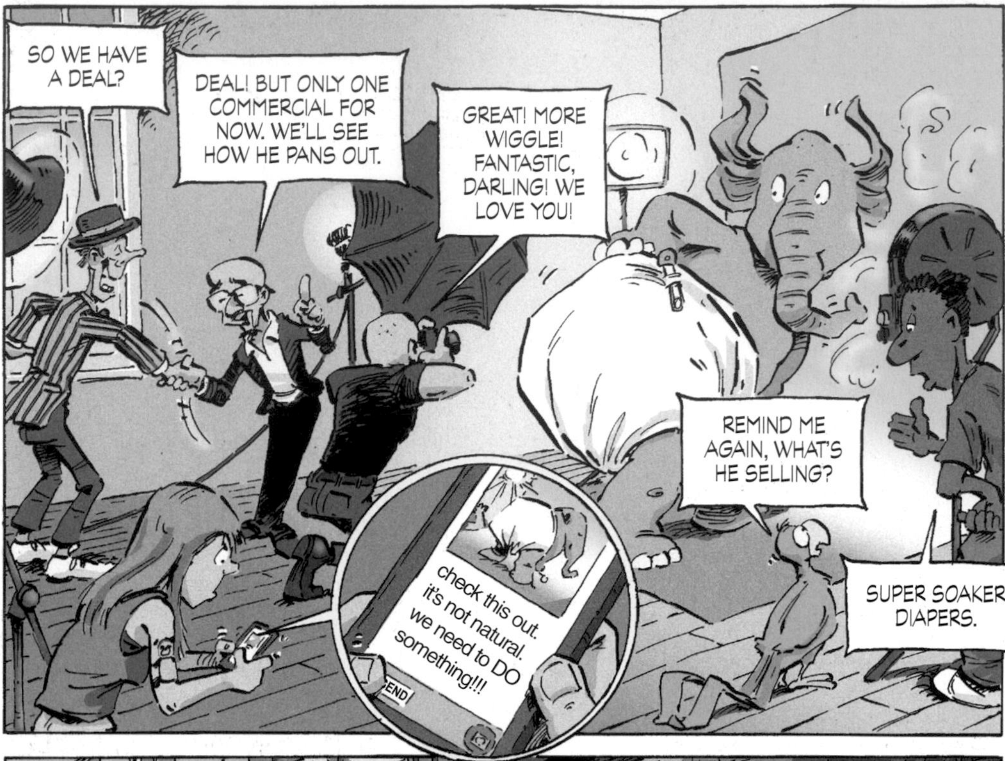
SO WE HAVE A DEAL?
DEAL! BUT ONLY ONE COMMERCIAL FOR NOW. WE'LL SEE HOW HE PANS OUT.
GREAT! MORE WIGGLE! FANTASTIC, DARLING! WE LOVE YOU!
REMIND ME AGAIN, WHAT'S HE SELLING?
check this out. it's not natural. we need to DO something!!!
END
SUPER SOAKER DIAPERS.

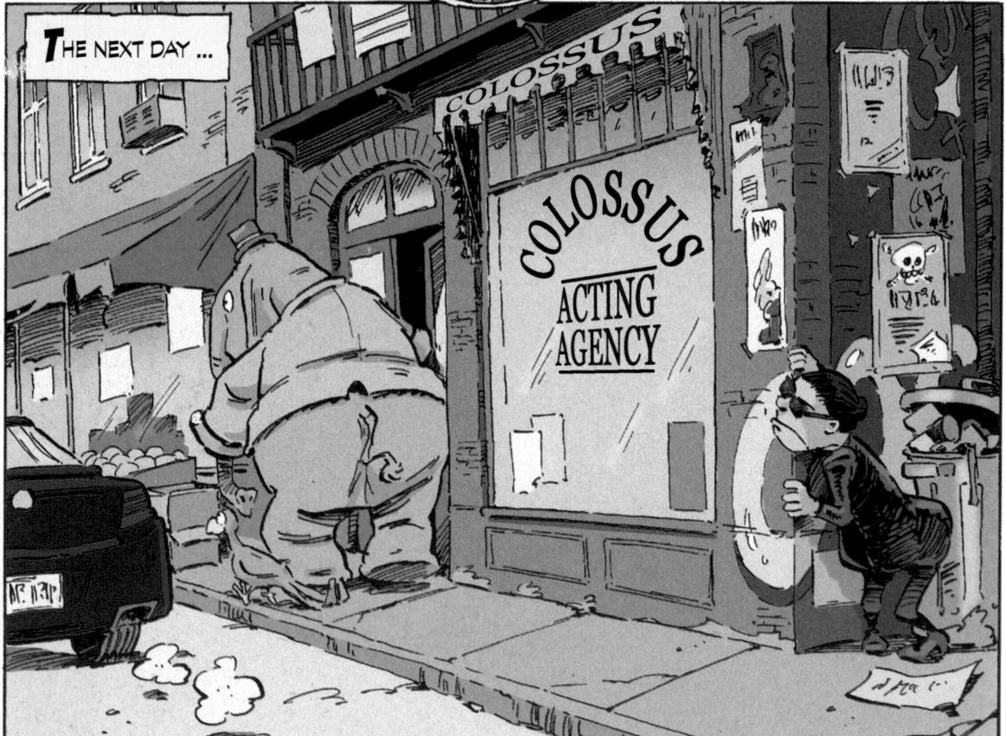
THE NEXT DAY ...
COLOSSUS
COLOSSUS
COLOSSUS
ACTING AGENCY

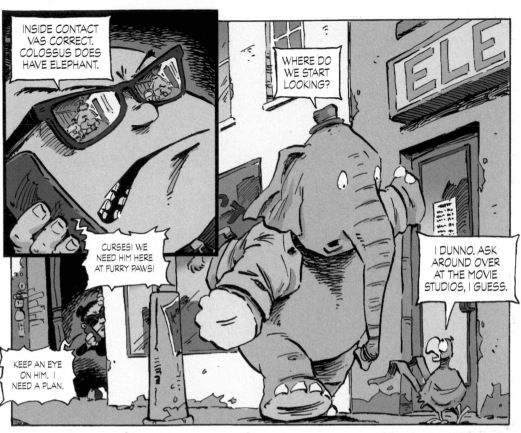

INSIDE CONTACT VAS CORRECT. COLOSSUS DOES HAVE ELEPHANT.

WHERE DO WE START LOOKING?

CURSES! WE NEED HIM HERE AT FURRY PAWS!

KEEP AN EYE ON HIM. I NEED A PLAN.

I DUNNO. ASK AROUND OVER AT THE MOVIE STUDIOS, I GUESS.

I THINK RUPERT KNOWS MORE ABOUT GEORGIE THAN HE'S LETTING ON. DIDN'T HE LOOK A BIT SHIFTY WHEN WE MENTIONED HIM?

RUPERT? D'YOU THINK? HE SEEMS LIKE SUCH A NICE GUY!

A SHORT WHILE LATER ...

I DON'T CARE WHO YOU'RE LOOKING FOR. IF YOU WANT IN, YOU LINE UP AND PAY LIKE EVERYONE ELSE.

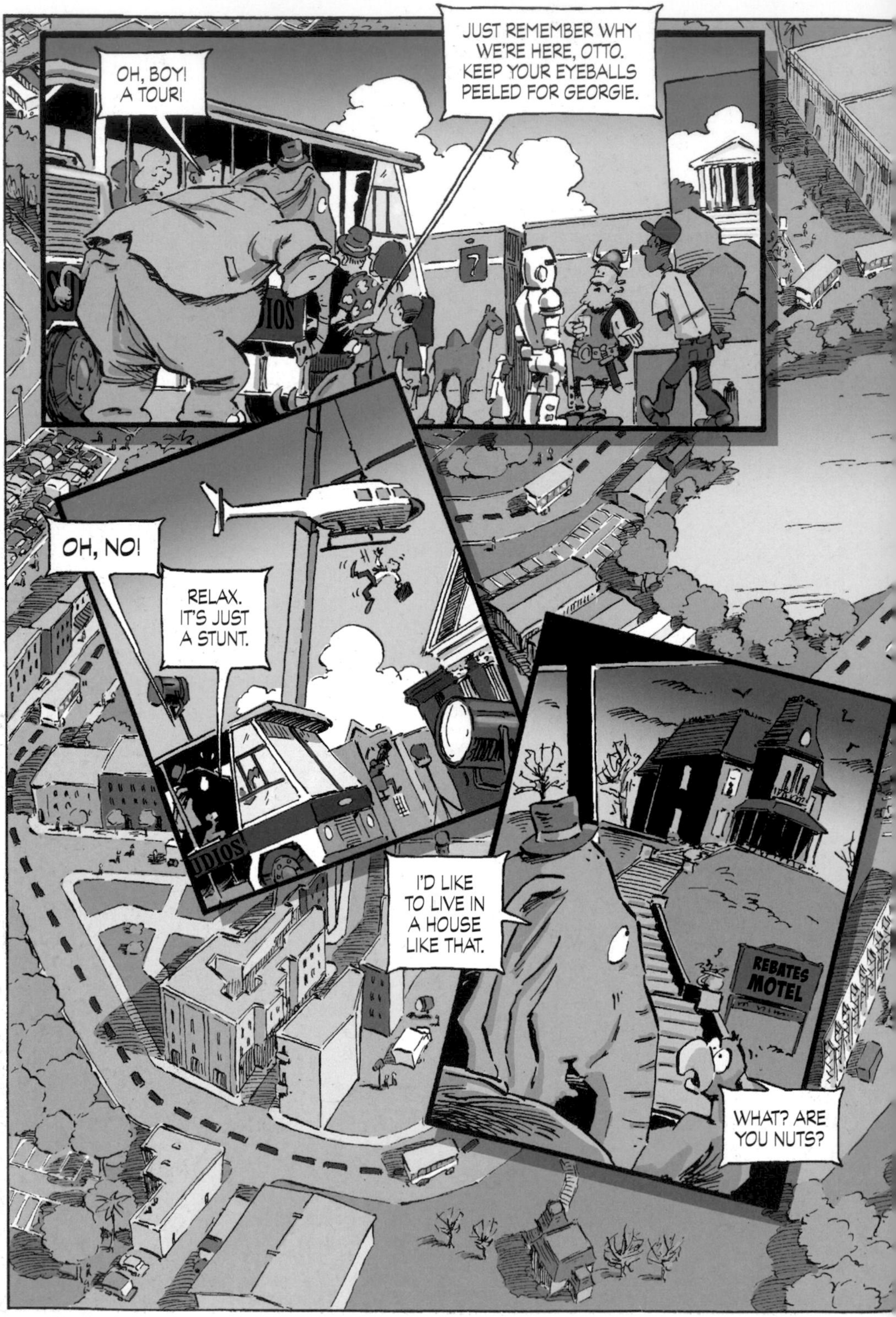
OH, BOY! A TOUR!
JUST REMEMBER WHY WE'RE HERE, OTTO. KEEP YOUR EYEBALLS PEELED FOR GEORGIE.
OH, NO!
RELAX. IT'S JUST A STUNT.
I'D LIKE TO LIVE IN A HOUSE LIKE THAT.
REBATES MOTEL
WHAT? ARE YOU NUTS?

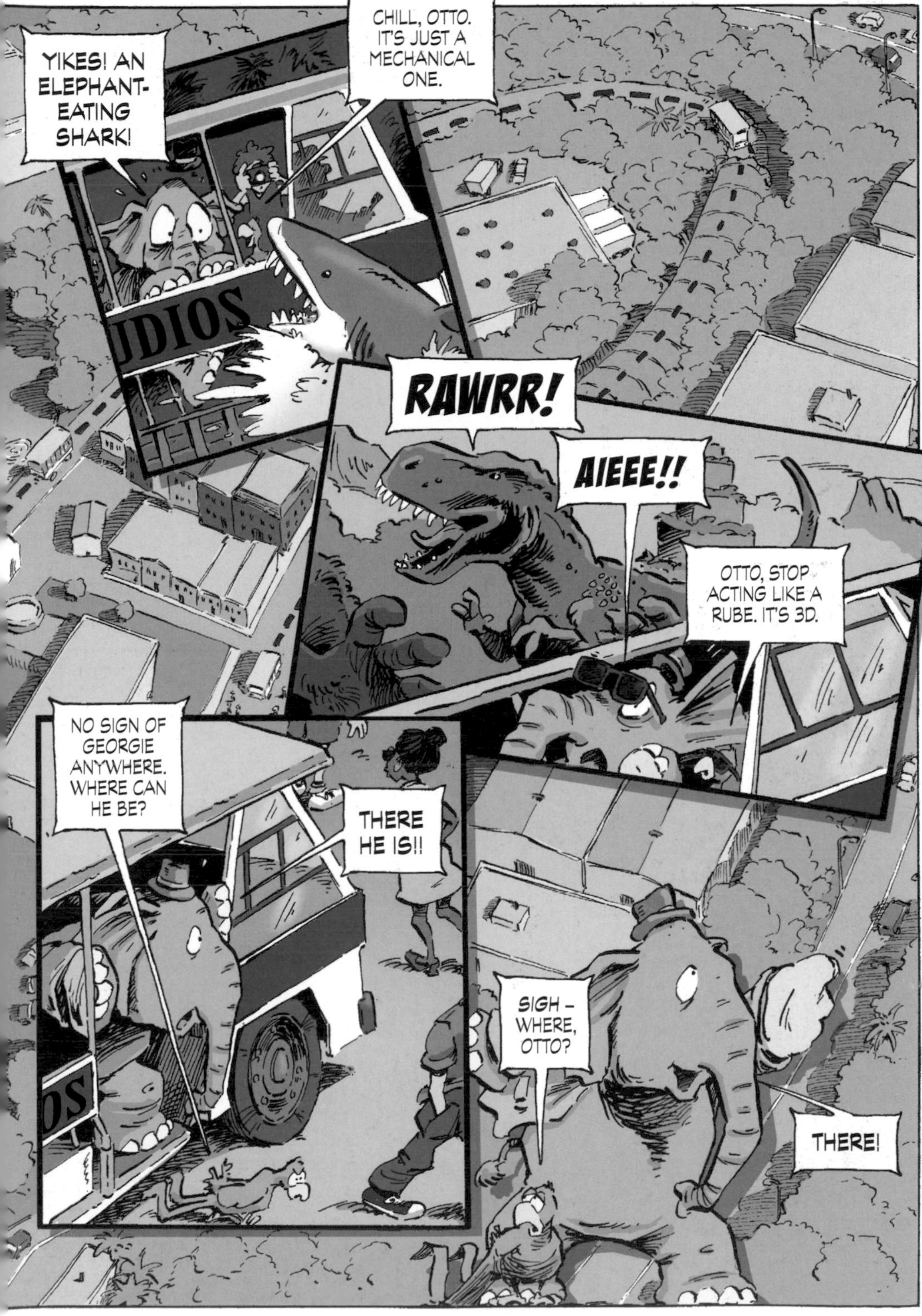
YIKES! AN ELEPHANT-EATING SHARK!
CHILL, OTTO. IT'S JUST A MECHANICAL ONE.
UDIOS
RAWRR!
AIEEE!!
OTTO, STOP ACTING LIKE A RUBE. IT'S 3D.
NO SIGN OF GEORGIE ANYWHERE. WHERE CAN HE BE?
THERE HE IS!!
OS
SIGH – WHERE, OTTO?
THERE!

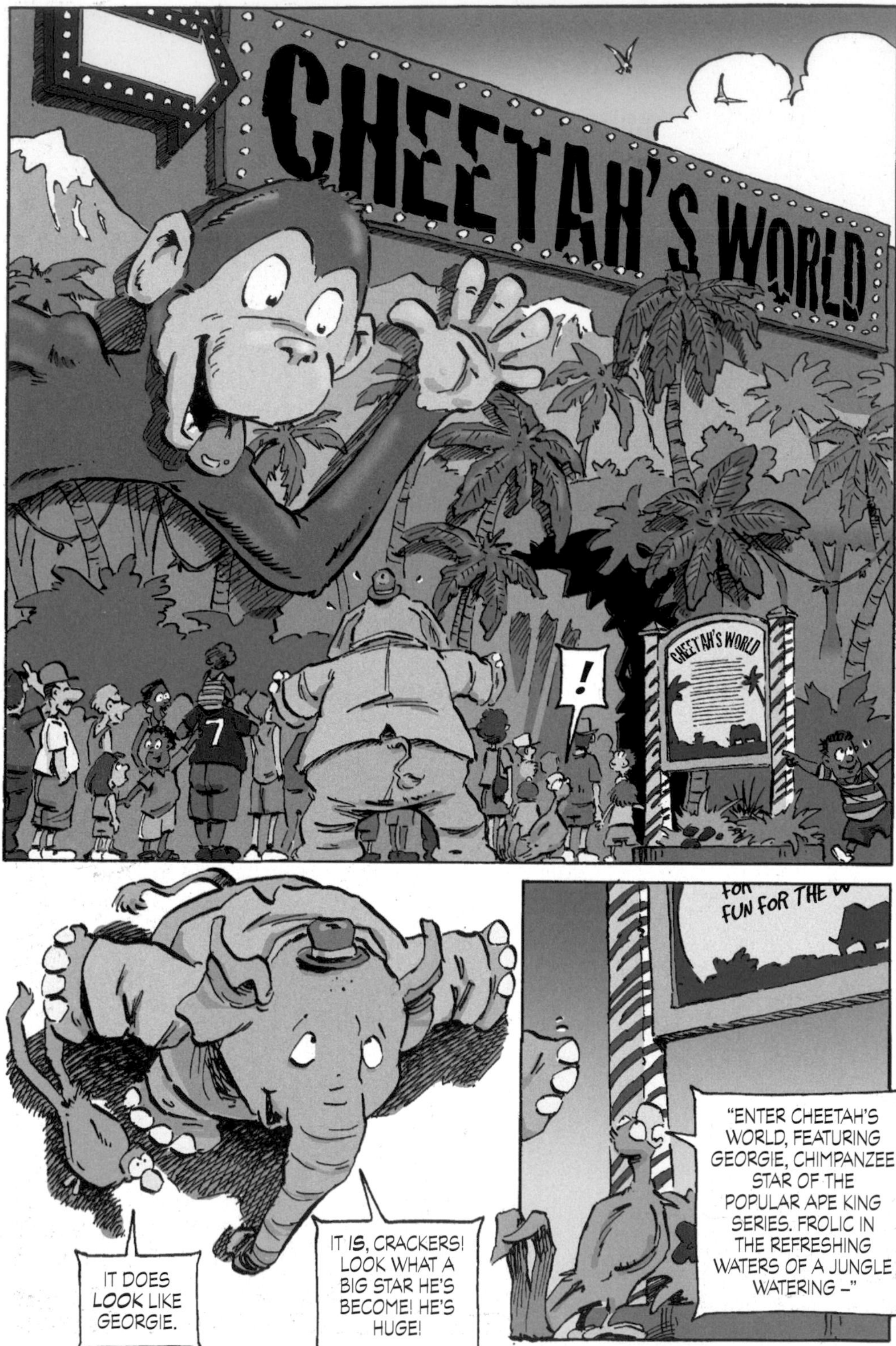
CHEETAH'S WORLD
CHEETAH'S WORLD
!
IT DOES LOOK LIKE GEORGIE.
IT IS, CRACKERS! LOOK WHAT A BIG STAR HE'S BECOME! HE'S HUGE!
"ENTER CHEETAH'S WORLD, FEATURING GEORGIE, CHIMPANZEE STAR OF THE POPULAR APE KING SERIES. FROLIC IN THE REFRESHING WATERS OF A JUNGLE WATERING –"

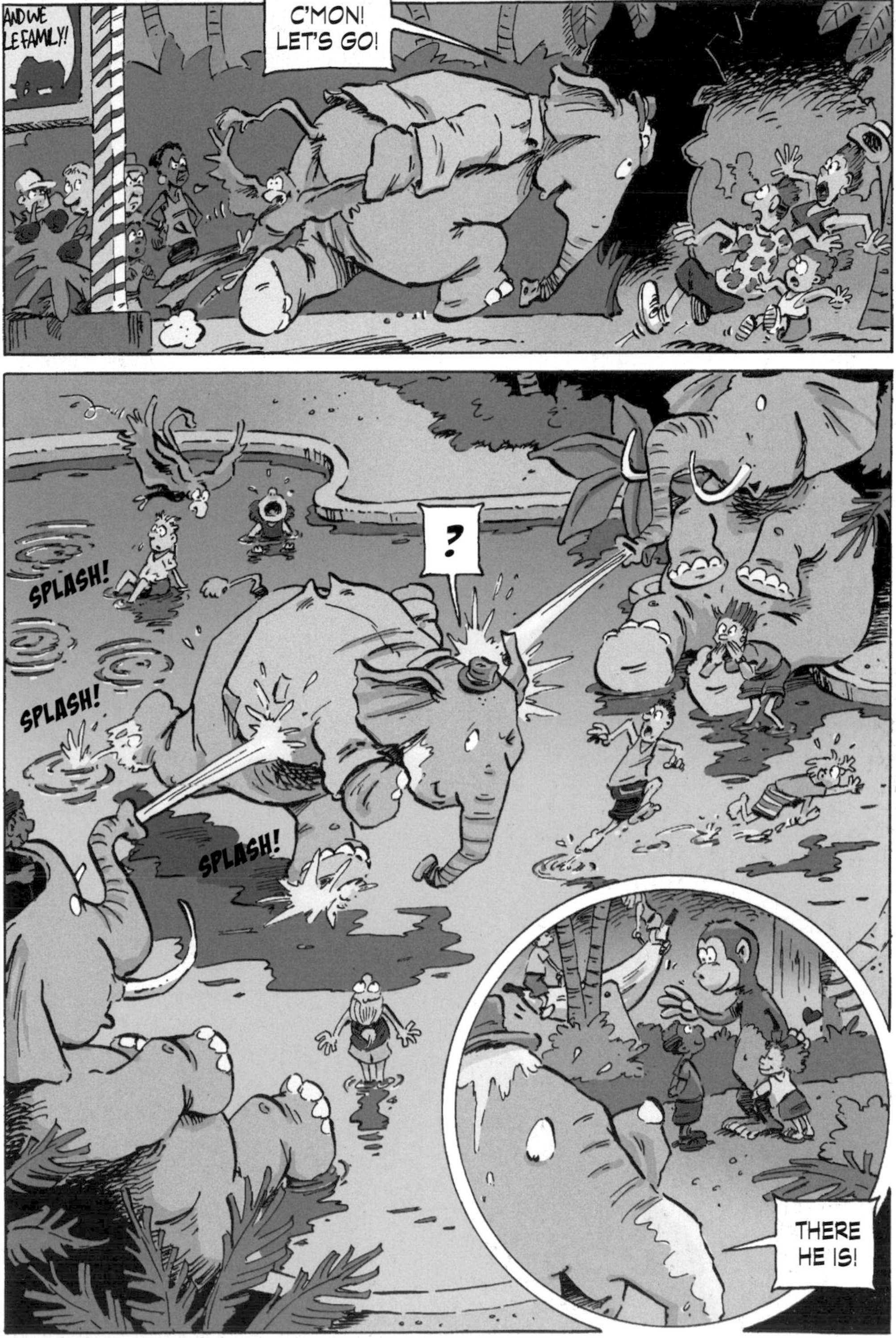
AND WE
LE FAMILY!
C'MON! LET'S GO!
?
SPLASH!
SPLASH!
SPLASH!
THERE HE IS!

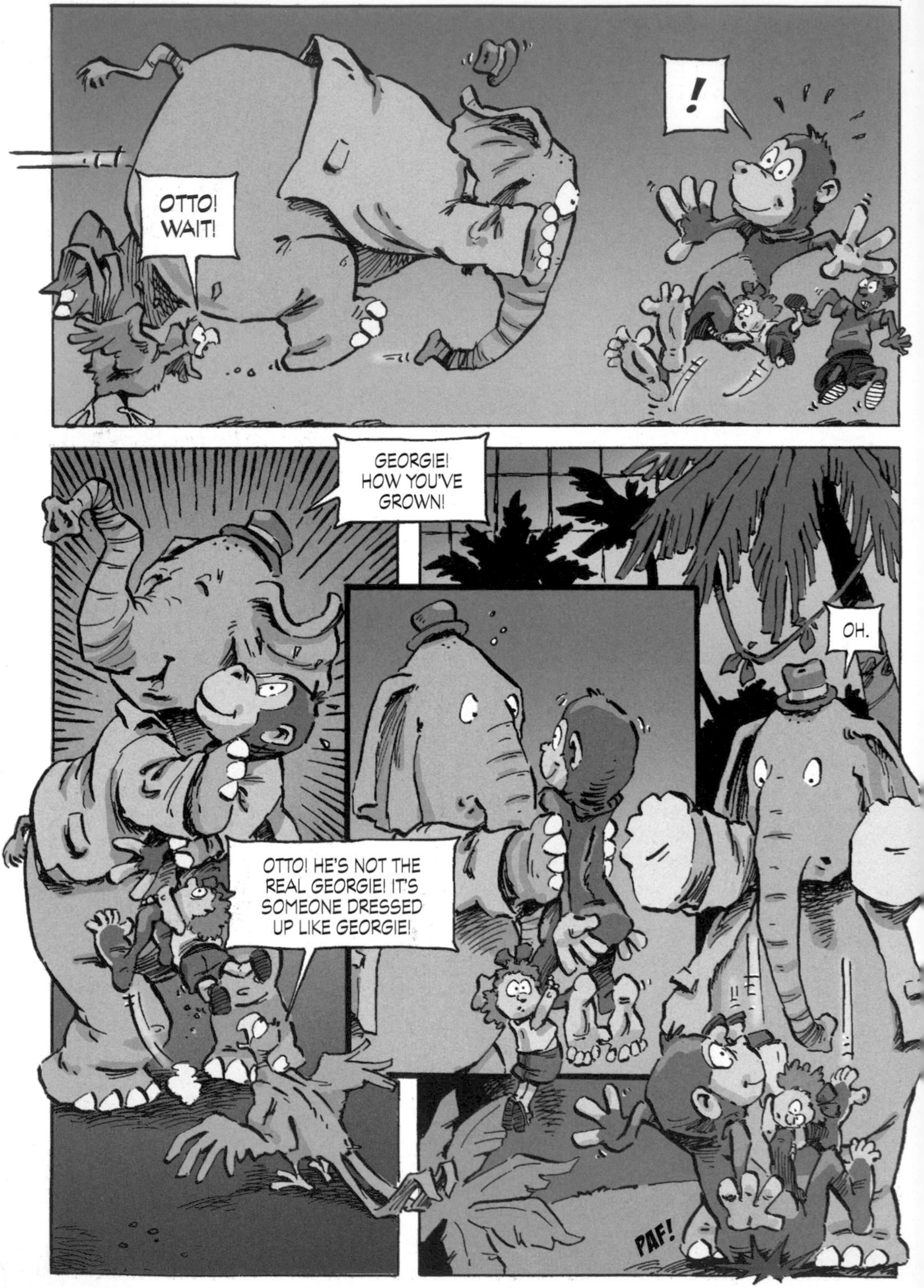
OTTO! WAIT!
!
GEORGIE! HOW YOU'VE GROWN!
OTTO! HE'S NOT THE REAL GEORGIE! IT'S SOMEONE DRESSED UP LIKE GEORGIE!
OH.
PAF!

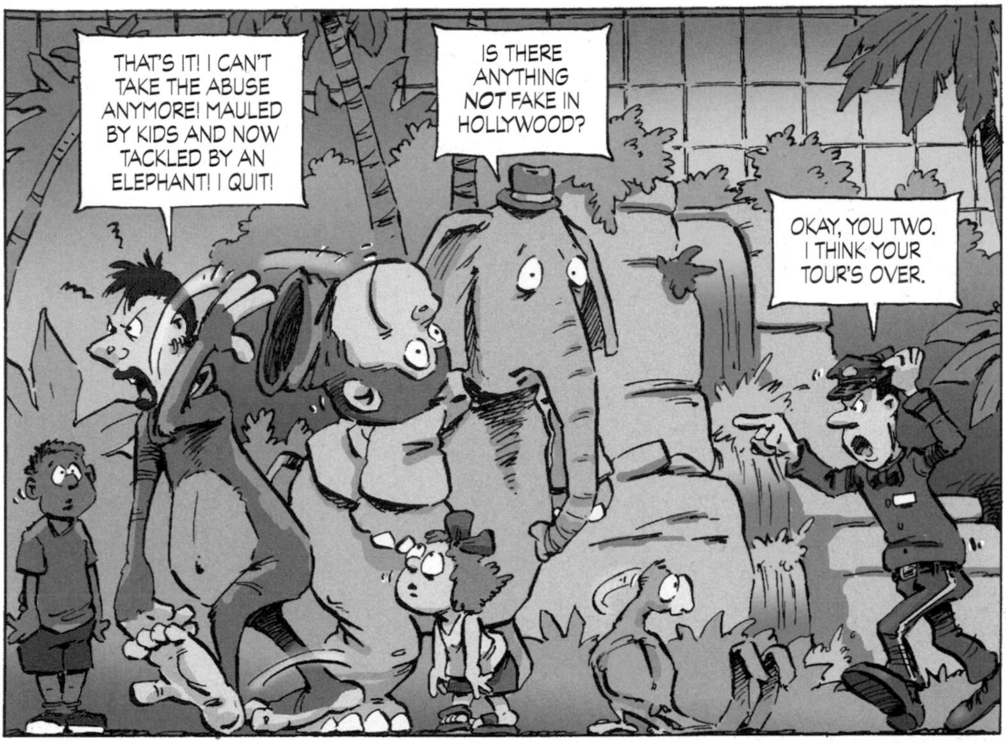
THAT'S IT! I CAN'T TAKE THE ABUSE ANYMORE! MAULED BY KIDS AND NOW TACKLED BY AN ELEPHANT! I QUIT!
IS THERE ANYTHING NOT FAKE IN HOLLYWOOD?
OKAY, YOU TWO. I THINK YOUR TOUR'S OVER.

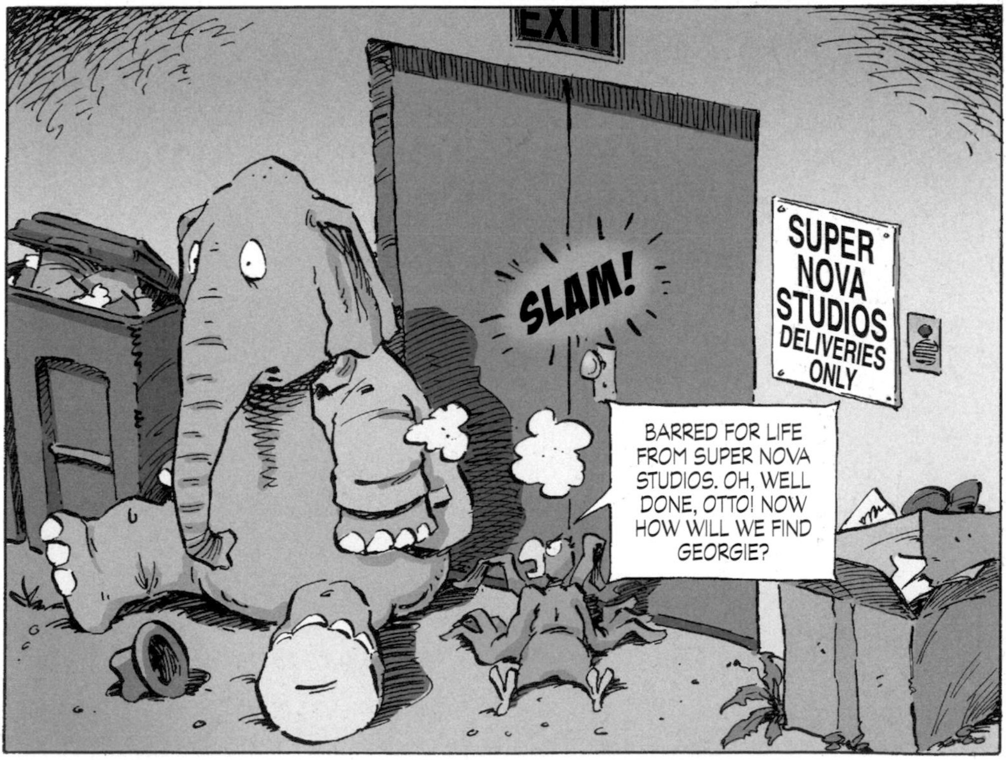
EXIT
SUPER NOVA STUDIOS DELIVERIES ONLY
SLAM!
BARRED FOR LIFE FROM SUPER NOVA STUDIOS. OH, WELL DONE, OTTO! NOW HOW WILL WE FIND GEORGIE?

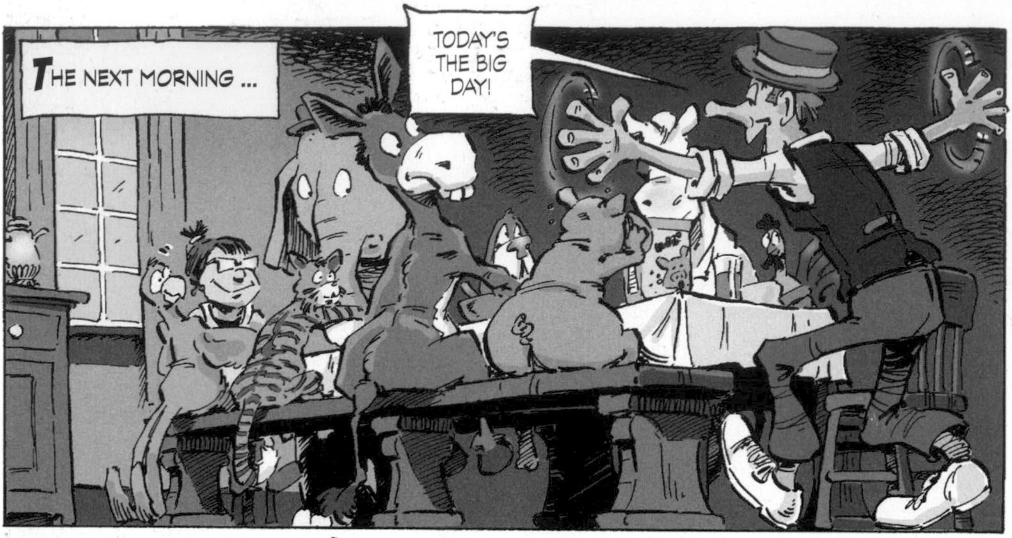
THE NEXT MORNING ...
TODAY'S THE BIG DAY!

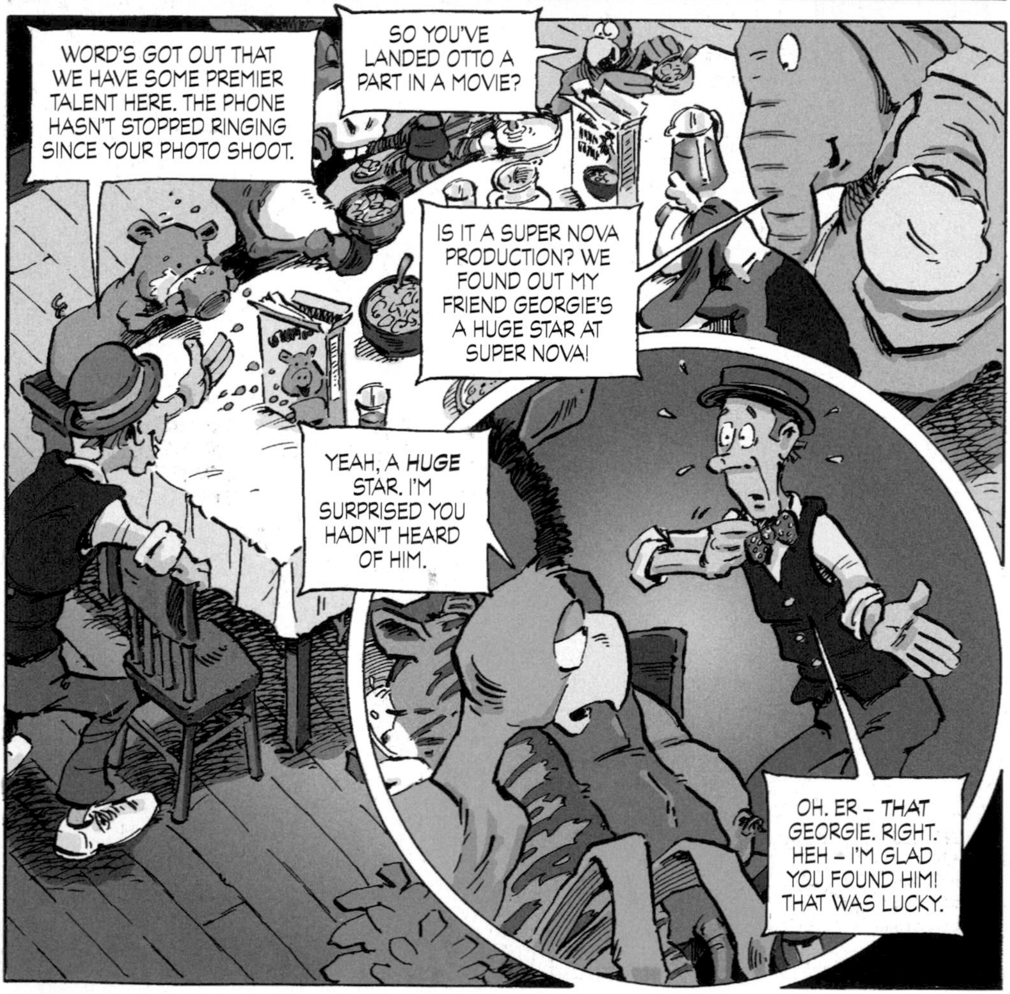
WORD'S GOT OUT THAT WE HAVE SOME PREMIER TALENT HERE. THE PHONE HASN'T STOPPED RINGING SINCE YOUR PHOTO SHOOT.
SO YOU'VE LANDED OTTO A PART IN A MOVIE?
IS IT A SUPER NOVA PRODUCTION? WE FOUND OUT MY FRIEND GEORGIE'S A HUGE STAR AT SUPER NOVA!
YEAH, A *HUGE* STAR. I'M SURPRISED YOU HADN'T HEARD OF HIM.
OH. ER – *THAT* GEORGIE. RIGHT. HEH – I'M GLAD YOU FOUND HIM! THAT WAS LUCKY.

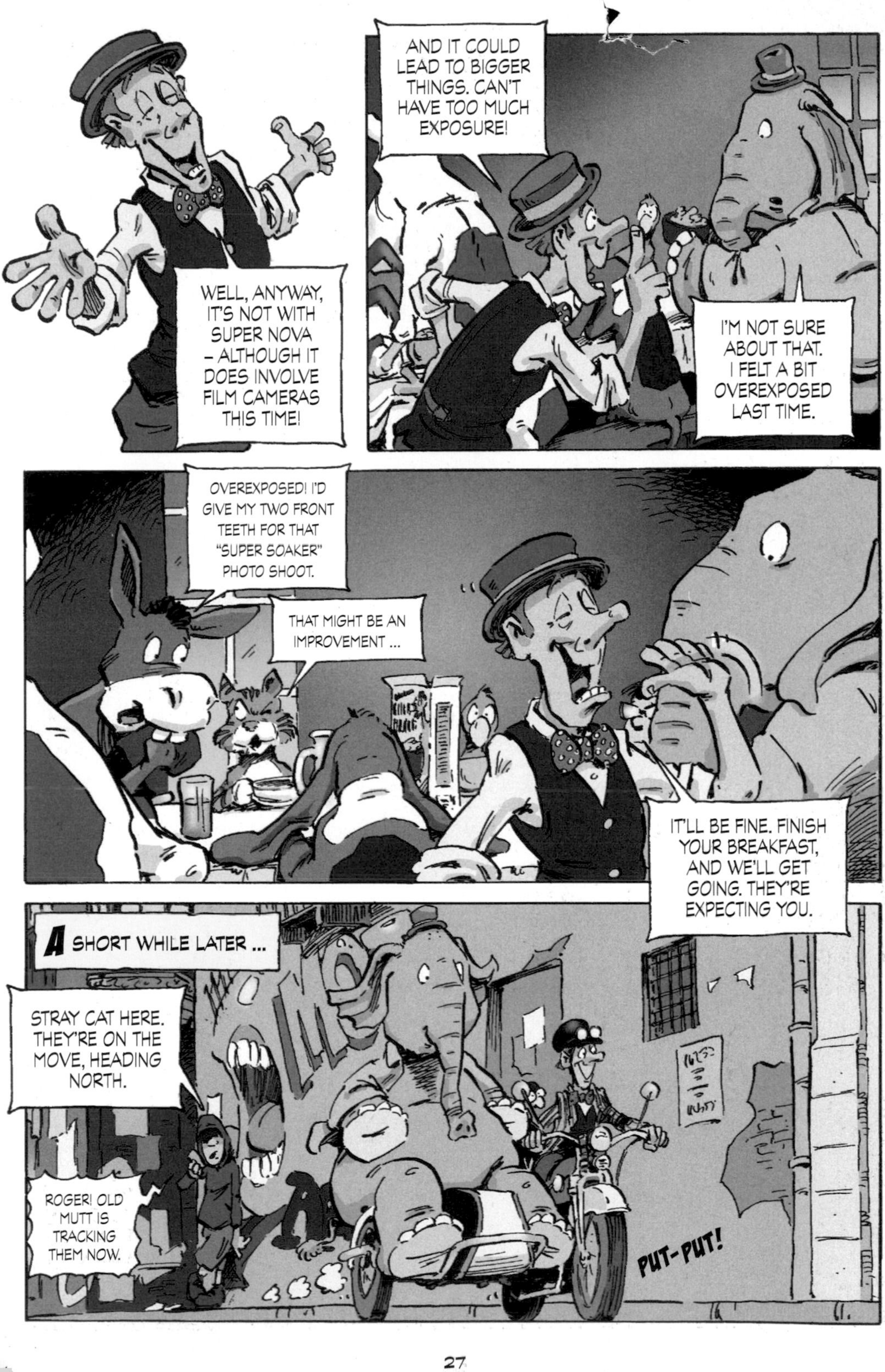
WELL, ANYWAY, IT'S NOT WITH SUPER NOVA – ALTHOUGH IT DOES INVOLVE FILM CAMERAS THIS TIME!
AND IT COULD LEAD TO BIGGER THINGS. CAN'T HAVE TOO MUCH EXPOSURE!
I'M NOT SURE ABOUT THAT. I FELT A BIT OVEREXPOSED LAST TIME.
OVEREXPOSED! I'D GIVE MY TWO FRONT TEETH FOR THAT "SUPER SOAKER" PHOTO SHOOT.
THAT MIGHT BE AN IMPROVEMENT ...
IT'LL BE FINE. FINISH YOUR BREAKFAST, AND WE'LL GET GOING. THEY'RE EXPECTING YOU.
A SHORT WHILE LATER ...
STRAY CAT HERE. THEY'RE ON THE MOVE, HEADING NORTH.
ROGER! OLD MUTT IS TRACKING THEM NOW.
PUT-PUT!

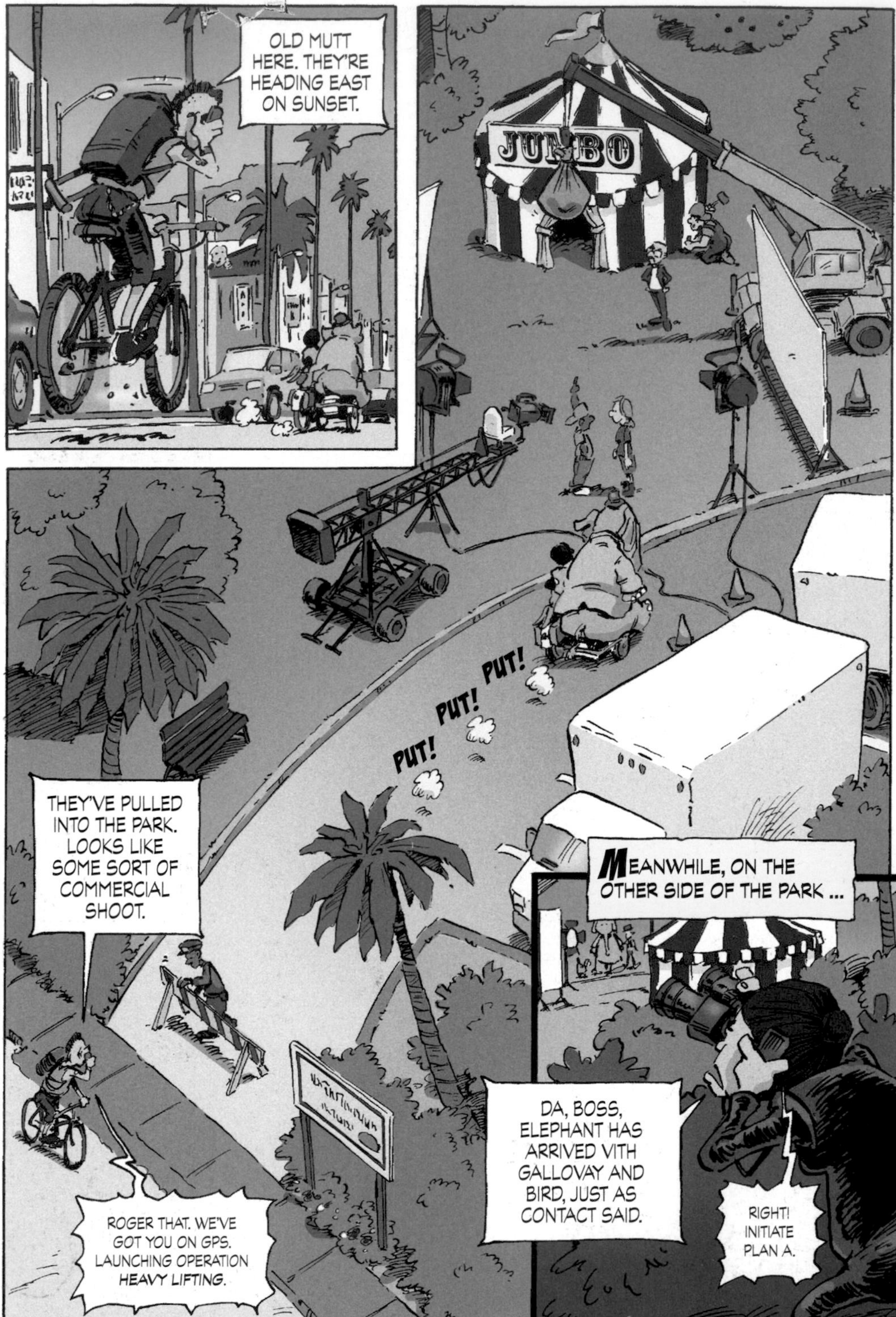
OLD MUTT HERE. THEY'RE HEADING EAST ON SUNSET.
JUMBO
PUT!
PUT!
PUT!
THEY'VE PULLED INTO THE PARK. LOOKS LIKE SOME SORT OF COMMERCIAL SHOOT.
ROGER THAT. WE'VE GOT YOU ON GPS. LAUNCHING OPERATION HEAVY LIFTING.
MEANWHILE, ON THE OTHER SIDE OF THE PARK ...
DA, BOSS, ELEPHANT HAS ARRIVED VITH GALLOVAY AND BIRD, JUST AS CONTACT SAID.
RIGHT! INITIATE PLAN A.

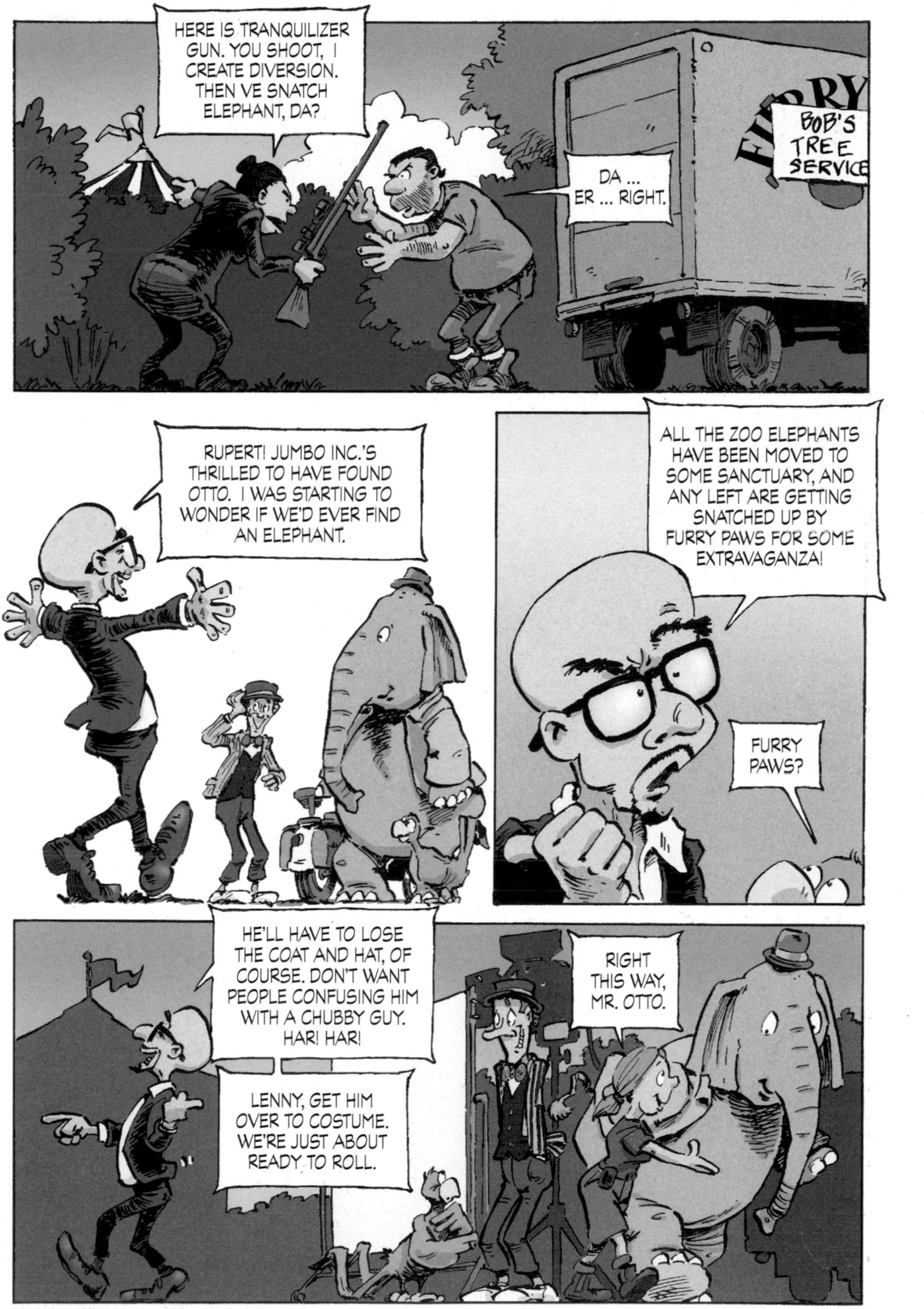
HERE IS TRANQUILIZER GUN. YOU SHOOT, I CREATE DIVERSION. THEN VE SNATCH ELEPHANT, DA?
FURRY
BOB'S TREE SERVICE
DA ... ER ... RIGHT.
RUPERT! JUMBO INC.'S THRILLED TO HAVE FOUND OTTO. I WAS STARTING TO WONDER IF WE'D EVER FIND AN ELEPHANT.
ALL THE ZOO ELEPHANTS HAVE BEEN MOVED TO SOME SANCTUARY, AND ANY LEFT ARE GETTING SNATCHED UP BY FURRY PAWS FOR SOME EXTRAVAGANZA!
FURRY PAWS?
HE'LL HAVE TO LOSE THE COAT AND HAT, OF COURSE. DON'T WANT PEOPLE CONFUSING HIM WITH A CHUBBY GUY. HAR! HAR!
LENNY, GET HIM OVER TO COSTUME. WE'RE JUST ABOUT READY TO ROLL.
RIGHT THIS WAY, MR. OTTO.

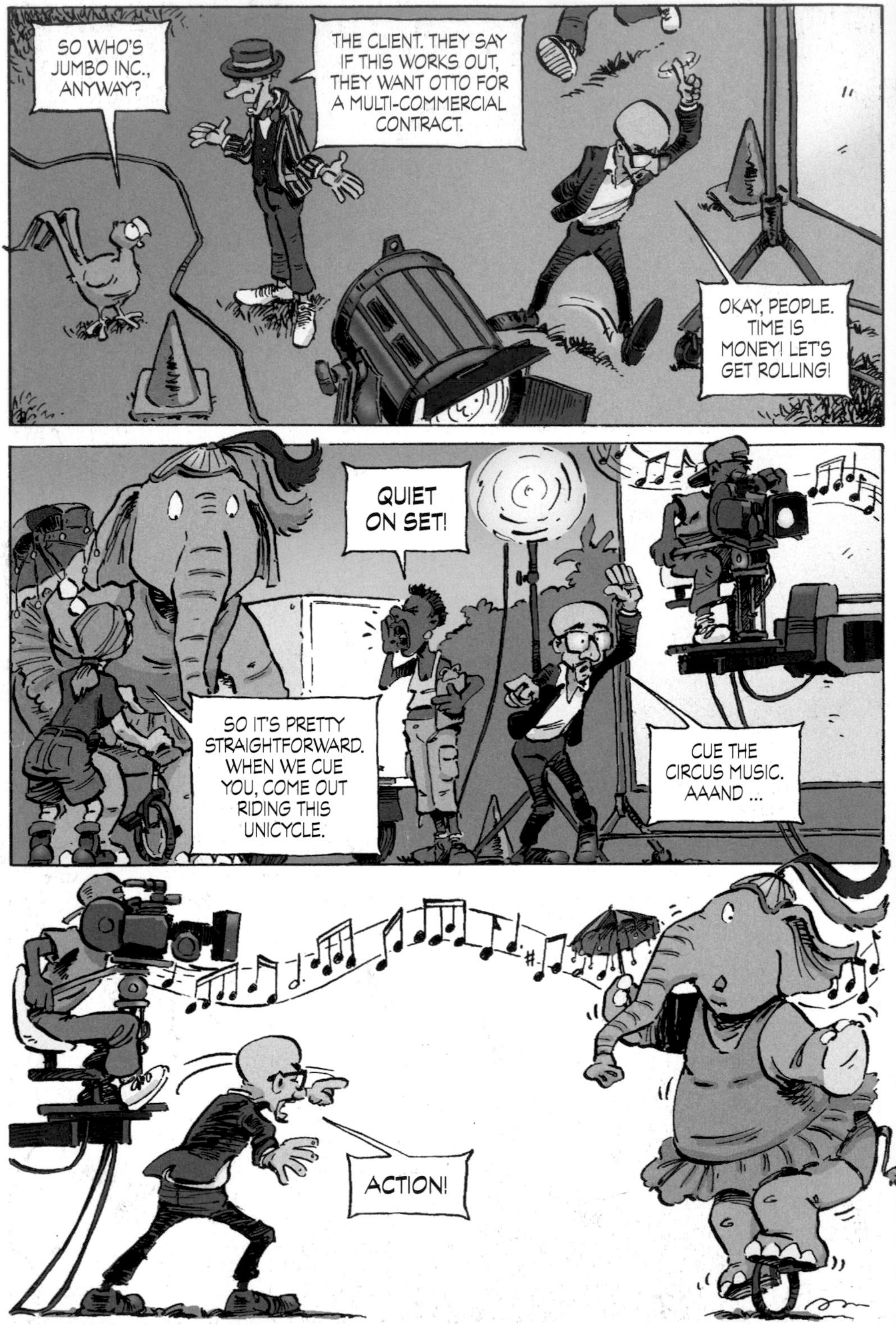
SO WHO'S JUMBO INC., ANYWAY?
THE CLIENT. THEY SAY IF THIS WORKS OUT, THEY WANT OTTO FOR A MULTI-COMMERCIAL CONTRACT.
OKAY, PEOPLE. TIME IS MONEY! LET'S GET ROLLING!
QUIET ON SET!
SO IT'S PRETTY STRAIGHTFORWARD. WHEN WE CUE YOU, COME OUT RIDING THIS UNICYCLE.
CUE THE CIRCUS MUSIC. AAAND ...
ACTION!

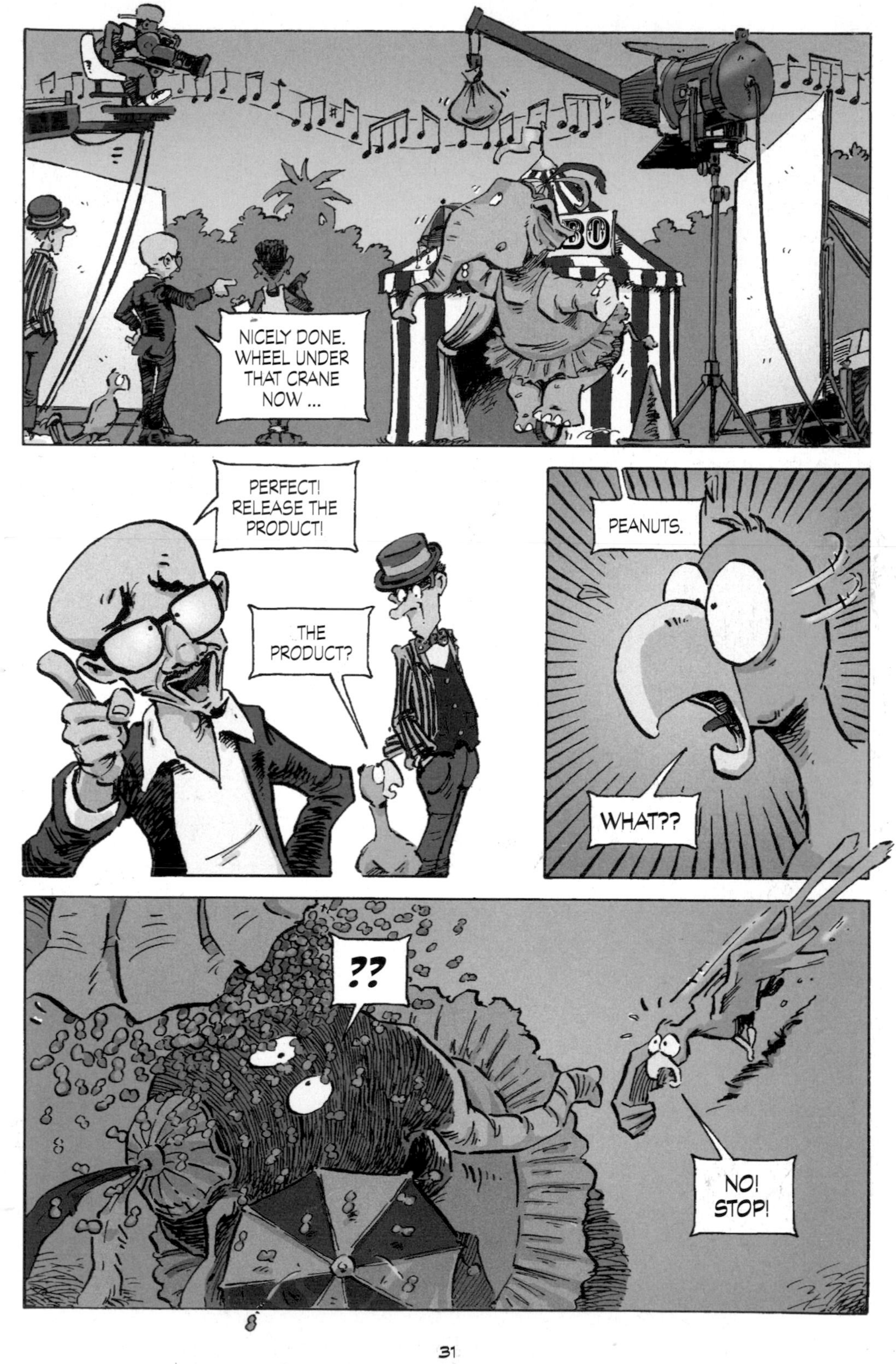
NICELY DONE. WHEEL UNDER THAT CRANE NOW ...
30
PERFECT! RELEASE THE PRODUCT!
THE PRODUCT?
PEANUTS.
WHAT??
??
NO! STOP!

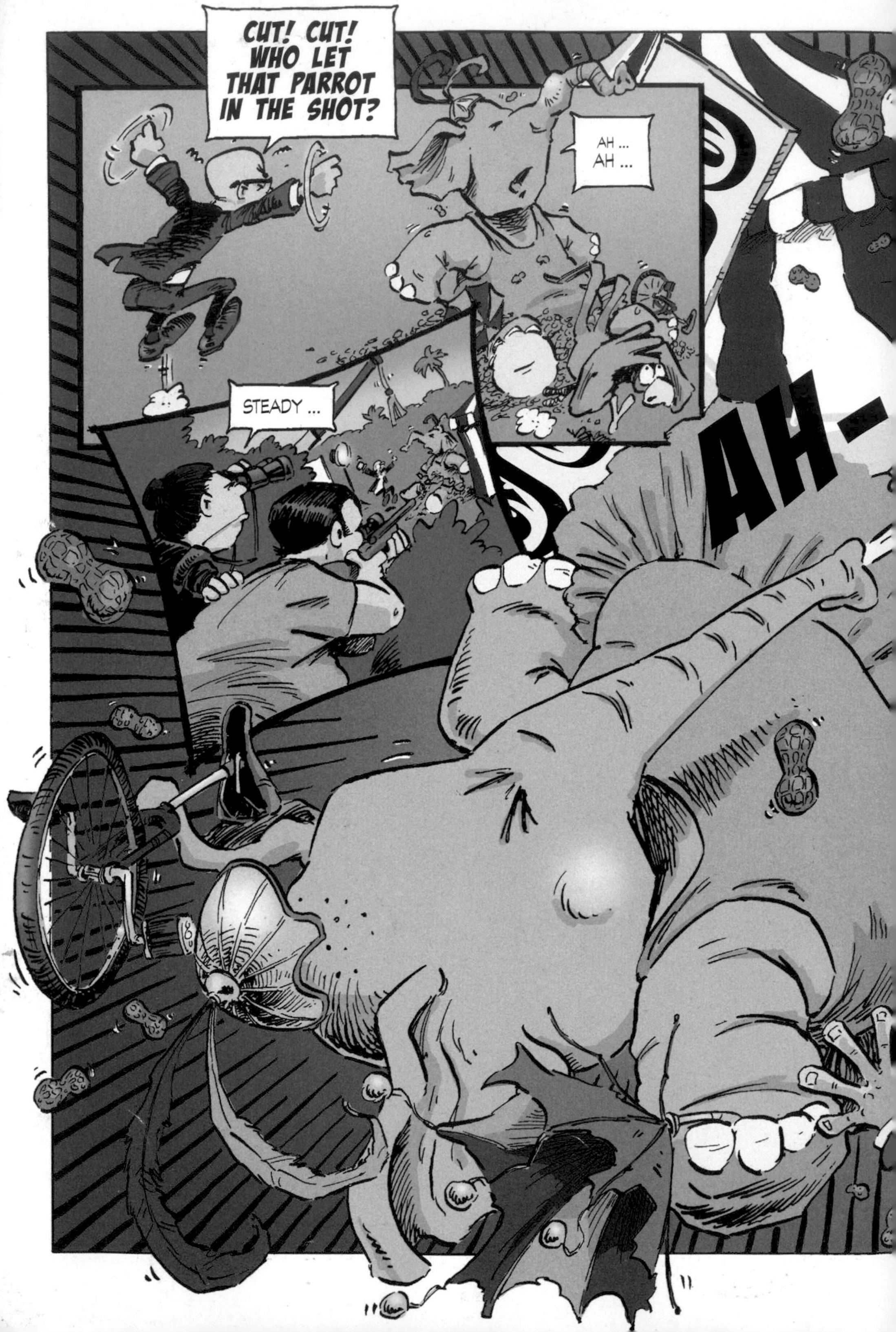
CUT! CUT! WHO LET THAT PARROT IN THE SHOT?
AH ... AH ...
STEADY ...
AH -

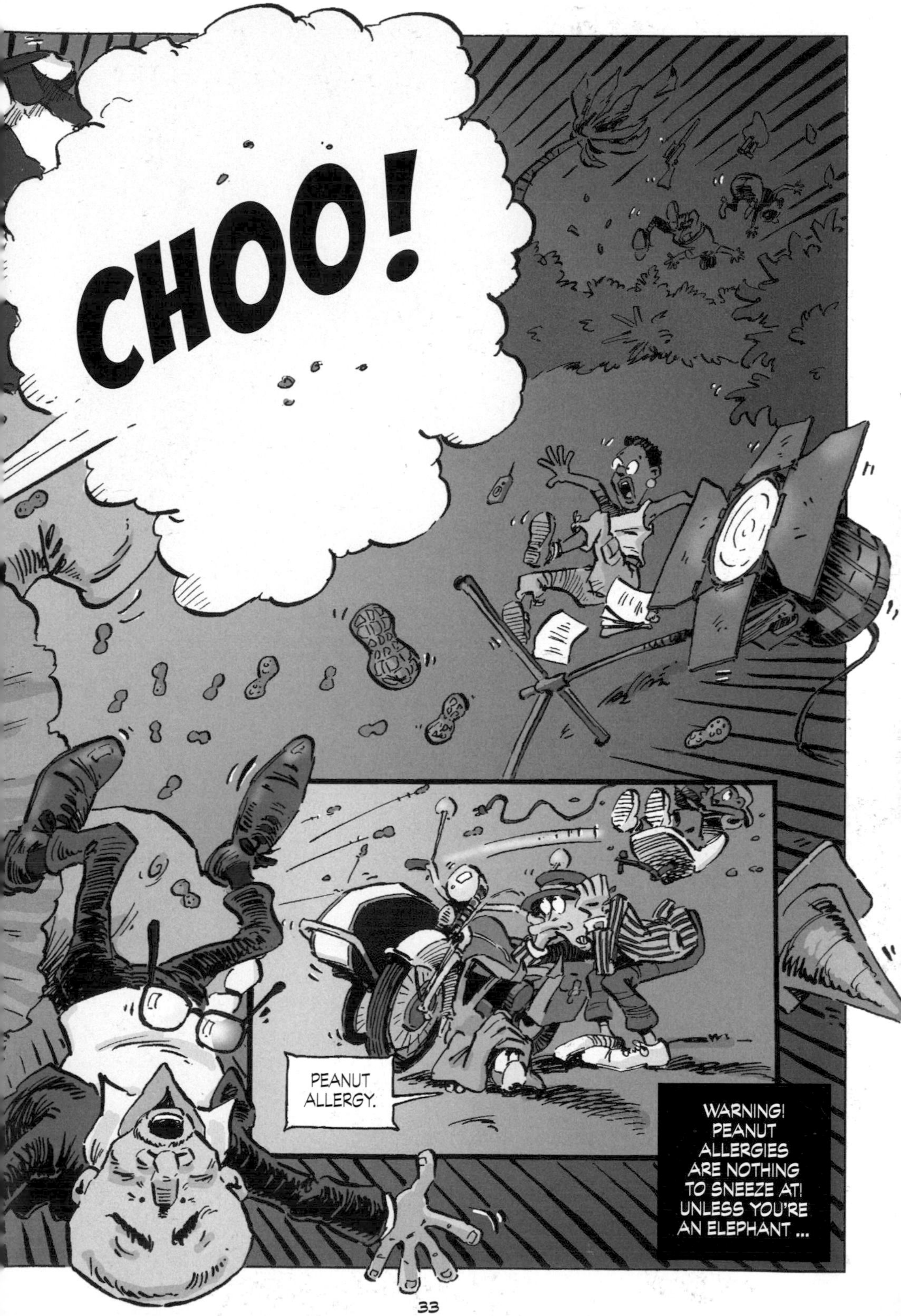
CHOO!
PEANUT ALLERGY.
WARNING! PEANUT ALLERGIES ARE NOTHING TO SNEEZE AT! UNLESS YOU'RE AN ELEPHANT ...

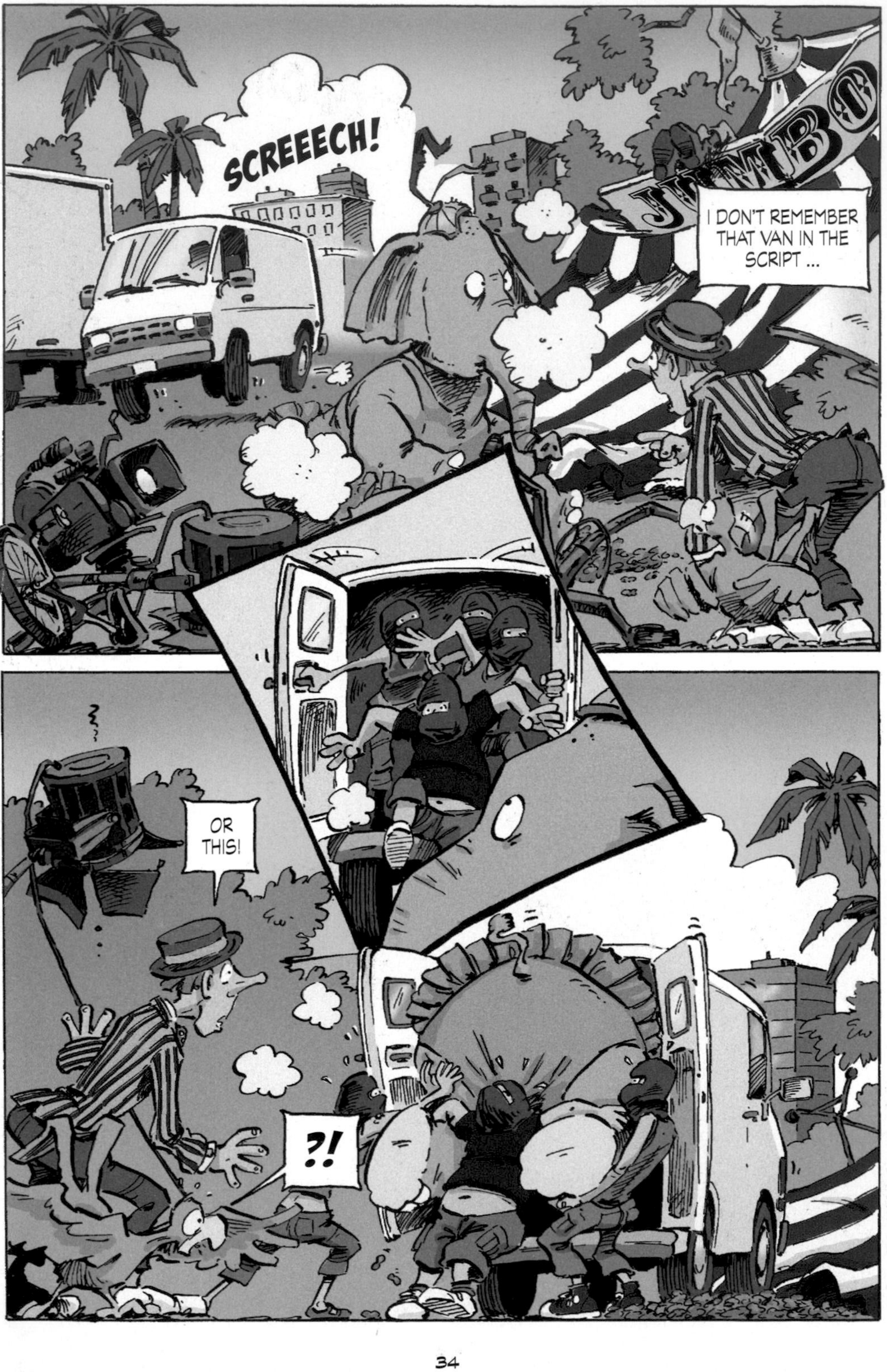
SCREEECH!
JUMBO
I DON'T REMEMBER THAT VAN IN THE SCRIPT ...
OR THIS!
?!

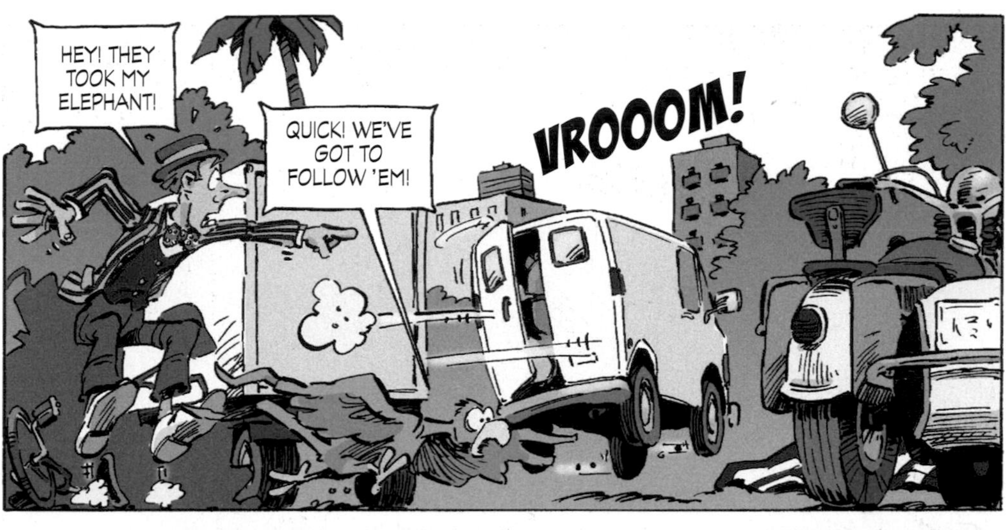
HEY! THEY TOOK MY ELEPHANT!
QUICK! WE'VE GOT TO FOLLOW 'EM!
VROOOM!

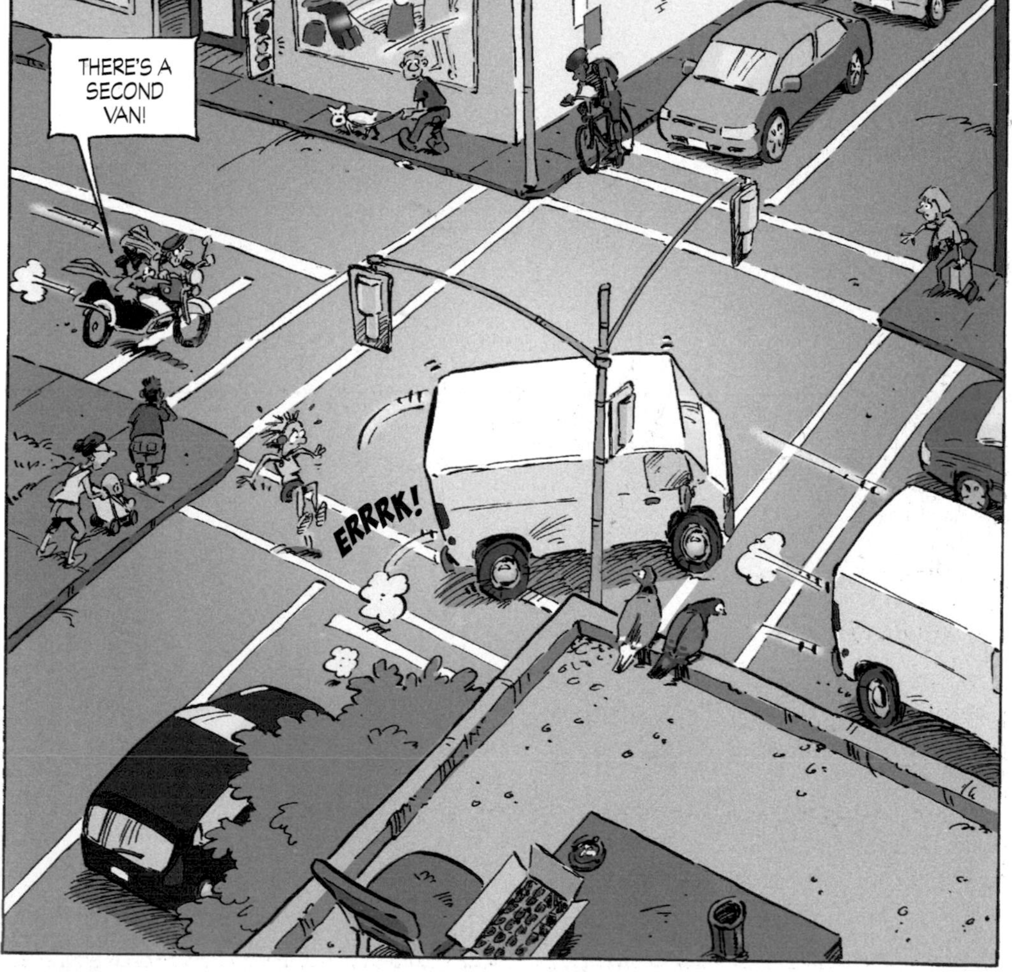
THERE'S A SECOND VAN!
ERRRK!

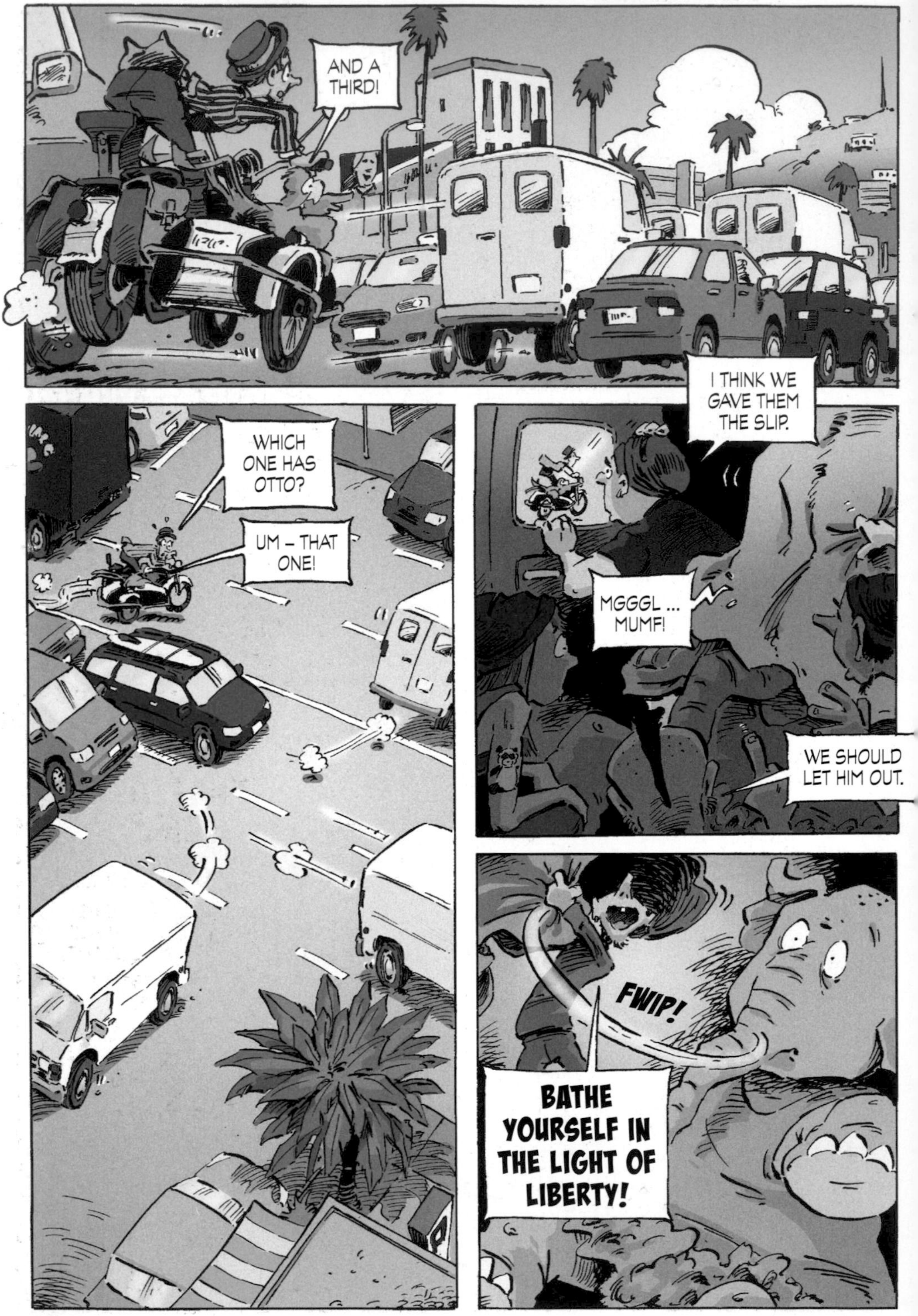
AND A THIRD!
WHICH ONE HAS OTTO?
UM – THAT ONE!
I THINK WE GAVE THEM THE SLIP.
MGGGL ... MUMF!
WE SHOULD LET HIM OUT.
FWIP!
BATHE YOURSELF IN THE LIGHT OF LIBERTY!

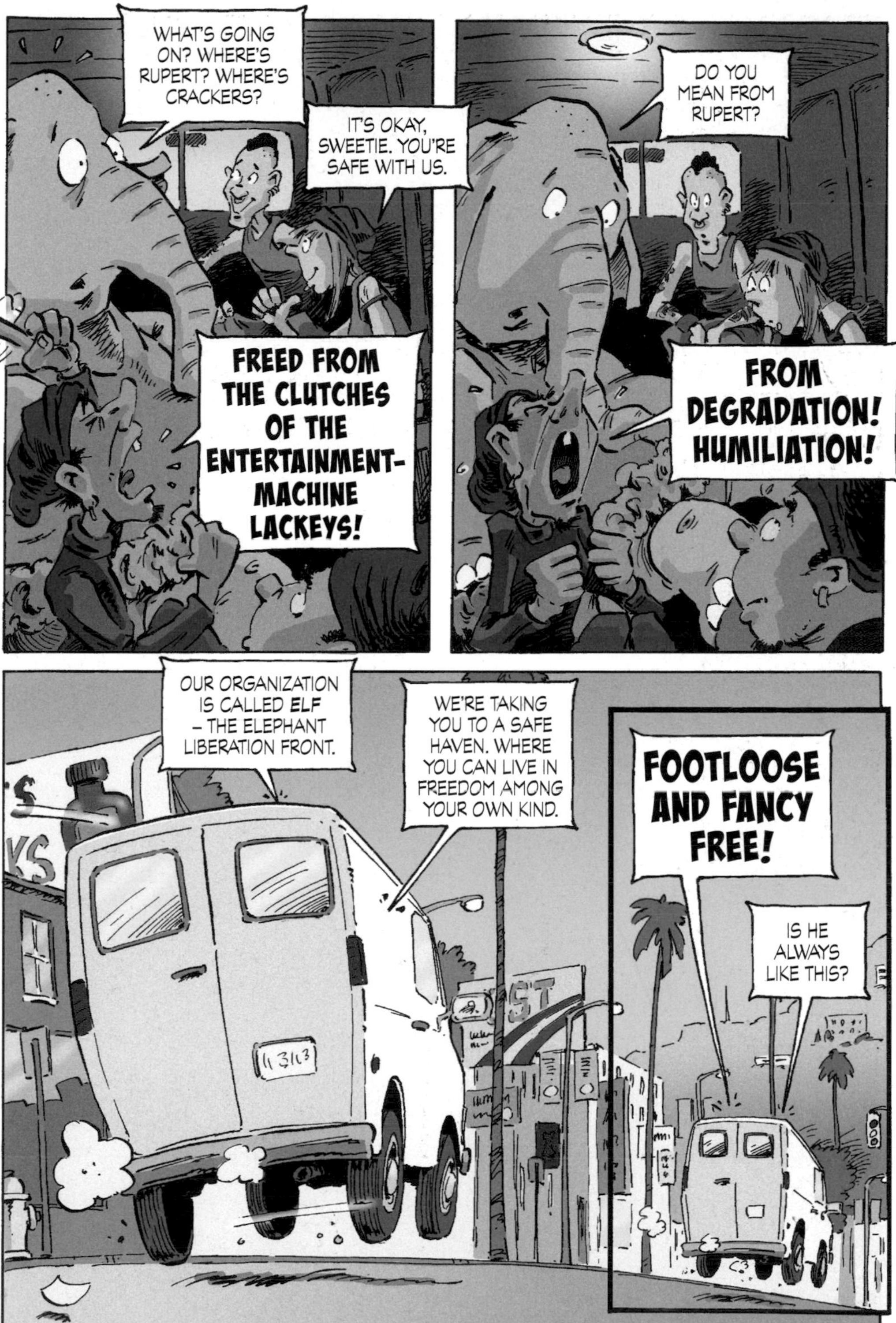
WHAT'S GOING ON? WHERE'S RUPERT? WHERE'S CRACKERS?
IT'S OKAY, SWEETIE. YOU'RE SAFE WITH US.
FREED FROM THE CLUTCHES OF THE ENTERTAINMENT-MACHINE LACKEYS!
DO YOU MEAN FROM RUPERT?
FROM DEGRADATION! HUMILIATION!
OUR ORGANIZATION IS CALLED ELF – THE ELEPHANT LIBERATION FRONT.
WE'RE TAKING YOU TO A SAFE HAVEN. WHERE YOU CAN LIVE IN FREEDOM AMONG YOUR OWN KIND.
FOOTLOOSE AND FANCY FREE!
IS HE ALWAYS LIKE THIS?

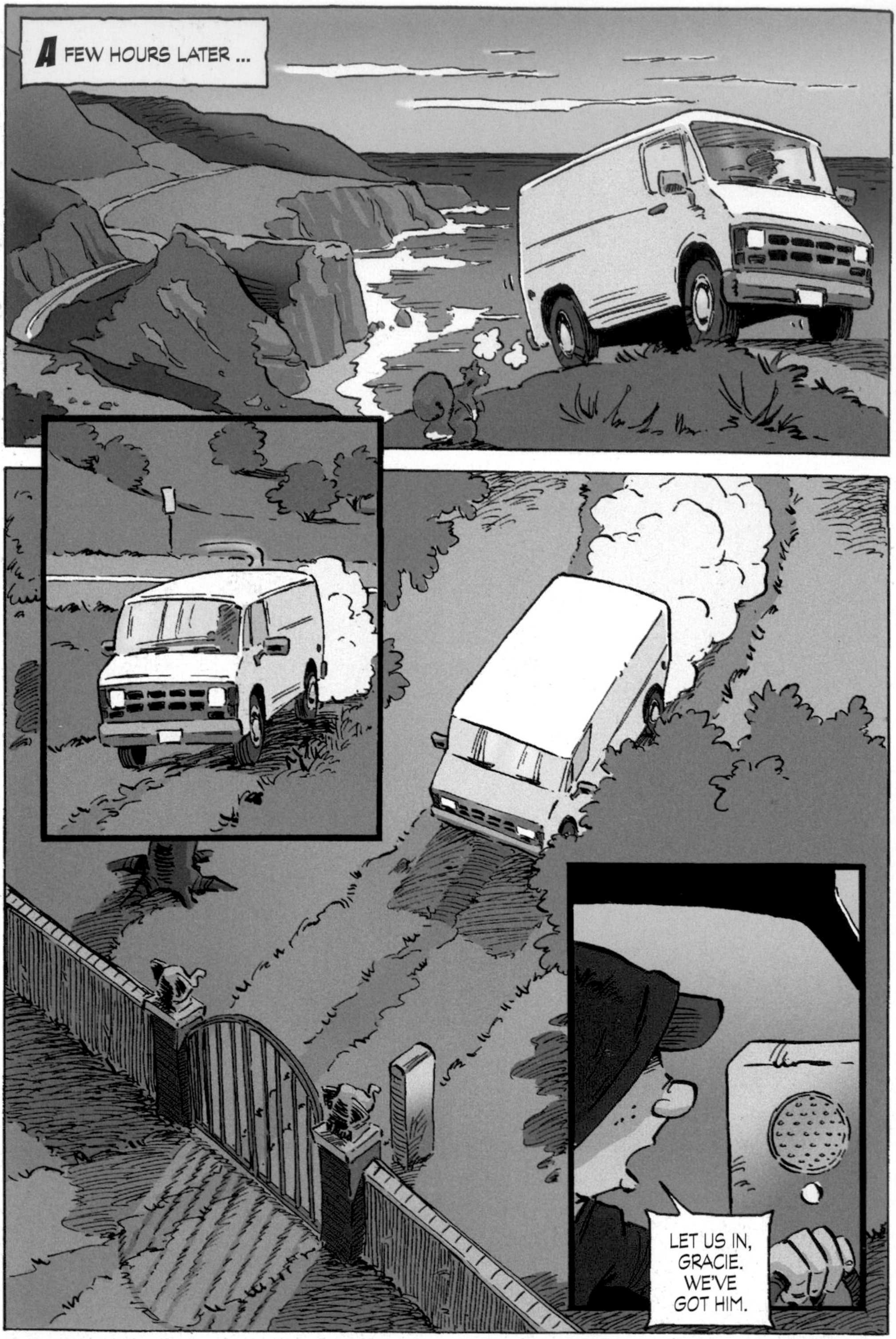
A FEW HOURS LATER ...
LET US IN, GRACIE. WE'VE GOT HIM.

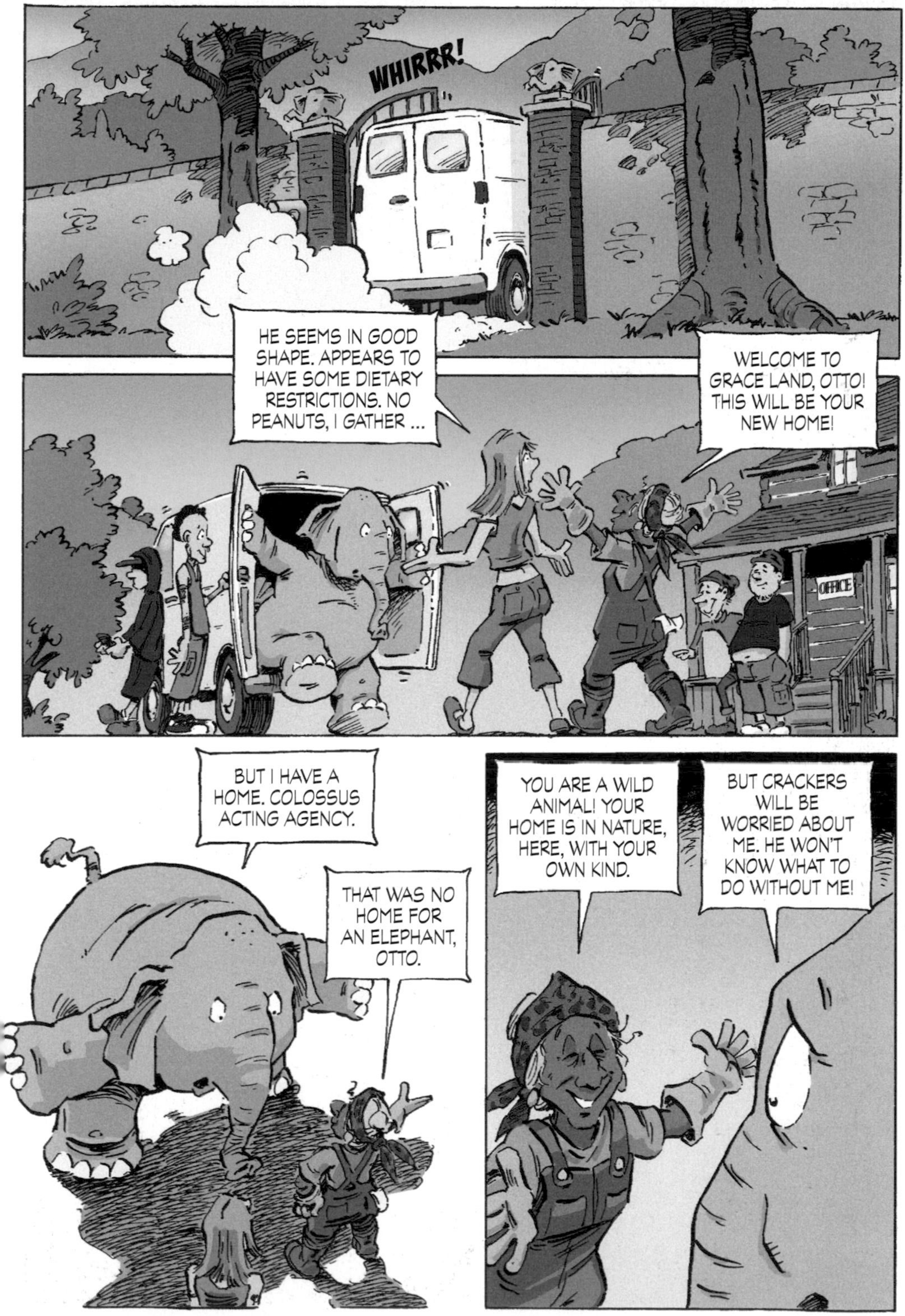
WHIRRR!
HE SEEMS IN GOOD SHAPE. APPEARS TO HAVE SOME DIETARY RESTRICTIONS. NO PEANUTS, I GATHER ...
WELCOME TO GRACE LAND, OTTO! THIS WILL BE YOUR NEW HOME!
OFFICE
BUT I HAVE A HOME. COLOSSUS ACTING AGENCY.
THAT WAS NO HOME FOR AN ELEPHANT, OTTO.
YOU ARE A WILD ANIMAL! YOUR HOME IS IN NATURE, HERE, WITH YOUR OWN KIND.
BUT CRACKERS WILL BE WORRIED ABOUT ME. HE WON'T KNOW WHAT TO DO WITHOUT ME!

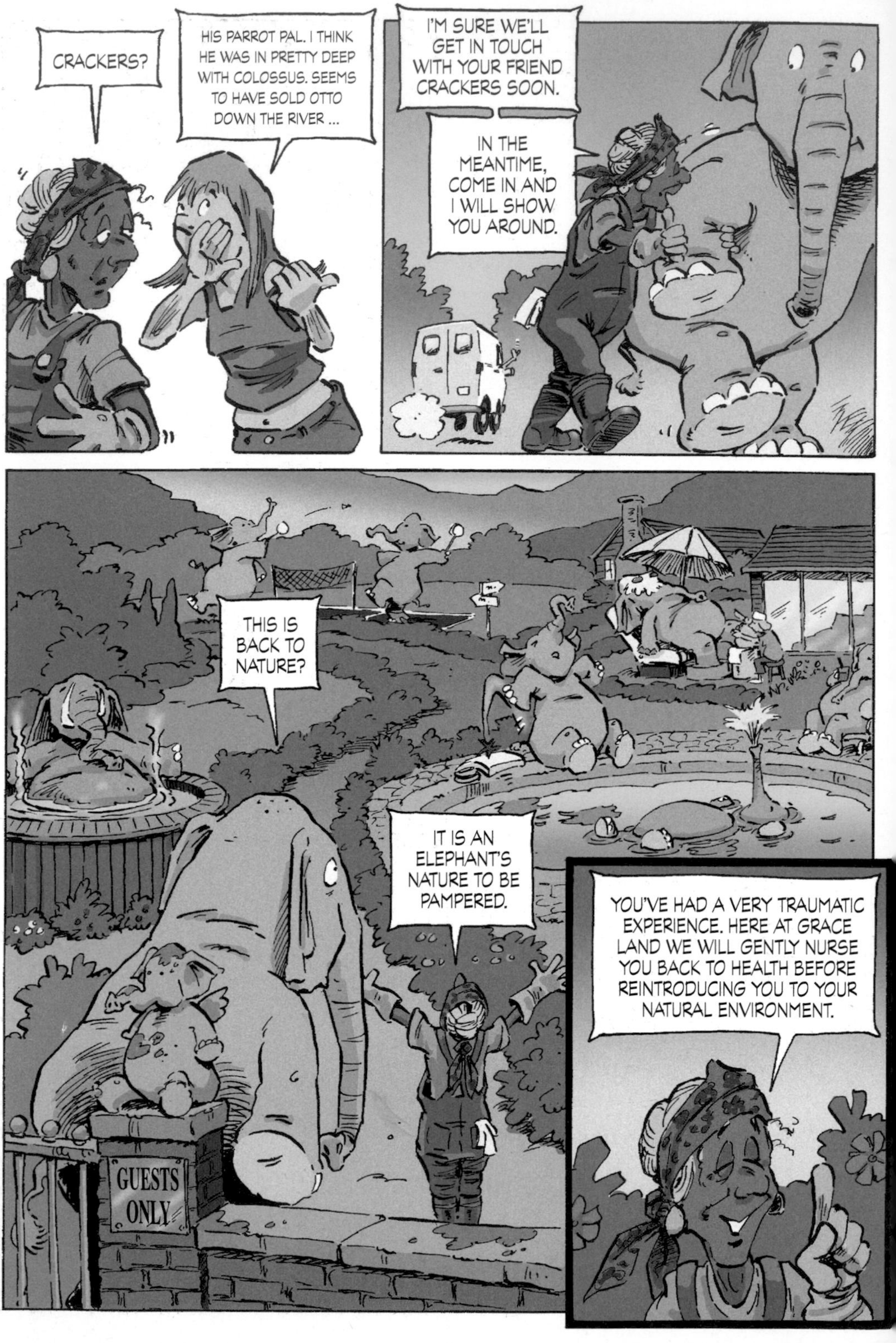
CRACKERS?
HIS PARROT PAL. I THINK HE WAS IN PRETTY DEEP WITH COLOSSUS. SEEMS TO HAVE SOLD OTTO DOWN THE RIVER ...
I'M SURE WE'LL GET IN TOUCH WITH YOUR FRIEND CRACKERS SOON.
IN THE MEANTIME, COME IN AND I WILL SHOW YOU AROUND.
THIS IS BACK TO NATURE?
IT IS AN ELEPHANT'S NATURE TO BE PAMPERED.
YOU'VE HAD A VERY TRAUMATIC EXPERIENCE. HERE AT GRACE LAND WE WILL GENTLY NURSE YOU BACK TO HEALTH BEFORE REINTRODUCING YOU TO YOUR NATURAL ENVIRONMENT.
GUESTS ONLY

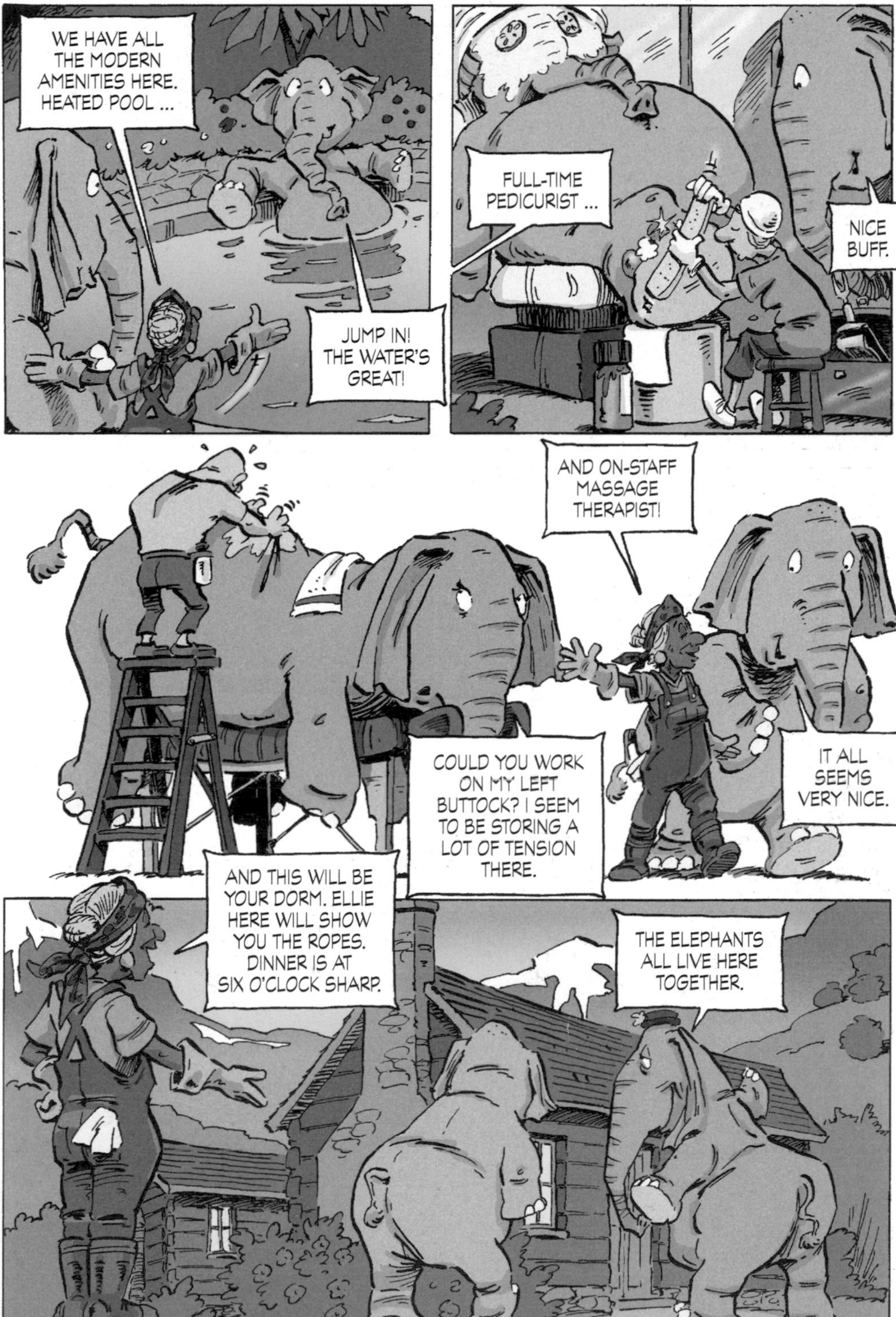
WE HAVE ALL THE MODERN AMENITIES HERE. HEATED POOL ...
JUMP IN! THE WATER'S GREAT!
FULL-TIME PEDICURIST ...
NICE BUFF.
AND ON-STAFF MASSAGE THERAPIST!
COULD YOU WORK ON MY LEFT BUTTOCK? I SEEM TO BE STORING A LOT OF TENSION THERE.
IT ALL SEEMS VERY NICE.
AND THIS WILL BE YOUR DORM. ELLIE HERE WILL SHOW YOU THE ROPES. DINNER IS AT SIX O'CLOCK SHARP.
THE ELEPHANTS ALL LIVE HERE TOGETHER.

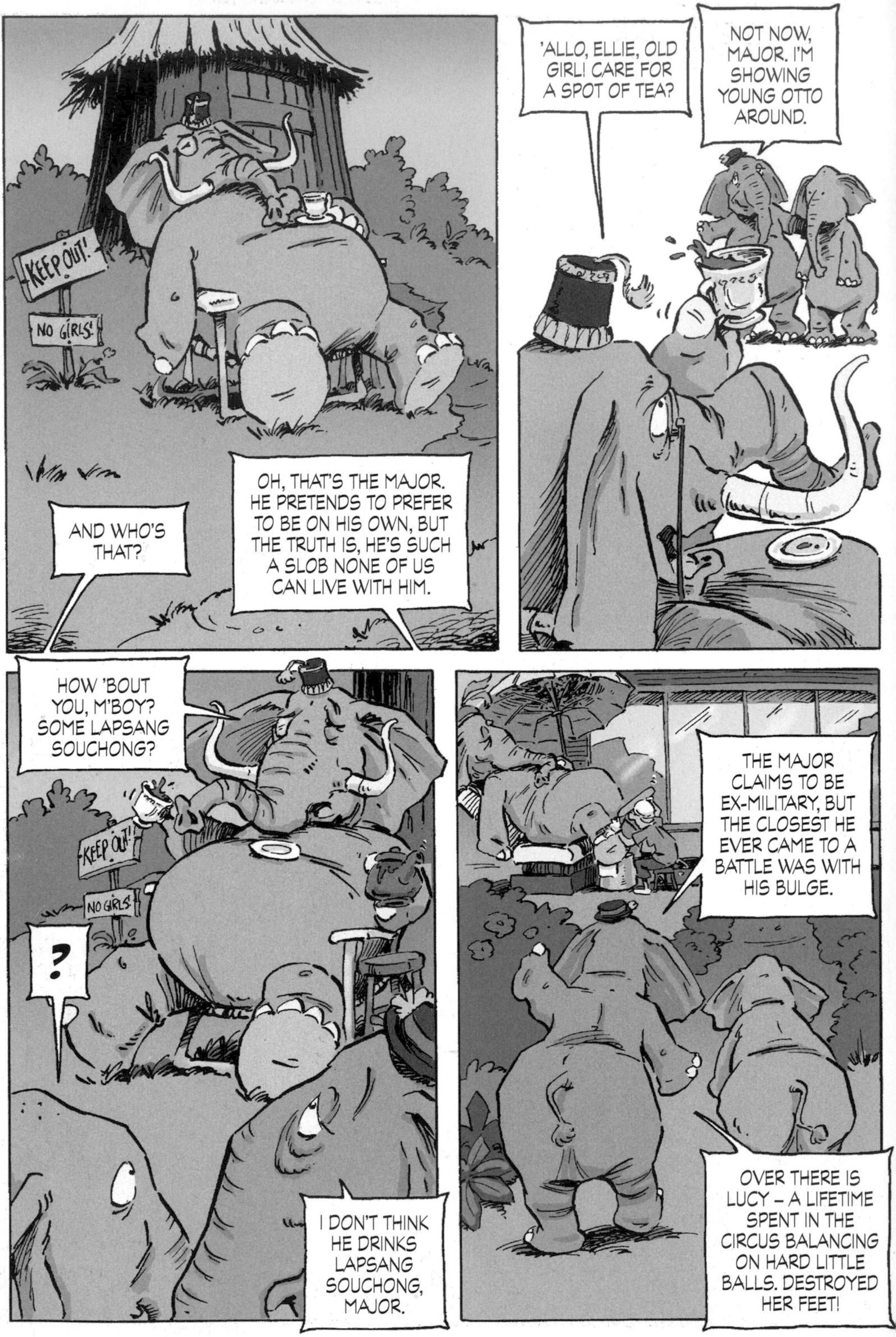
KEEP OUT!
NO GIRLS!
AND WHO'S THAT?
OH, THAT'S THE MAJOR. HE PRETENDS TO PREFER TO BE ON HIS OWN, BUT THE TRUTH IS, HE'S SUCH A SLOB NONE OF US CAN LIVE WITH HIM.
'ALLO, ELLIE, OLD GIRL! CARE FOR A SPOT OF TEA?
NOT NOW, MAJOR. I'M SHOWING YOUNG OTTO AROUND.
HOW 'BOUT YOU, M'BOY? SOME LAPSANG SOUCHONG?
KEEP OUT!
NO GIRLS!
?
I DON'T THINK HE DRINKS LAPSANG SOUCHONG, MAJOR.
THE MAJOR CLAIMS TO BE EX-MILITARY, BUT THE CLOSEST HE EVER CAME TO A BATTLE WAS WITH HIS BULGE.
OVER THERE IS LUCY – A LIFETIME SPENT IN THE CIRCUS BALANCING ON HARD LITTLE BALLS. DESTROYED HER FEET!

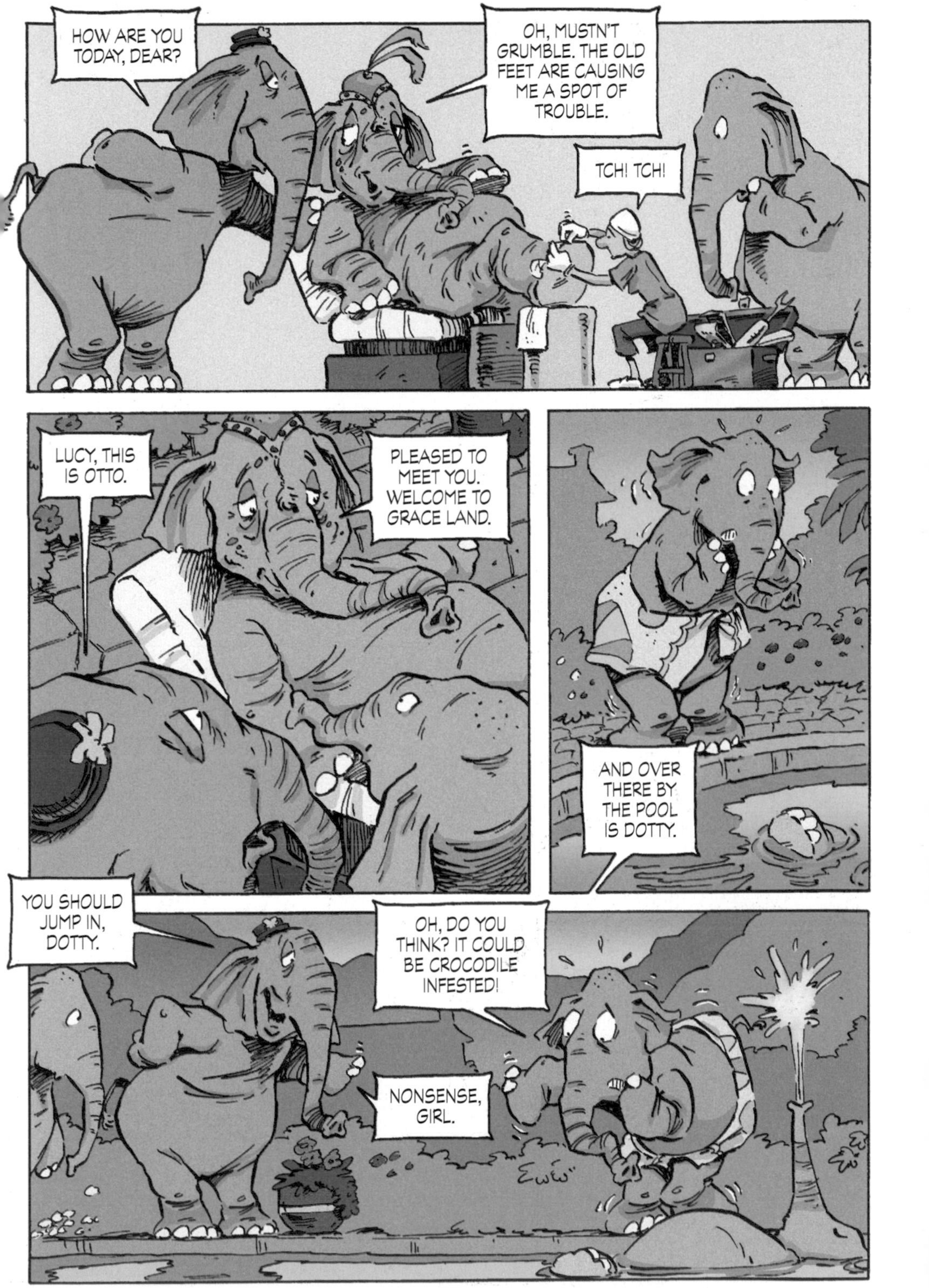
HOW ARE YOU TODAY, DEAR?
OH, MUSTN'T GRUMBLE. THE OLD FEET ARE CAUSING ME A SPOT OF TROUBLE.
TCH! TCH!
LUCY, THIS IS OTTO.
PLEASED TO MEET YOU. WELCOME TO GRACE LAND.
AND OVER THERE BY THE POOL IS DOTTY.
YOU SHOULD JUMP IN, DOTTY.
OH, DO YOU THINK? IT COULD BE CROCODILE INFESTED!
NONSENSE, GIRL.
EWW

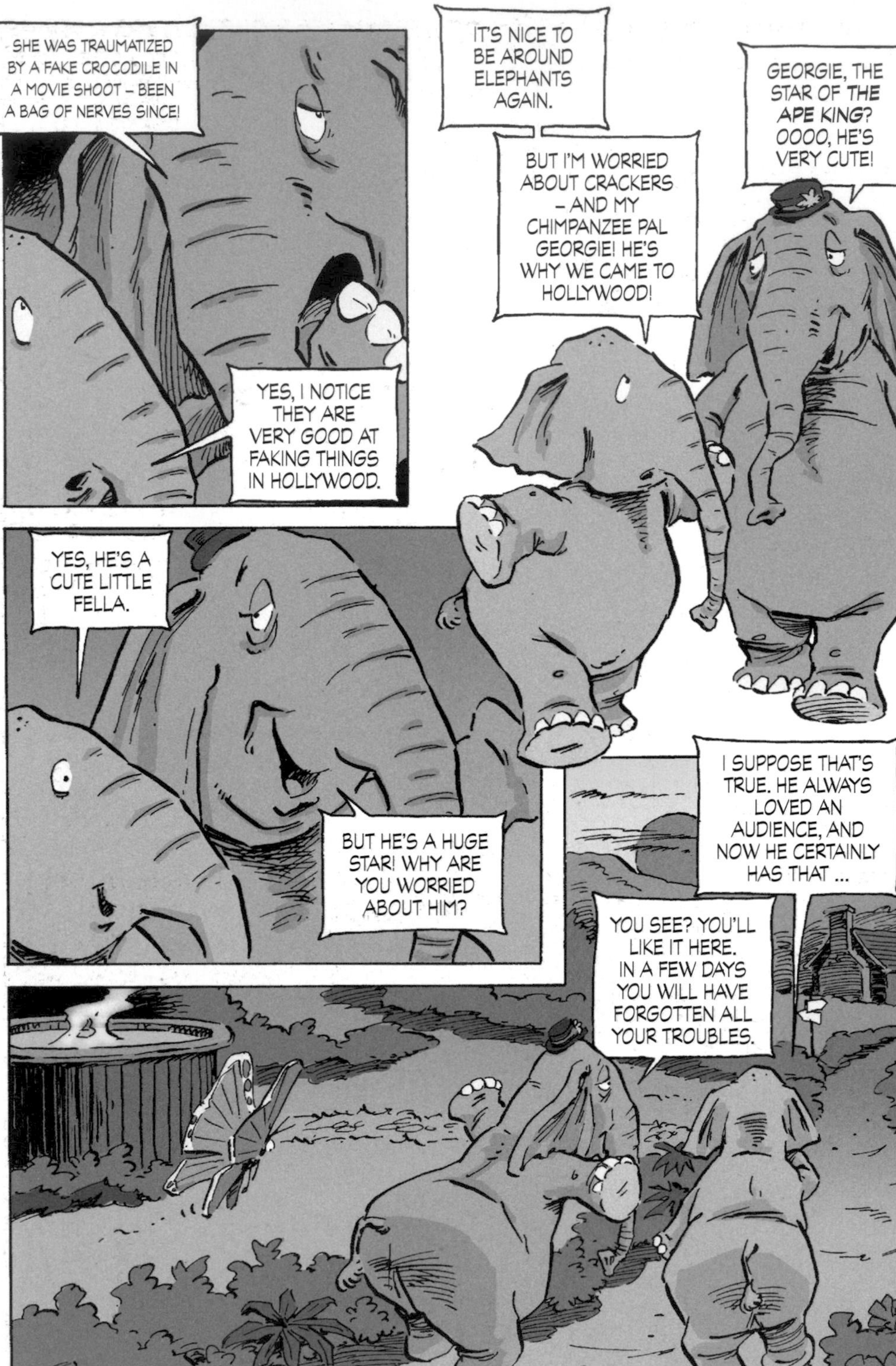
SHE WAS TRAUMATIZED BY A FAKE CROCODILE IN A MOVIE SHOOT – BEEN A BAG OF NERVES SINCE!
YES, I NOTICE THEY ARE VERY GOOD AT FAKING THINGS IN HOLLYWOOD.
IT'S NICE TO BE AROUND ELEPHANTS AGAIN.
BUT I'M WORRIED ABOUT CRACKERS – AND MY CHIMPANZEE PAL GEORGIE! HE'S WHY WE CAME TO HOLLYWOOD!
GEORGIE, THE STAR OF THE APE KING? OOOO, HE'S VERY CUTE!
YES, HE'S A CUTE LITTLE FELLA.
BUT HE'S A HUGE STAR! WHY ARE YOU WORRIED ABOUT HIM?
I SUPPOSE THAT'S TRUE. HE ALWAYS LOVED AN AUDIENCE, AND NOW HE CERTAINLY HAS THAT ...
YOU SEE? YOU'LL LIKE IT HERE. IN A FEW DAYS YOU WILL HAVE FORGOTTEN ALL YOUR TROUBLES.

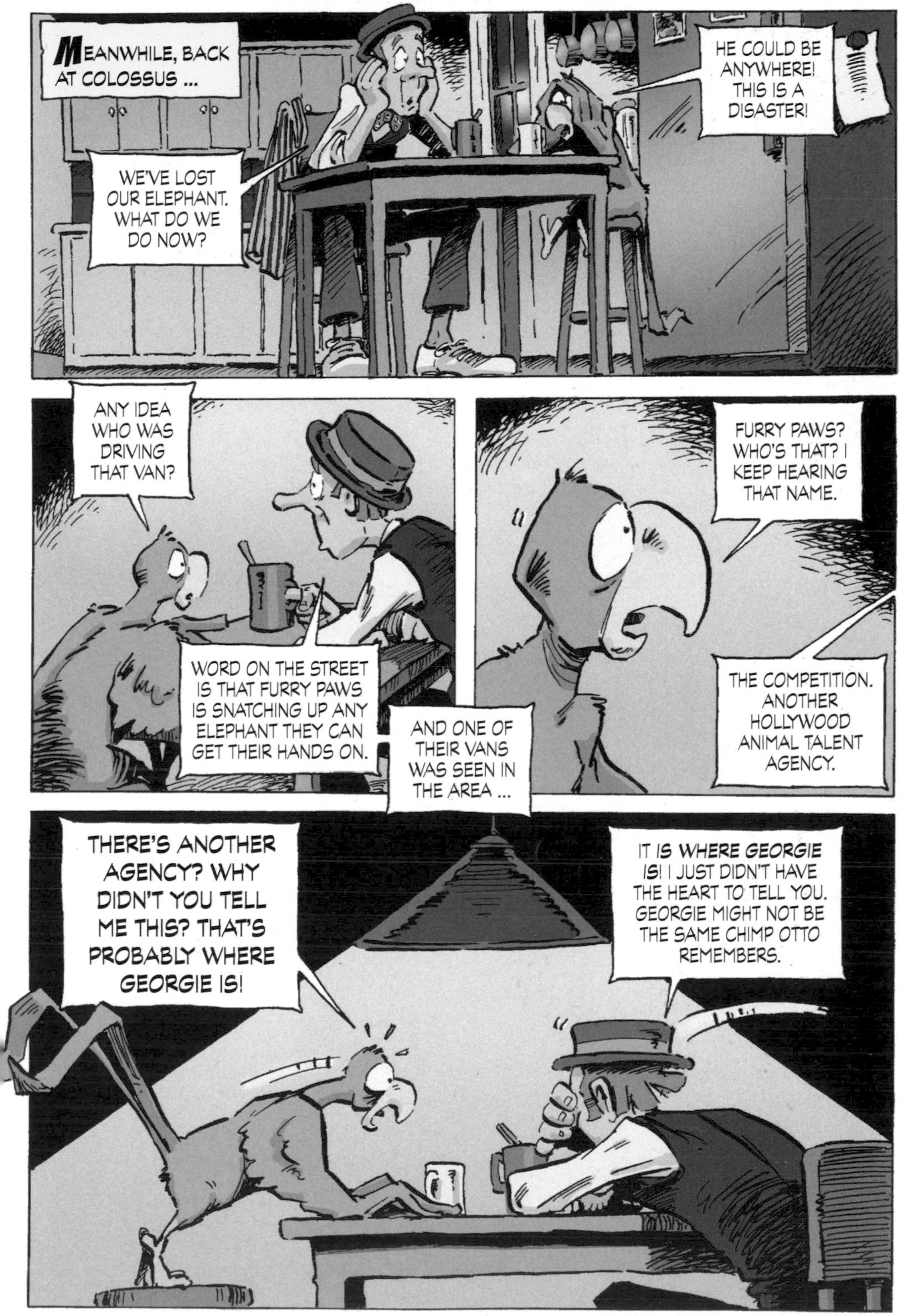
MEANWHILE, BACK AT COLOSSUS ...
WE'VE LOST OUR ELEPHANT. WHAT DO WE DO NOW?
HE COULD BE ANYWHERE! THIS IS A DISASTER!
ANY IDEA WHO WAS DRIVING THAT VAN?
WORD ON THE STREET IS THAT FURRY PAWS IS SNATCHING UP ANY ELEPHANT THEY CAN GET THEIR HANDS ON.
AND ONE OF THEIR VANS WAS SEEN IN THE AREA ...
FURRY PAWS? WHO'S THAT? I KEEP HEARING THAT NAME.
THE COMPETITION. ANOTHER HOLLYWOOD ANIMAL TALENT AGENCY.
THERE'S ANOTHER AGENCY? WHY DIDN'T YOU TELL ME THIS? THAT'S PROBABLY WHERE GEORGIE IS!
IT IS WHERE GEORGIE IS! I JUST DIDN'T HAVE THE HEART TO TELL YOU. GEORGIE MIGHT NOT BE THE SAME CHIMP OTTO REMEMBERS.

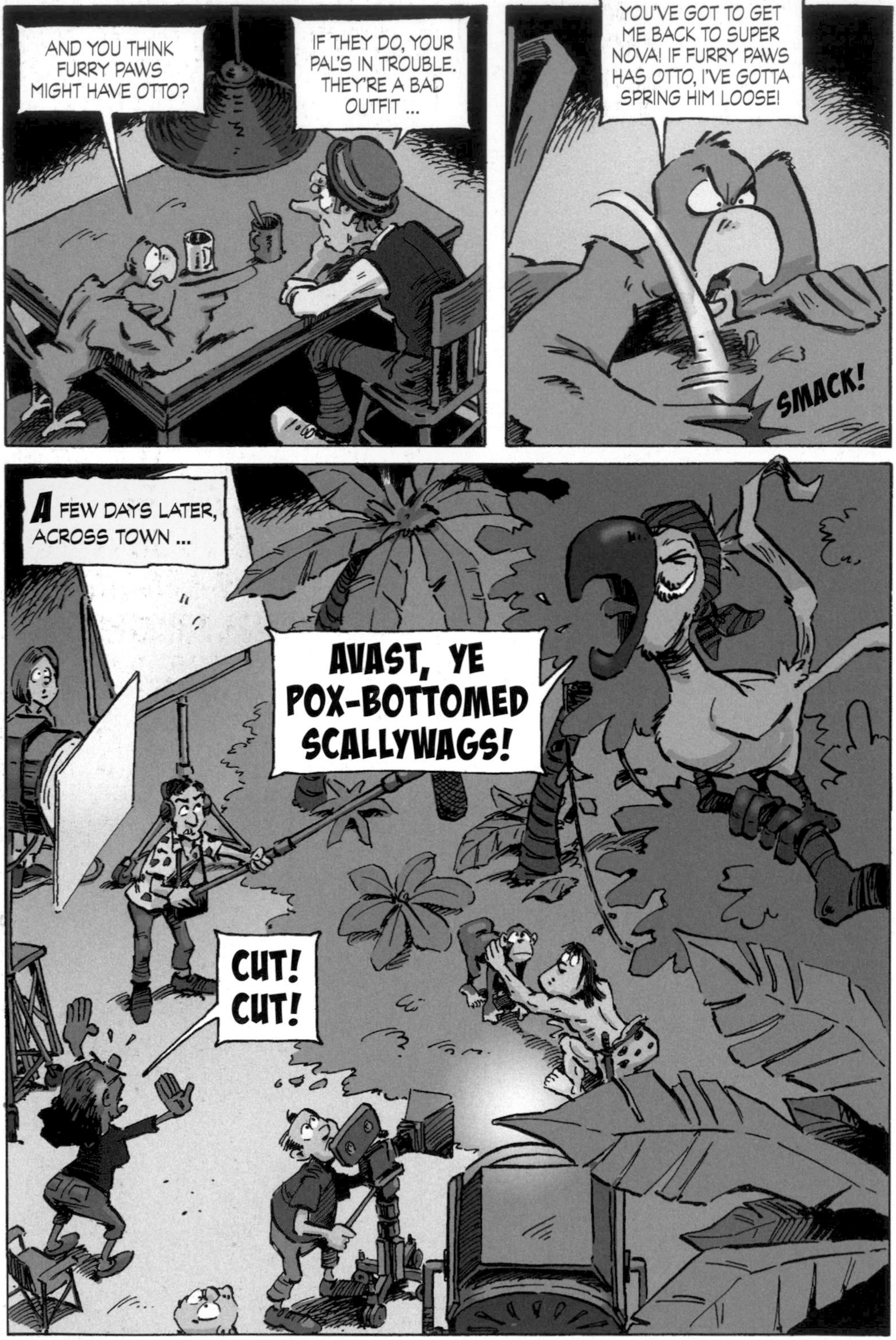
AND YOU THINK FURRY PAWS MIGHT HAVE OTTO?
IF THEY DO, YOUR PAL'S IN TROUBLE. THEY'RE A BAD OUTFIT ...
YOU'VE GOT TO GET ME BACK TO SUPER NOVA! IF FURRY PAWS HAS OTTO, I'VE GOTTA SPRING HIM LOOSE!
SMACK!
A FEW DAYS LATER, ACROSS TOWN ...
AVAST, YE POX-BOTTOMED SCALLYWAGS!
CUT! CUT!

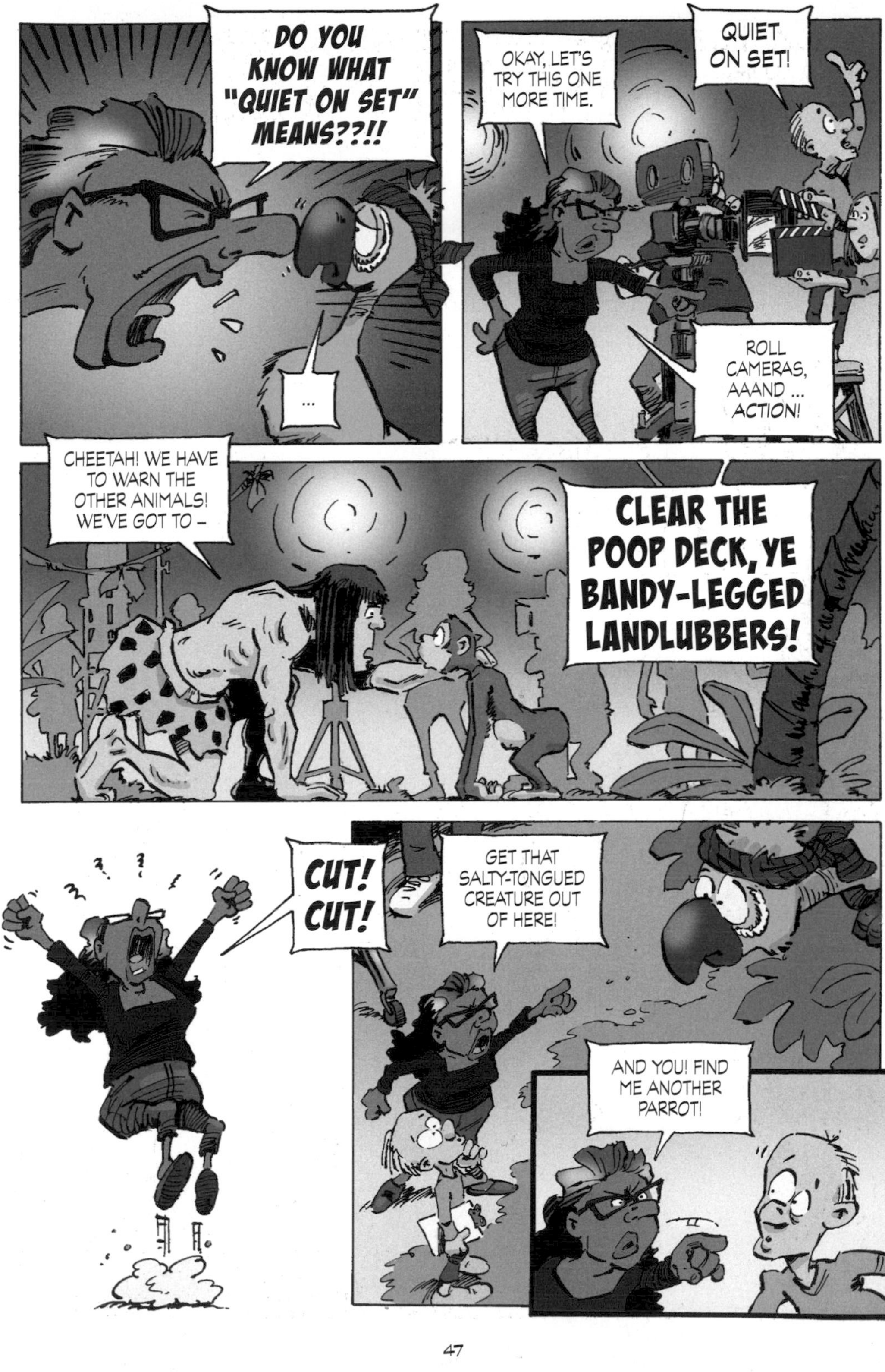
DO YOU KNOW WHAT "QUIET ON SET" MEANS??!!
...
OKAY, LET'S TRY THIS ONE MORE TIME.
QUIET ON SET!
ROLL CAMERAS, AAAND ... ACTION!
CHEETAH! WE HAVE TO WARN THE OTHER ANIMALS! WE'VE GOT TO –
CLEAR THE POOP DECK, YE BANDY-LEGGED LANDLUBBERS!
CUT! CUT!
GET THAT SALTY-TONGUED CREATURE OUT OF HERE!
AND YOU! FIND ME ANOTHER PARROT!

THAT PIRATIC SQUAB WAS THE ONLY GREEN PARROT FURRY PAWS HAD! WHAT DO I DO NOW?

BZZT!

WHAT?

CARLO, MY BOY! HOW ARE THINGS HANGING AT SUPER NOVA? WE NEED TO DO BUSINESS!

UNLESS YOU HAVE AN AFRICAN GREEN PARROT, GALLOWAY, I'VE BEEN HUNG OUT TO DRY!

AN AFRICAN GREEN? REALLY? WELL, AS A MATTER OF FACT, THIS MAY BE YOUR LUCKY DAY ...

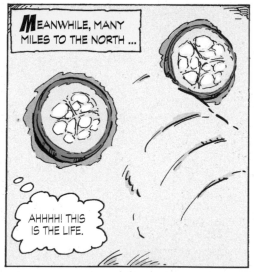

*M*EANWHILE, MANY MILES TO THE NORTH ...

AHHHH! THIS IS THE LIFE.

WAITER! ANOTHER GUAVA JUICE, PLEASE!

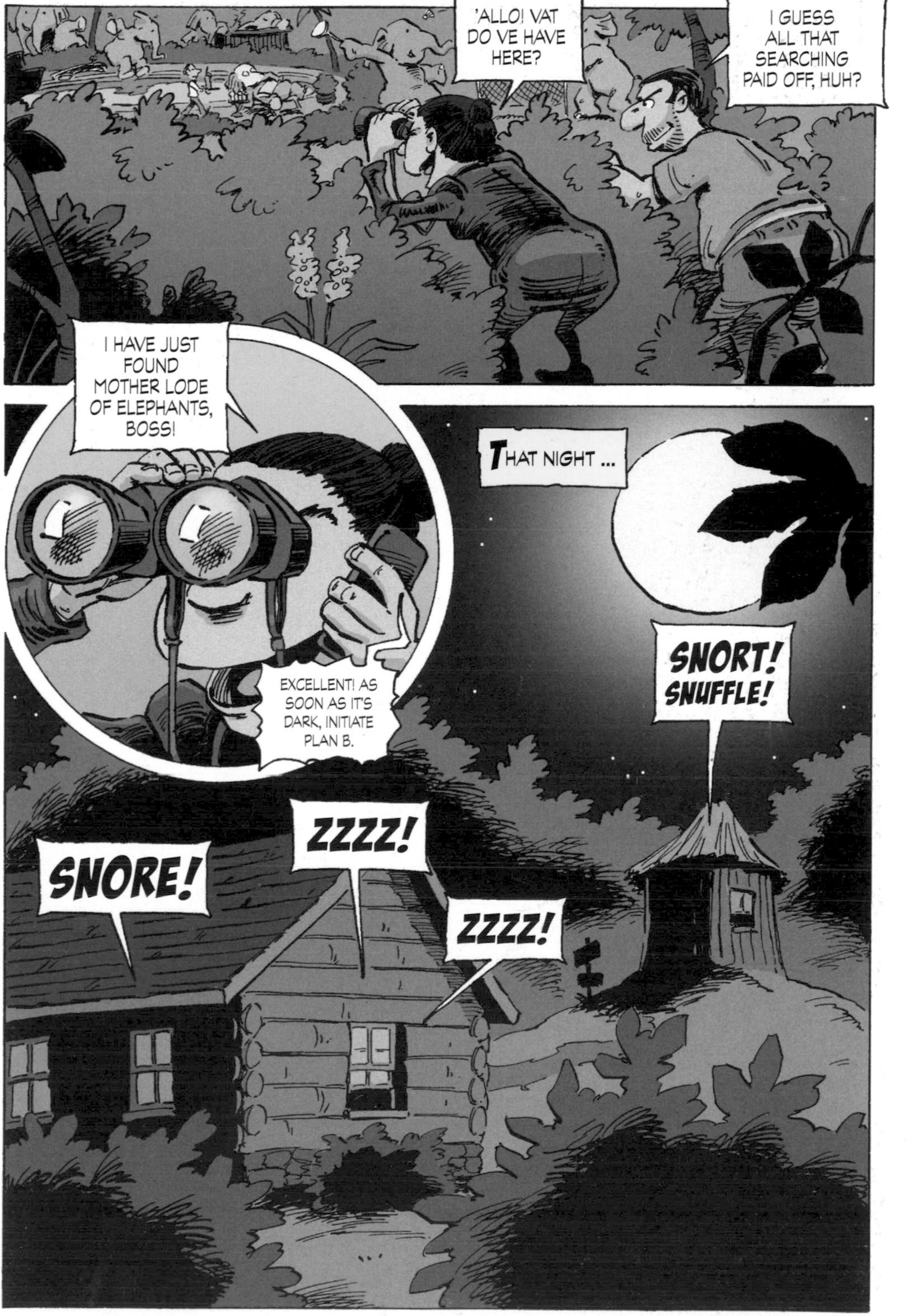
'ALLO! VAT DO VE HAVE HERE?
I GUESS ALL THAT SEARCHING PAID OFF, HUH?
I HAVE JUST FOUND MOTHER LODE OF ELEPHANTS, BOSS!
EXCELLENT! AS SOON AS IT'S DARK, INITIATE PLAN B.
THAT NIGHT ...
SNORT! SNUFFLE!
SNORE!
ZZZZ!
ZZZZ!

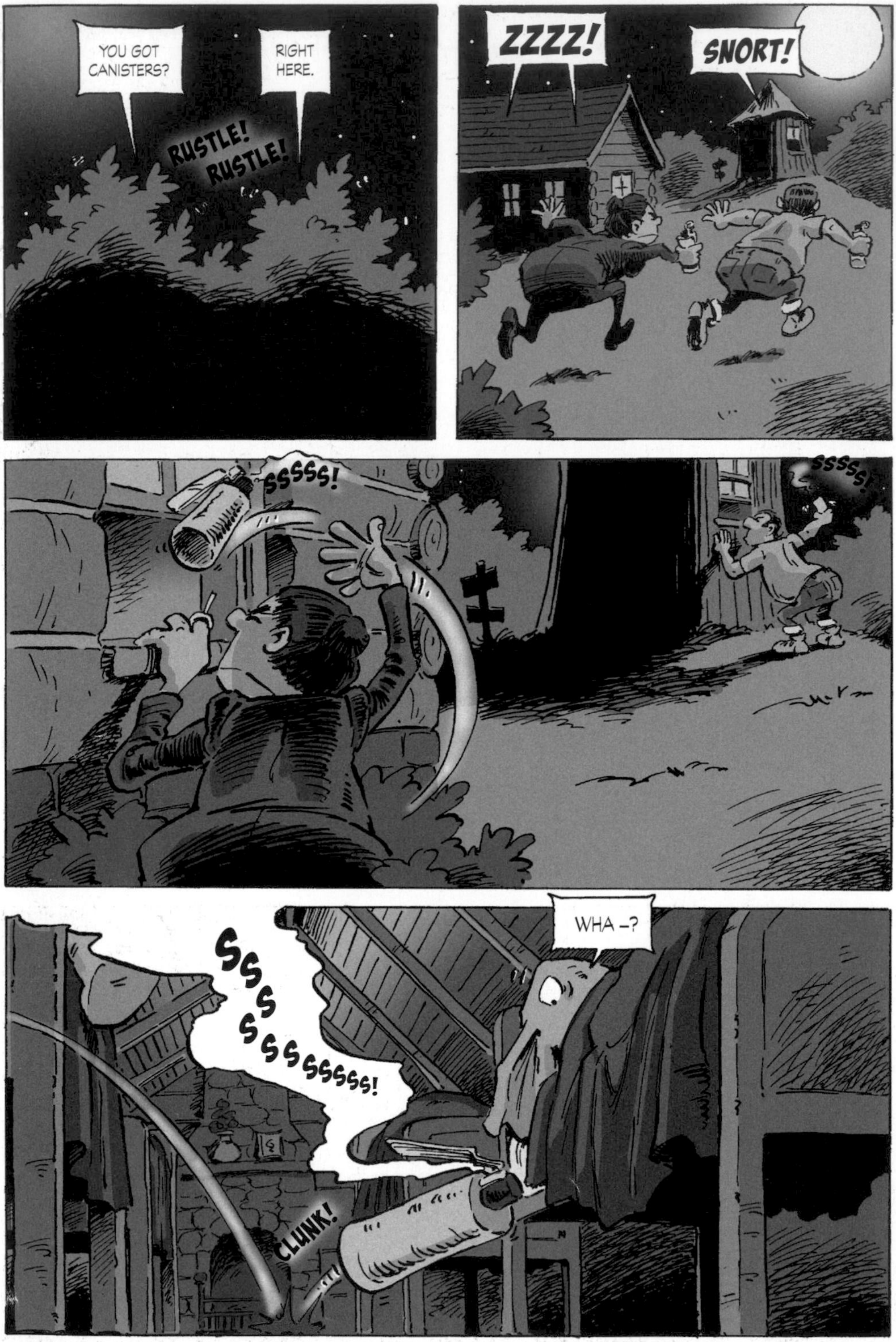
YOU GOT CANISTERS?
RIGHT HERE.
RUSTLE! RUSTLE!
ZZZZ!
SNORT!
SSSSS!
SSSSS!
WHA –?
SSSSSSSSSSS!
CLUNK!

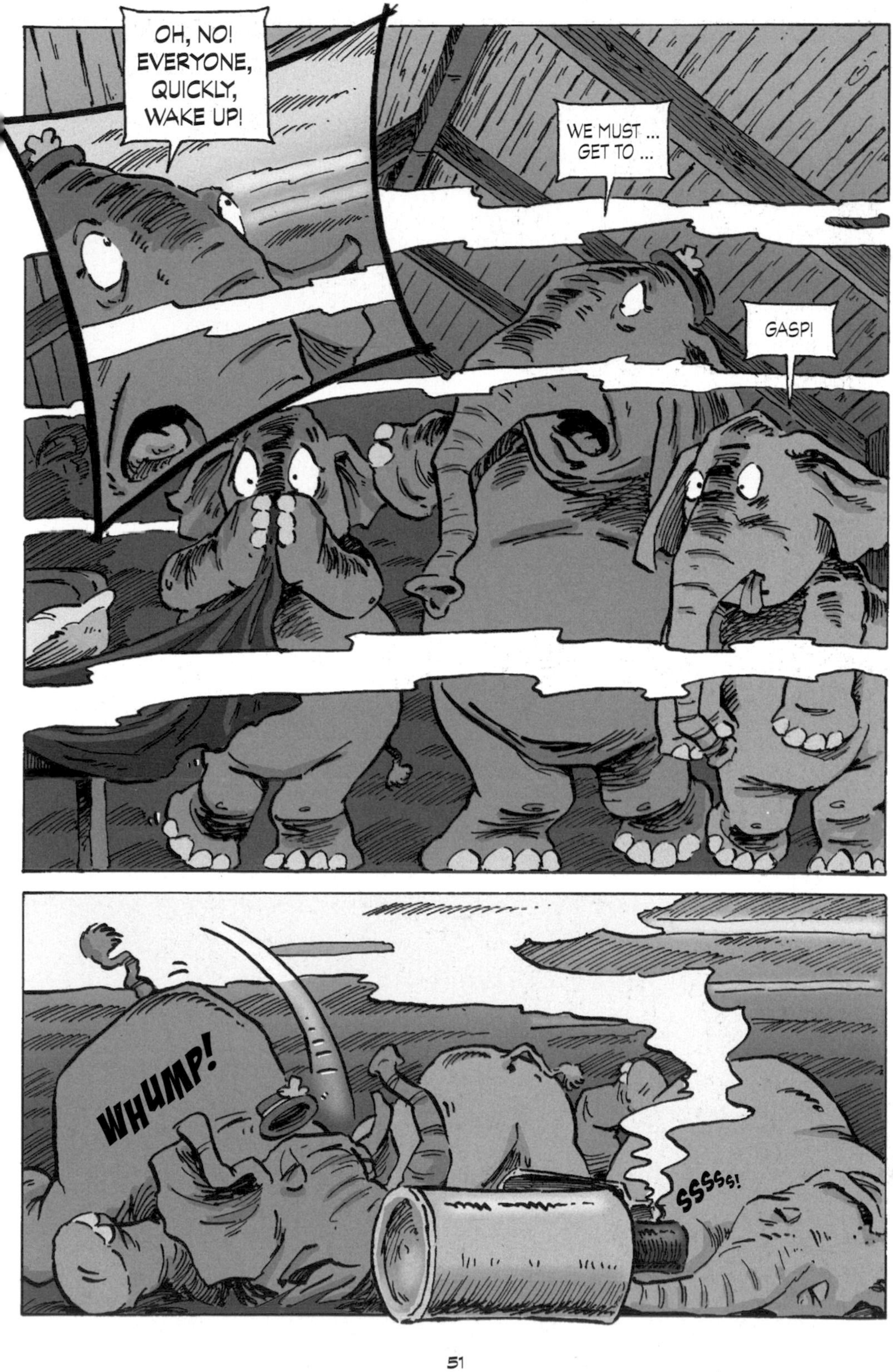
OH, NO! EVERYONE, QUICKLY, WAKE UP!
WE MUST ... GET TO ...
GASP!
WHUMP!
SSSSS!

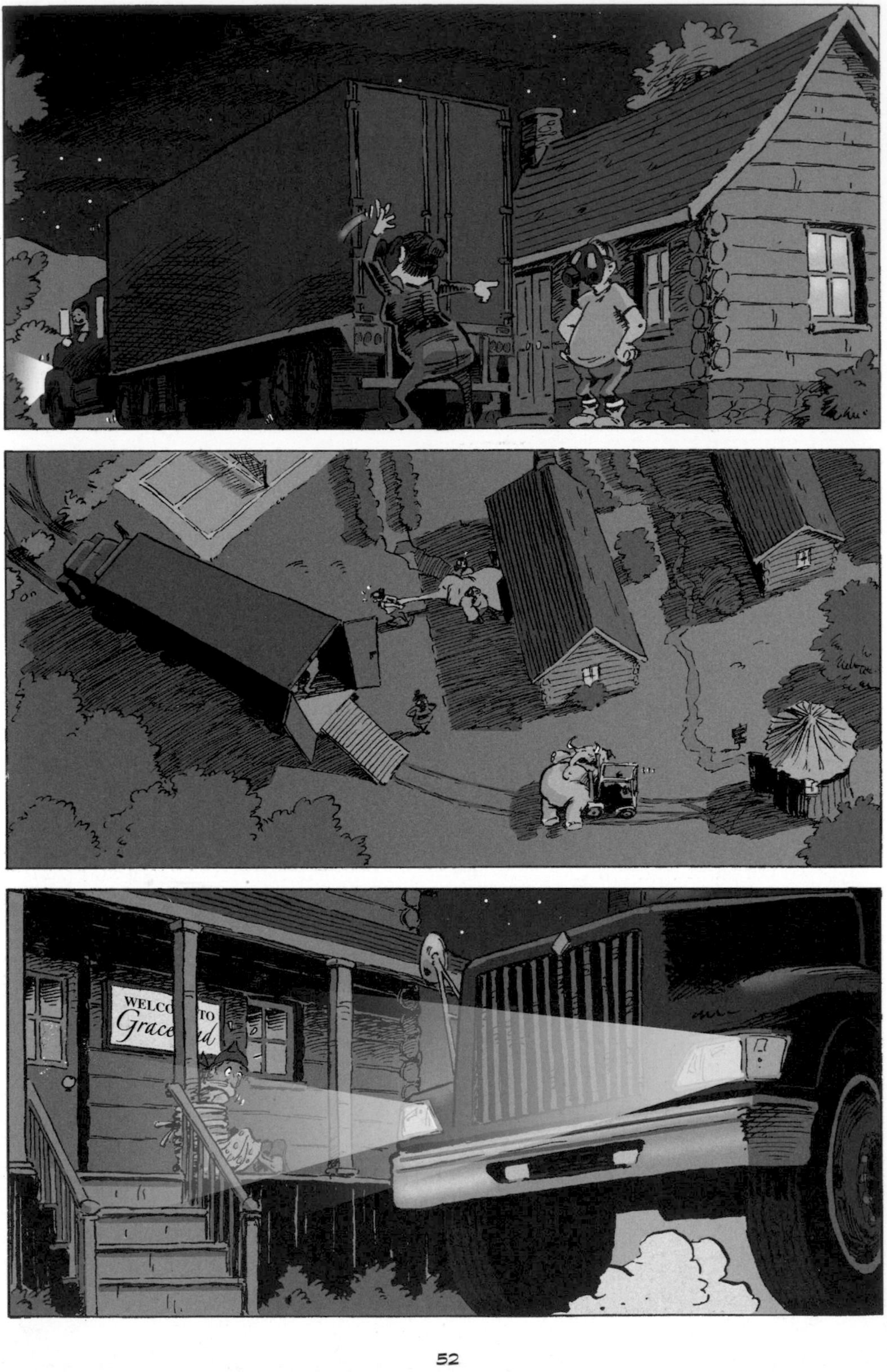
WELCO TO
Grace

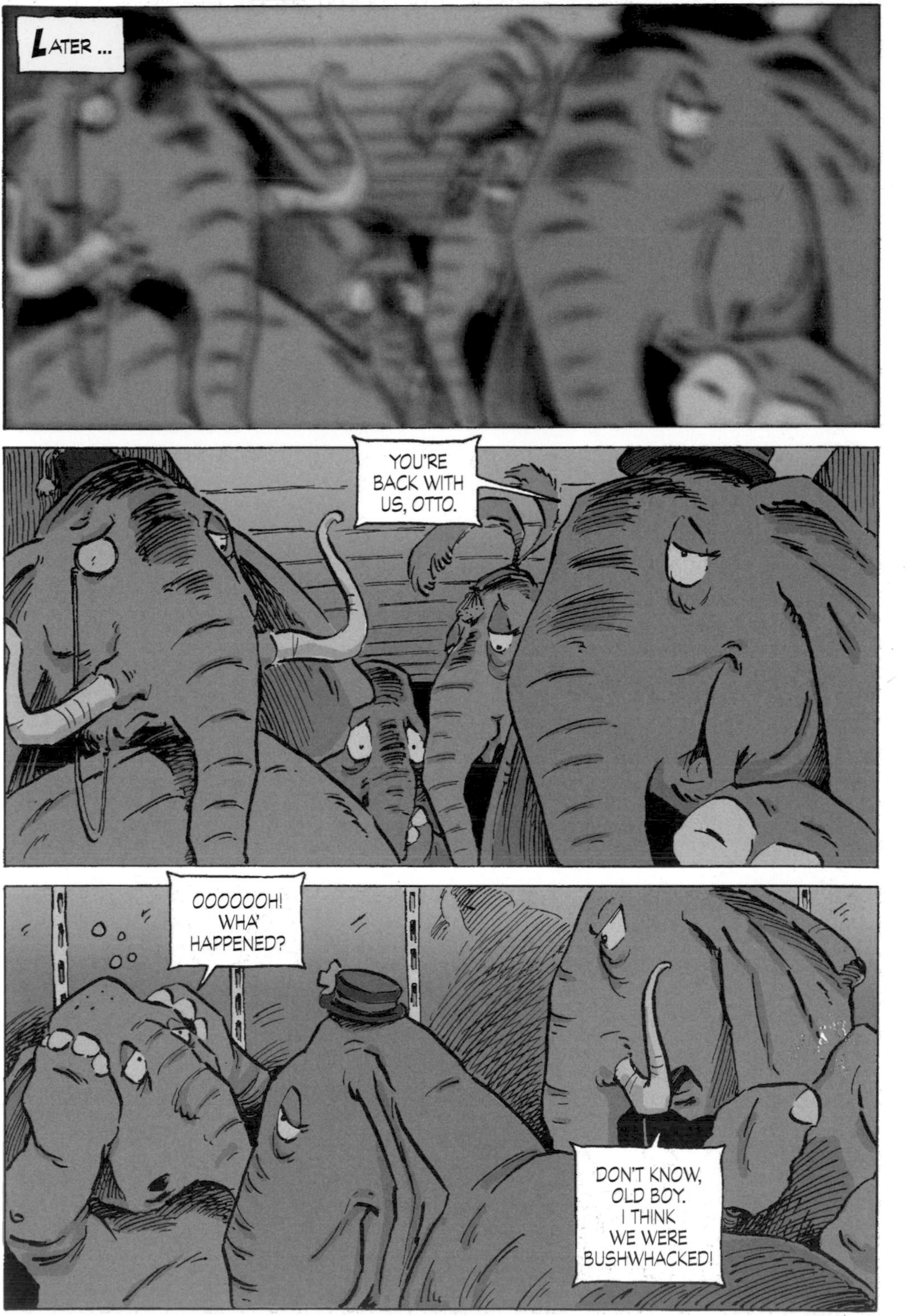
LATER ...
YOU'RE BACK WITH US, OTTO.
OOOOOOH! WHA' HAPPENED?
DON'T KNOW, OLD BOY. I THINK WE WERE BUSHWHACKED!

CREAK!

GOOD! ELEPHANTS NOT SLEEPINK? GET THEM OUT OF TRUCK. THEY HAVE VORK TO DO!

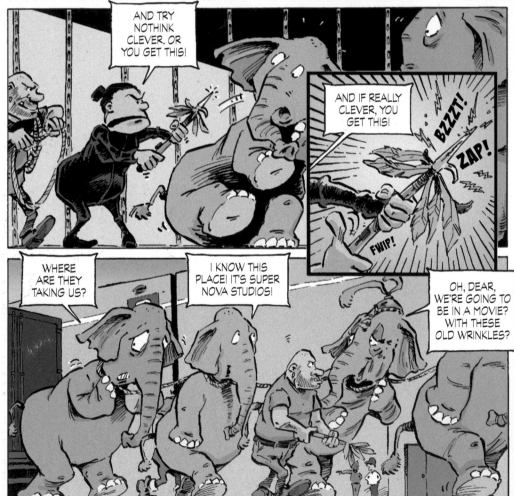

AND TRY NOTHINK CLEVER. OR YOU GET THIS!

AND IF REALLY CLEVER, YOU GET THIS!

BZZZT!

ZAP!

FWIP!

WHERE ARE THEY TAKING US?

I KNOW THIS PLACE! IT'S SUPER NOVA STUDIOS!

OH, DEAR, WE'RE GOING TO BE IN A MOVIE? WITH THESE OLD WRINKLES?

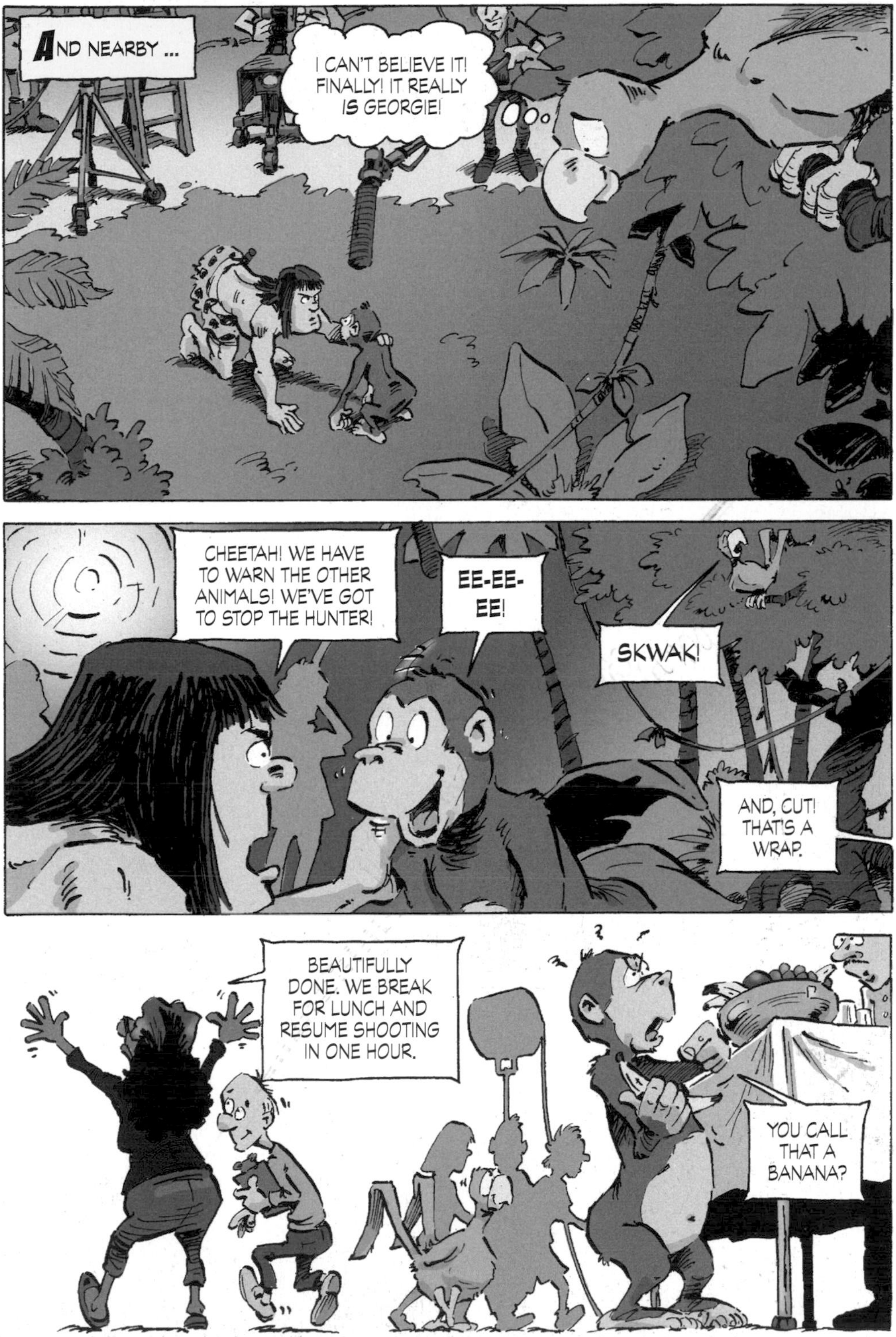
AND NEARBY ...
I CAN'T BELIEVE IT! FINALLY! IT REALLY IS GEORGIE!
CHEETAH! WE HAVE TO WARN THE OTHER ANIMALS! WE'VE GOT TO STOP THE HUNTER!
EE-EE-EE!
SKWAK!
AND, CUT! THAT'S A WRAP.
BEAUTIFULLY DONE. WE BREAK FOR LUNCH AND RESUME SHOOTING IN ONE HOUR.
YOU CALL THAT A BANANA?

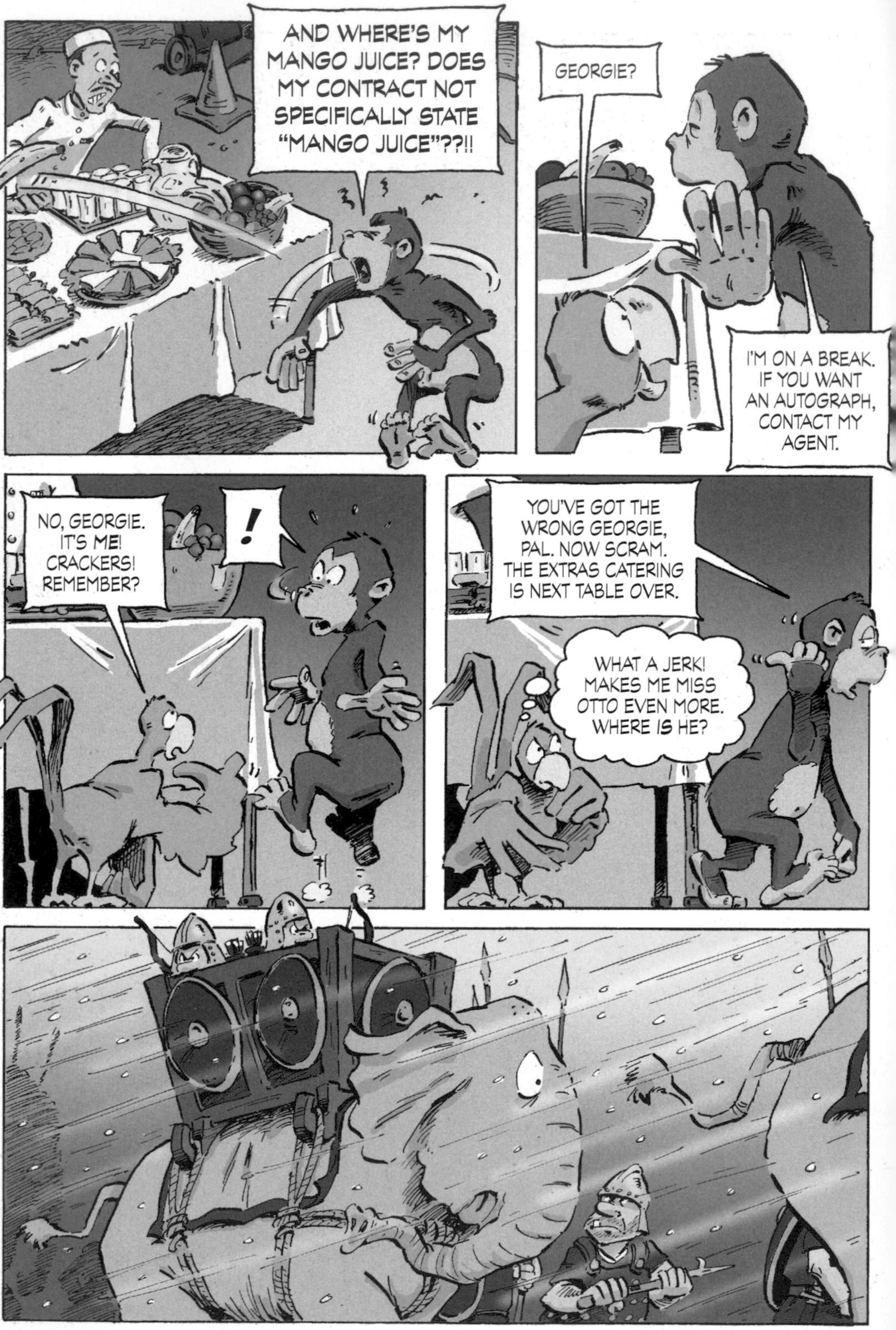
AND WHERE'S MY MANGO JUICE? DOES MY CONTRACT NOT SPECIFICALLY STATE "MANGO JUICE"??!!
GEORGIE?
I'M ON A BREAK. IF YOU WANT AN AUTOGRAPH, CONTACT MY AGENT.
NO, GEORGIE. IT'S ME! CRACKERS! REMEMBER?
!
YOU'VE GOT THE WRONG GEORGIE, PAL. NOW SCRAM. THE EXTRAS CATERING IS NEXT TABLE OVER.
WHAT A JERK! MAKES ME MISS OTTO EVEN MORE. WHERE IS HE?

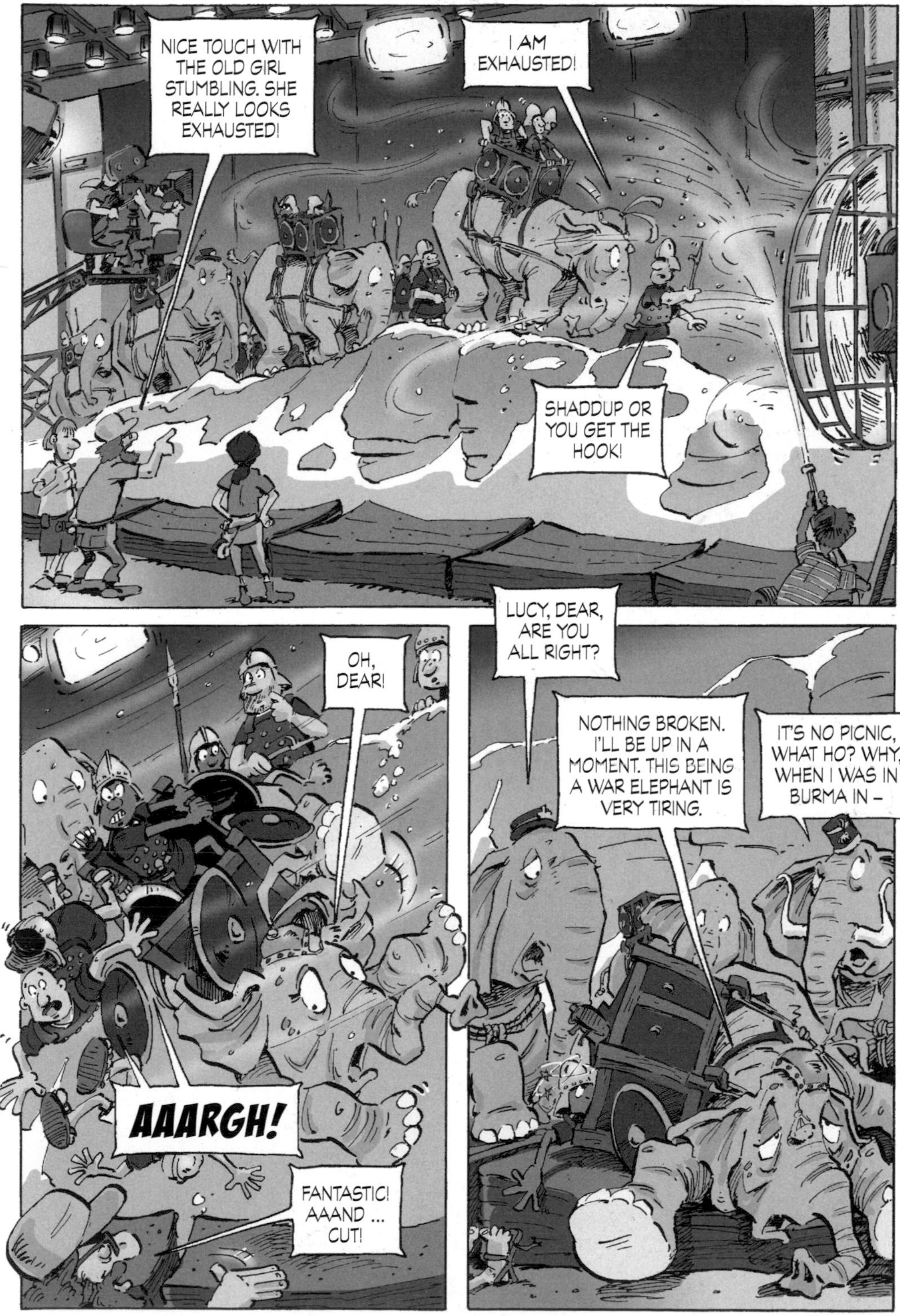
NICE TOUCH WITH THE OLD GIRL STUMBLING. SHE REALLY LOOKS EXHAUSTED!
I AM EXHAUSTED!
SHADDUP OR YOU GET THE HOOK!
OH, DEAR!
AAARGH!
FANTASTIC! AAAND ... CUT!
LUCY, DEAR, ARE YOU ALL RIGHT?
NOTHING BROKEN. I'LL BE UP IN A MOMENT. THIS BEING A WAR ELEPHANT IS VERY TIRING.
IT'S NO PICNIC, WHAT HO? WHY, WHEN I WAS IN BURMA IN –

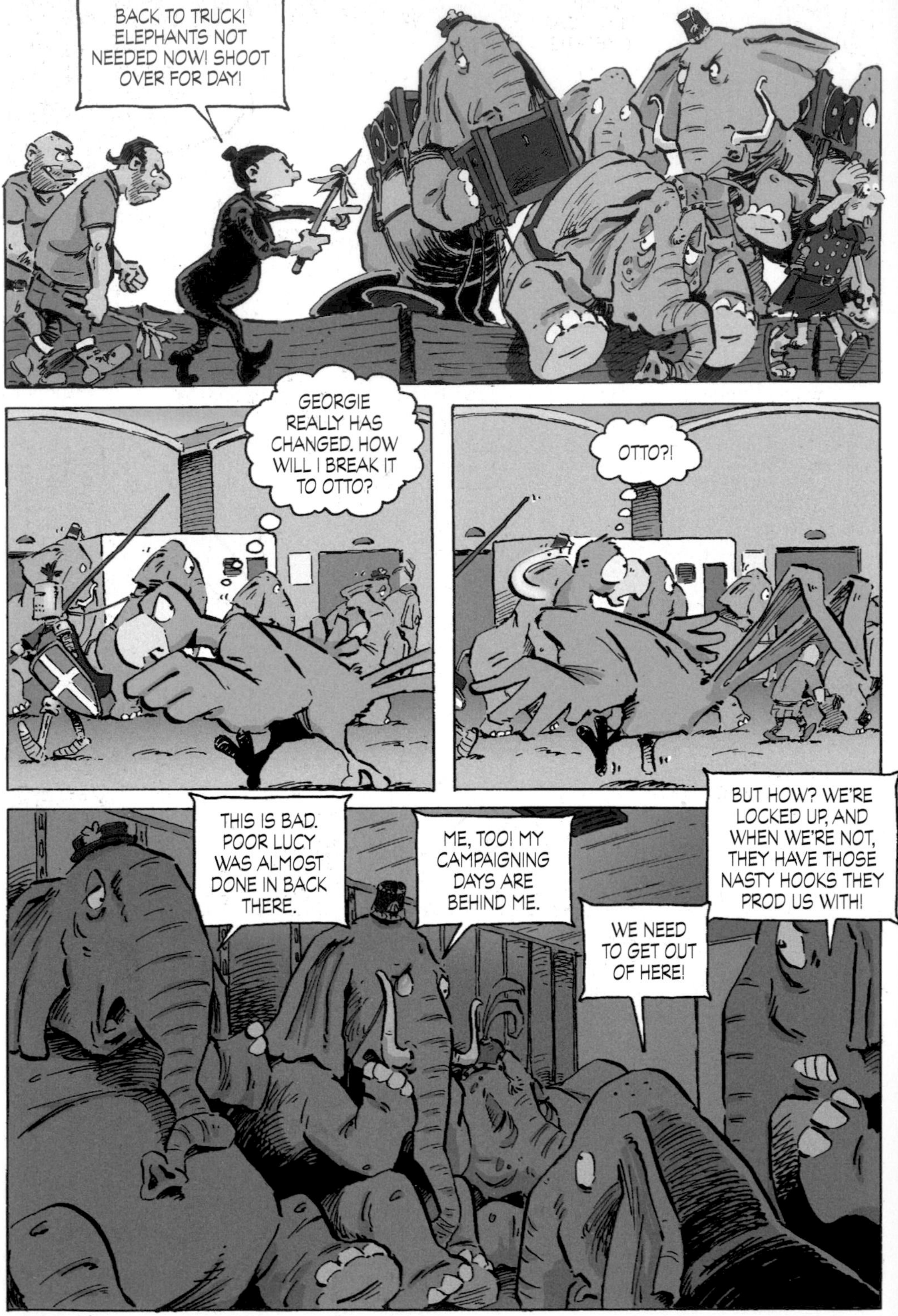
BACK TO TRUCK! ELEPHANTS NOT NEEDED NOW! SHOOT OVER FOR DAY!
GEORGIE REALLY HAS CHANGED. HOW WILL I BREAK IT TO OTTO?
OTTO?!
THIS IS BAD. POOR LUCY WAS ALMOST DONE IN BACK THERE.
ME, TOO! MY CAMPAIGNING DAYS ARE BEHIND ME.
WE NEED TO GET OUT OF HERE!
BUT HOW? WE'RE LOCKED UP, AND WHEN WE'RE NOT, THEY HAVE THOSE NASTY HOOKS THEY PROD US WITH!

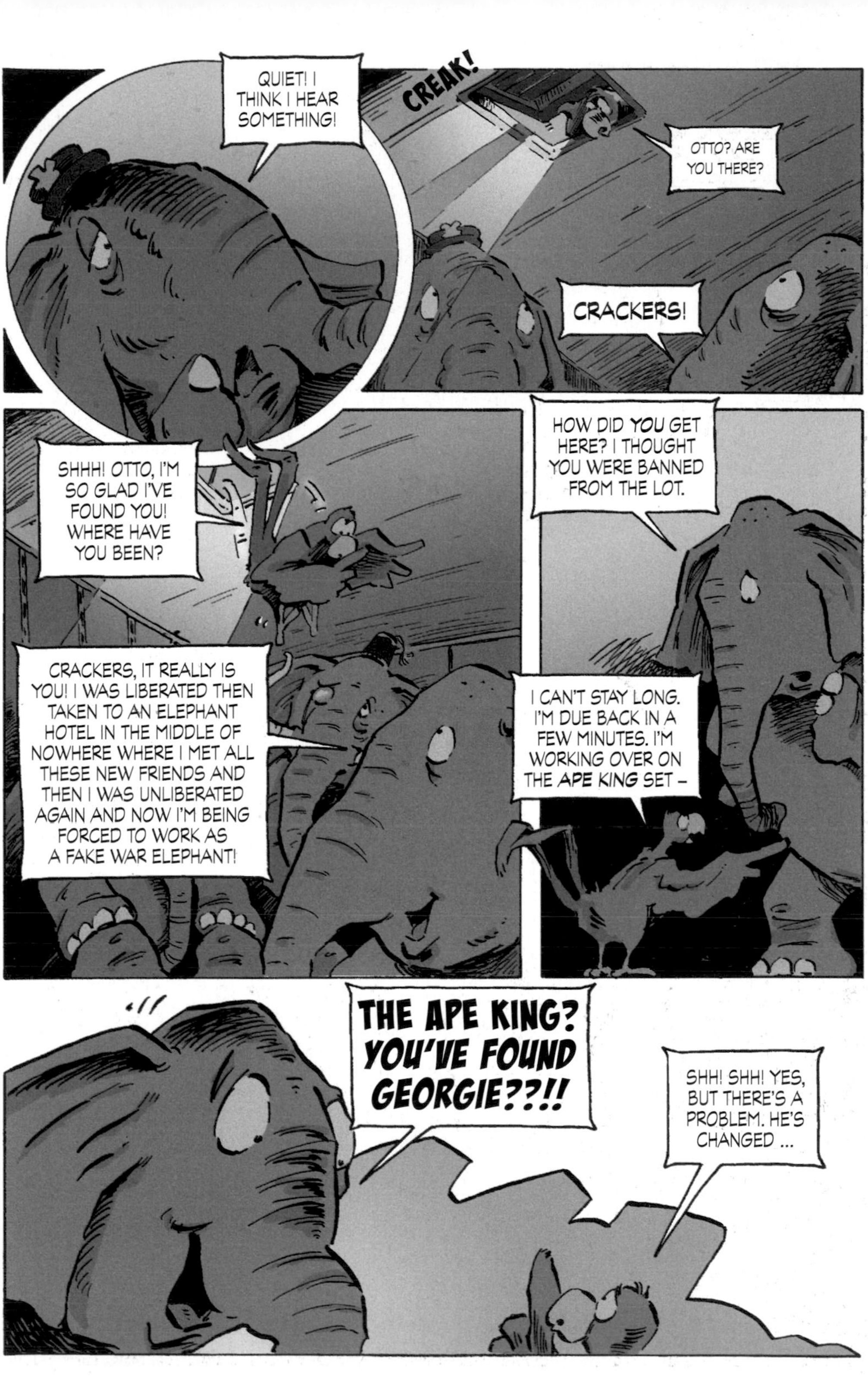
QUIET! I THINK I HEAR SOMETHING!
CREAK!
OTTO? ARE YOU THERE?
CRACKERS!
SHHH! OTTO, I'M SO GLAD I'VE FOUND YOU! WHERE HAVE YOU BEEN?
CRACKERS, IT REALLY IS YOU! I WAS LIBERATED THEN TAKEN TO AN ELEPHANT HOTEL IN THE MIDDLE OF NOWHERE WHERE I MET ALL THESE NEW FRIENDS AND THEN I WAS UNLIBERATED AGAIN AND NOW I'M BEING FORCED TO WORK AS A FAKE WAR ELEPHANT!
HOW DID YOU GET HERE? I THOUGHT YOU WERE BANNED FROM THE LOT.
I CAN'T STAY LONG. I'M DUE BACK IN A FEW MINUTES. I'M WORKING OVER ON THE APE KING SET –
THE APE KING? YOU'VE FOUND GEORGIE??!!
SHH! SHH! YES, BUT THERE'S A PROBLEM. HE'S CHANGED ...

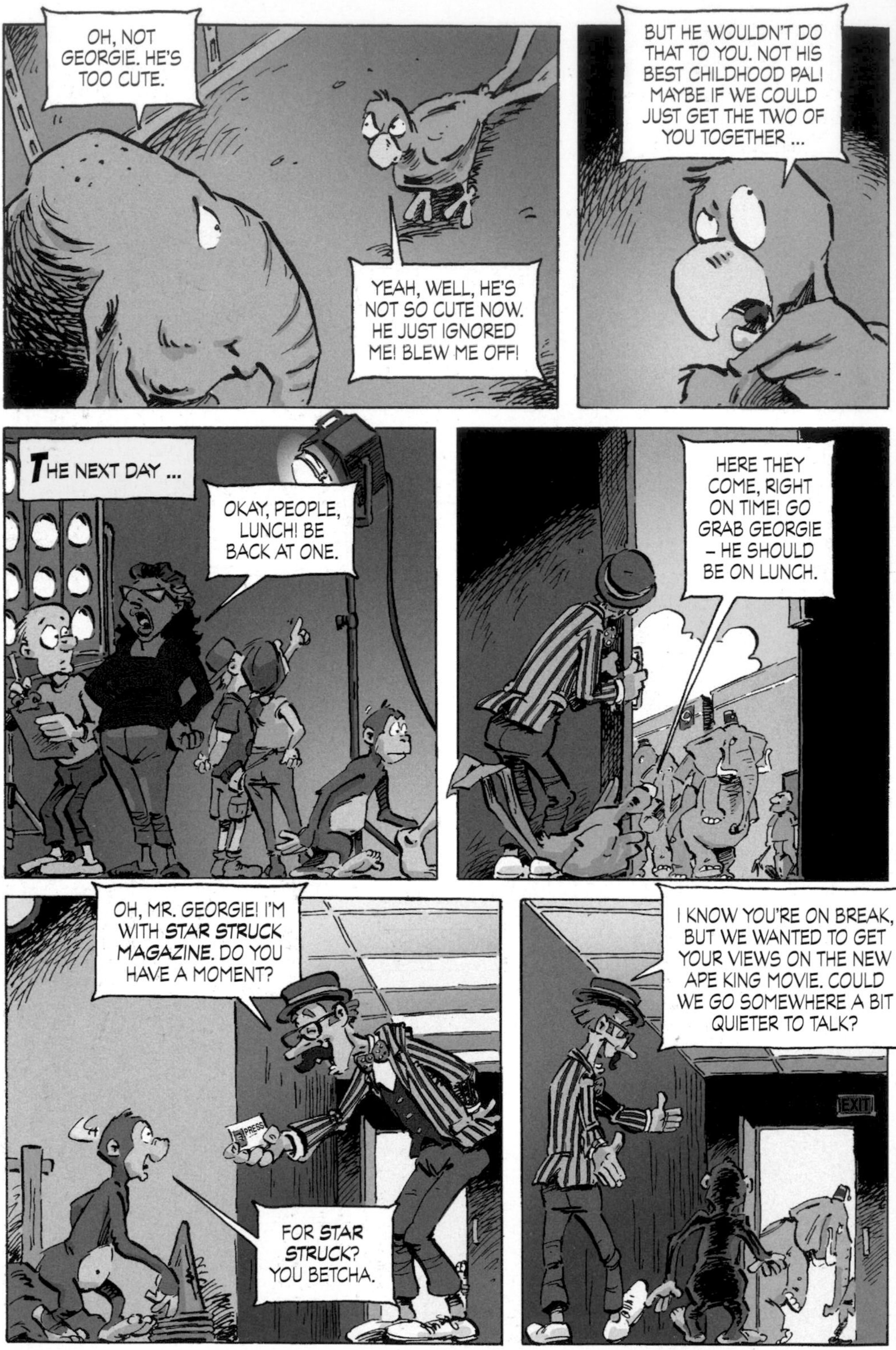
OH, NOT GEORGIE. HE'S TOO CUTE.
YEAH, WELL, HE'S NOT SO CUTE NOW. HE JUST IGNORED ME! BLEW ME OFF!
BUT HE WOULDN'T DO THAT TO YOU. NOT HIS BEST CHILDHOOD PAL! MAYBE IF WE COULD JUST GET THE TWO OF YOU TOGETHER ...
THE NEXT DAY ...
OKAY, PEOPLE, LUNCH! BE BACK AT ONE.
HERE THEY COME, RIGHT ON TIME! GO GRAB GEORGIE – HE SHOULD BE ON LUNCH.
OH, MR. GEORGIE! I'M WITH STAR STRUCK MAGAZINE. DO YOU HAVE A MOMENT?
PRESS
FOR STAR STRUCK? YOU BETCHA.
I KNOW YOU'RE ON BREAK, BUT WE WANTED TO GET YOUR VIEWS ON THE NEW APE KING MOVIE. COULD WE GO SOMEWHERE A BIT QUIETER TO TALK?
EXIT

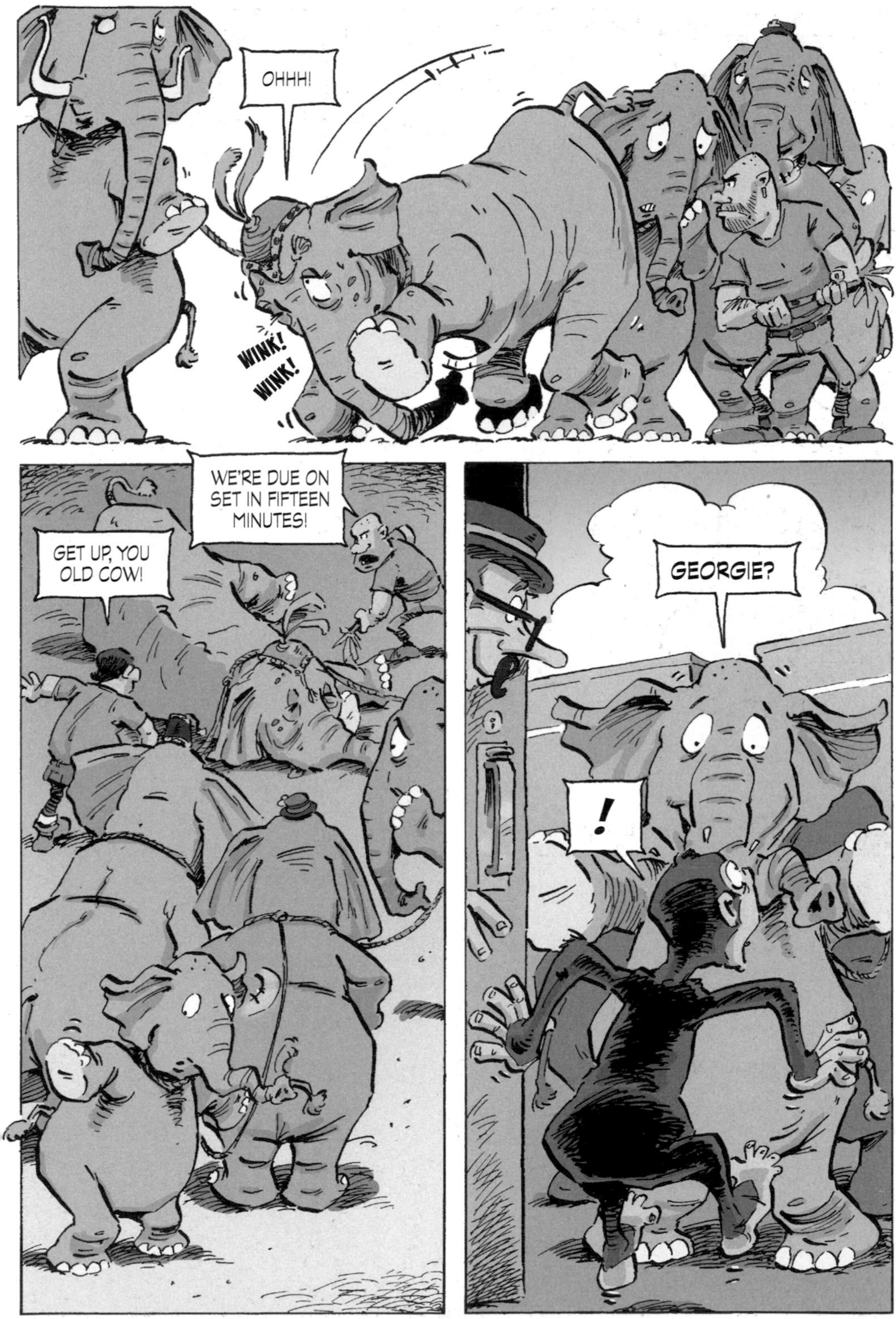
OHHH!
WINK!
WINK!
WE'RE DUE ON SET IN FIFTEEN MINUTES!
GET UP, YOU OLD COW!
GEORGIE?
!

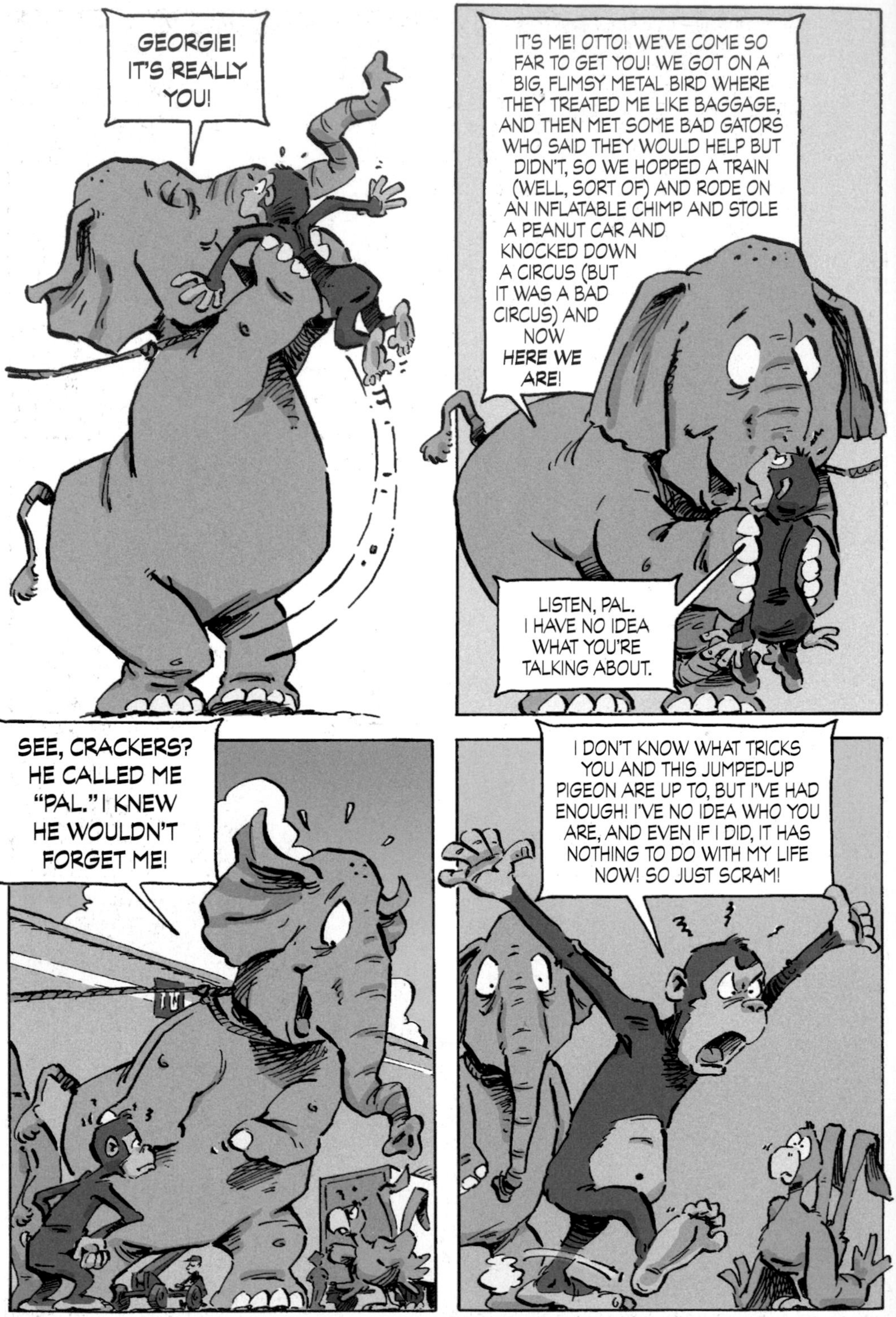
GEORGIE! IT'S REALLY YOU!
IT'S ME! OTTO! WE'VE COME SO FAR TO GET YOU! WE GOT ON A BIG, FLIMSY METAL BIRD WHERE THEY TREATED ME LIKE BAGGAGE, AND THEN MET SOME BAD GATORS WHO SAID THEY WOULD HELP BUT DIDN'T, SO WE HOPPED A TRAIN (WELL, SORT OF) AND RODE ON AN INFLATABLE CHIMP AND STOLE A PEANUT CAR AND KNOCKED DOWN A CIRCUS (BUT IT WAS A BAD CIRCUS) AND NOW HERE WE ARE!
LISTEN, PAL. I HAVE NO IDEA WHAT YOU'RE TALKING ABOUT.
SEE, CRACKERS? HE CALLED ME "PAL." I KNEW HE WOULDN'T FORGET ME!
I DON'T KNOW WHAT TRICKS YOU AND THIS JUMPED-UP PIGEON ARE UP TO, BUT I'VE HAD ENOUGH! I'VE NO IDEA WHO YOU ARE, AND EVEN IF I DID, IT HAS NOTHING TO DO WITH MY LIFE NOW! SO JUST SCRAM!

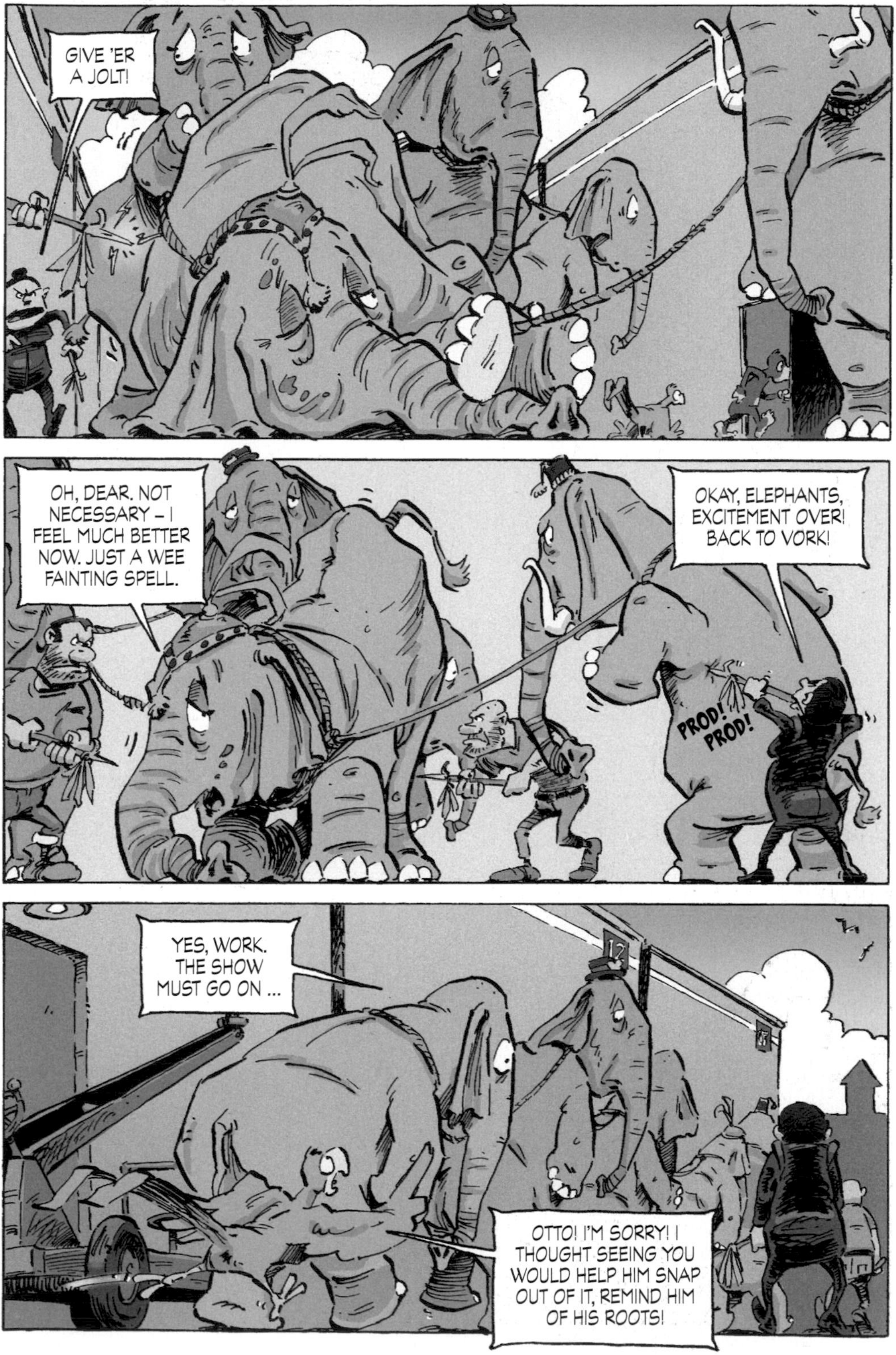
GIVE 'ER A JOLT!
OH, DEAR. NOT NECESSARY – I FEEL MUCH BETTER NOW. JUST A WEE FAINTING SPELL.
OKAY, ELEPHANTS, EXCITEMENT OVER! BACK TO VORK!
PROD! PROD!
YES, WORK. THE SHOW MUST GO ON ...
OTTO! I'M SORRY! I THOUGHT SEEING YOU WOULD HELP HIM SNAP OUT OF IT, REMIND HIM OF HIS ROOTS!

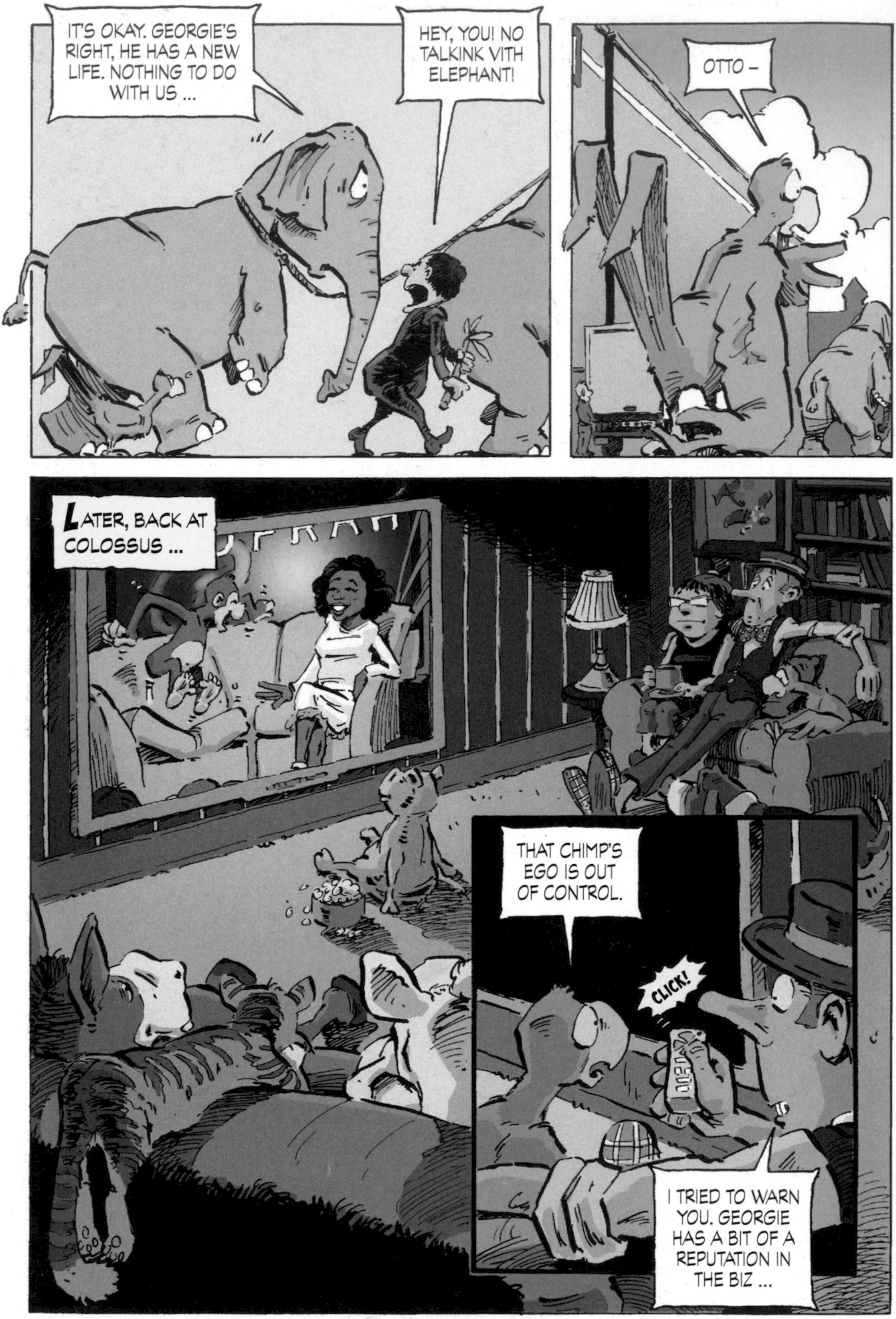
IT'S OKAY. GEORGIE'S RIGHT, HE HAS A NEW LIFE. NOTHING TO DO WITH US ...
HEY, YOU! NO TALKINK VITH ELEPHANT!
OTTO –
LATER, BACK AT COLOSSUS ...
THAT CHIMP'S EGO IS OUT OF CONTROL.
CLICK!
I TRIED TO WARN YOU. GEORGIE HAS A BIT OF A REPUTATION IN THE BIZ ...

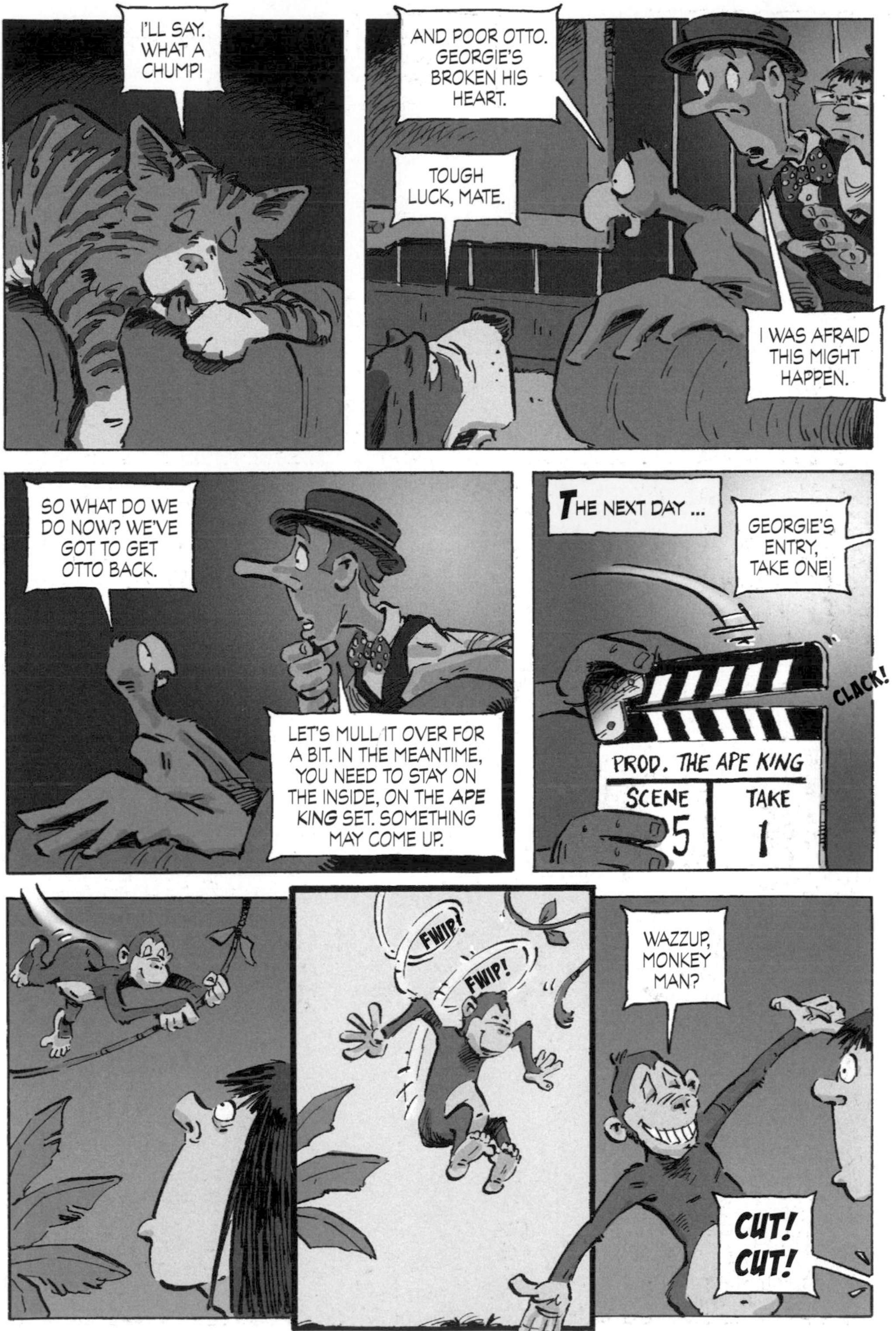
I'LL SAY. WHAT A CHUMP!
AND POOR OTTO. GEORGIE'S BROKEN HIS HEART.
TOUGH LUCK, MATE.
I WAS AFRAID THIS MIGHT HAPPEN.
SO WHAT DO WE DO NOW? WE'VE GOT TO GET OTTO BACK.
LET'S MULL IT OVER FOR A BIT. IN THE MEANTIME, YOU NEED TO STAY ON THE INSIDE, ON THE APE KING SET. SOMETHING MAY COME UP.
THE NEXT DAY ...
GEORGIE'S ENTRY, TAKE ONE!
CLACK!
PROD. THE APE KING
SCENE 5
TAKE 1
FWIP!
FWIP!
WAZZUP, MONKEY MAN?
CUT! CUT!

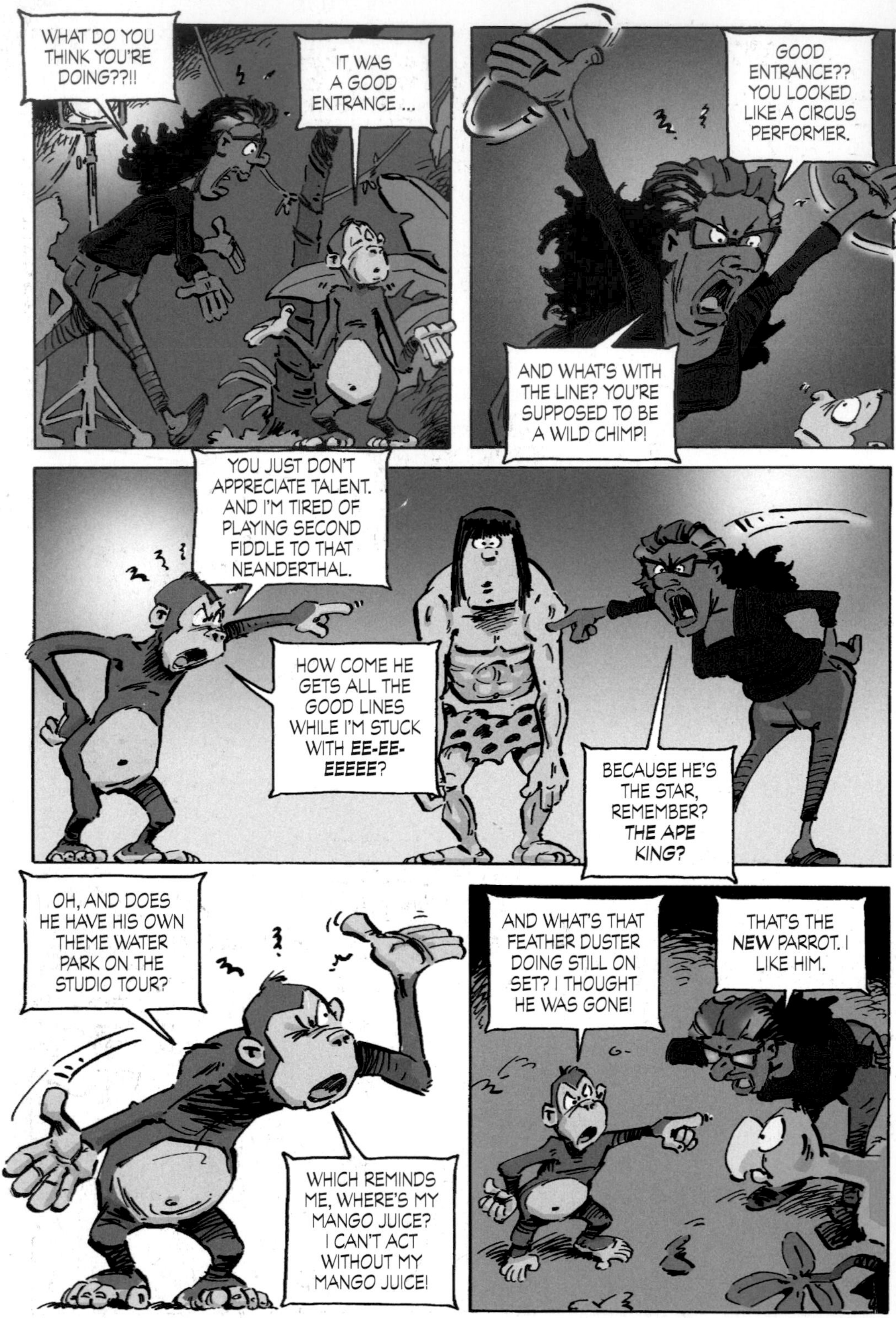

WHAT DO YOU THINK YOU'RE DOING??!!
IT WAS A GOOD ENTRANCE ...
GOOD ENTRANCE?? YOU LOOKED LIKE A CIRCUS PERFORMER.
AND WHAT'S WITH THE LINE? YOU'RE SUPPOSED TO BE A WILD CHIMP!
YOU JUST DON'T APPRECIATE TALENT. AND I'M TIRED OF PLAYING SECOND FIDDLE TO THAT NEANDERTHAL.
HOW COME HE GETS ALL THE GOOD LINES WHILE I'M STUCK WITH EE-EE-EEEEE?
BECAUSE HE'S THE STAR, REMEMBER? THE APE KING?
OH, AND DOES HE HAVE HIS OWN THEME WATER PARK ON THE STUDIO TOUR?
WHICH REMINDS ME, WHERE'S MY MANGO JUICE? I CAN'T ACT WITHOUT MY MANGO JUICE!
AND WHAT'S THAT FEATHER DUSTER DOING STILL ON SET? I THOUGHT HE WAS GONE!
THAT'S THE NEW PARROT. I LIKE HIM.

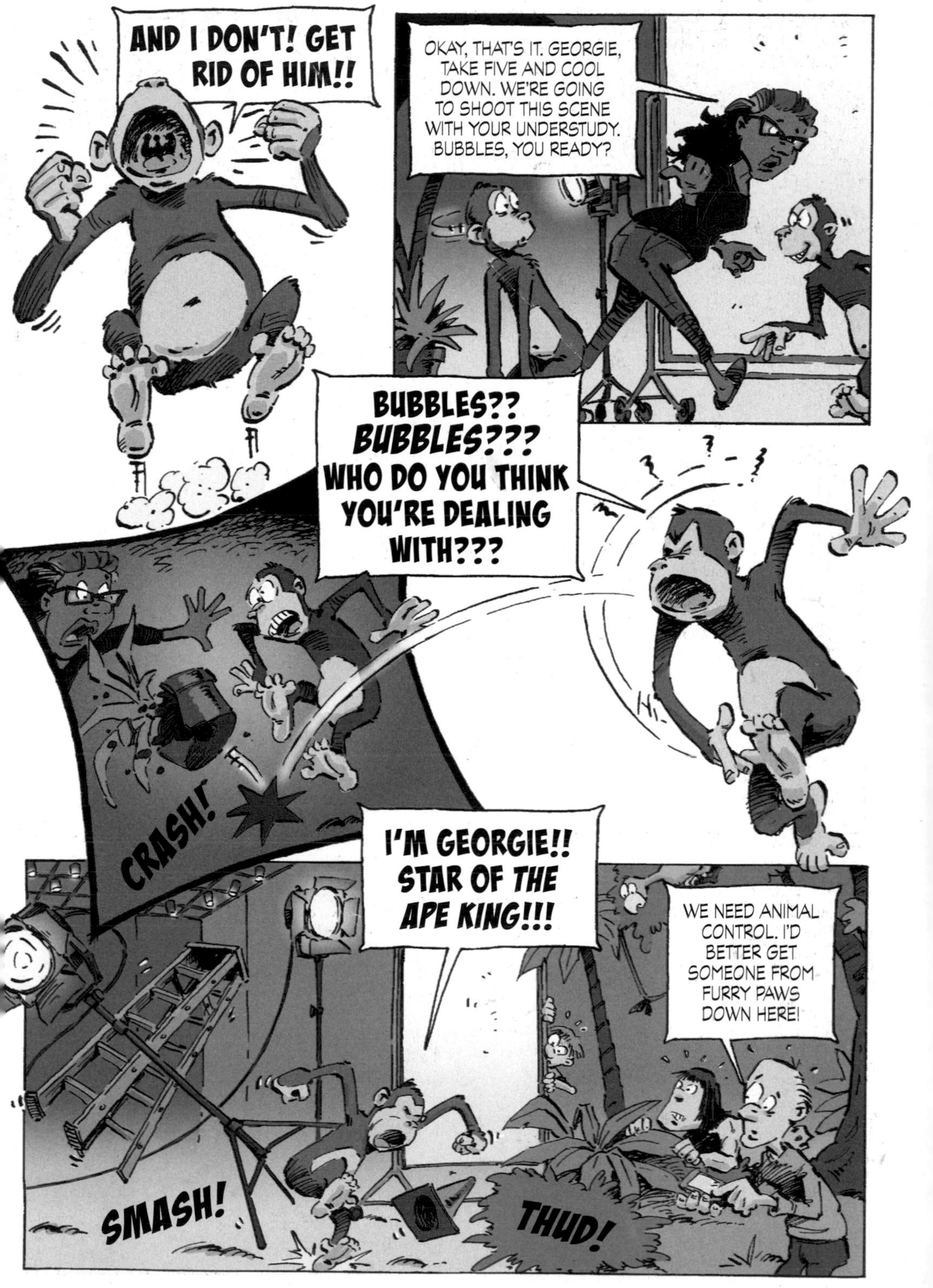
AND I DON'T! GET RID OF HIM!!
OKAY, THAT'S IT. GEORGIE, TAKE FIVE AND COOL DOWN. WE'RE GOING TO SHOOT THIS SCENE WITH YOUR UNDERSTUDY. BUBBLES, YOU READY?
BUBBLES?? *BUBBLES???* WHO DO YOU THINK YOU'RE DEALING WITH???
CRASH!
I'M GEORGIE!! STAR OF THE *APE KING!!!*
WE NEED ANIMAL CONTROL. I'D BETTER GET SOMEONE FROM FURRY PAWS DOWN HERE!
SMASH!
THUD!

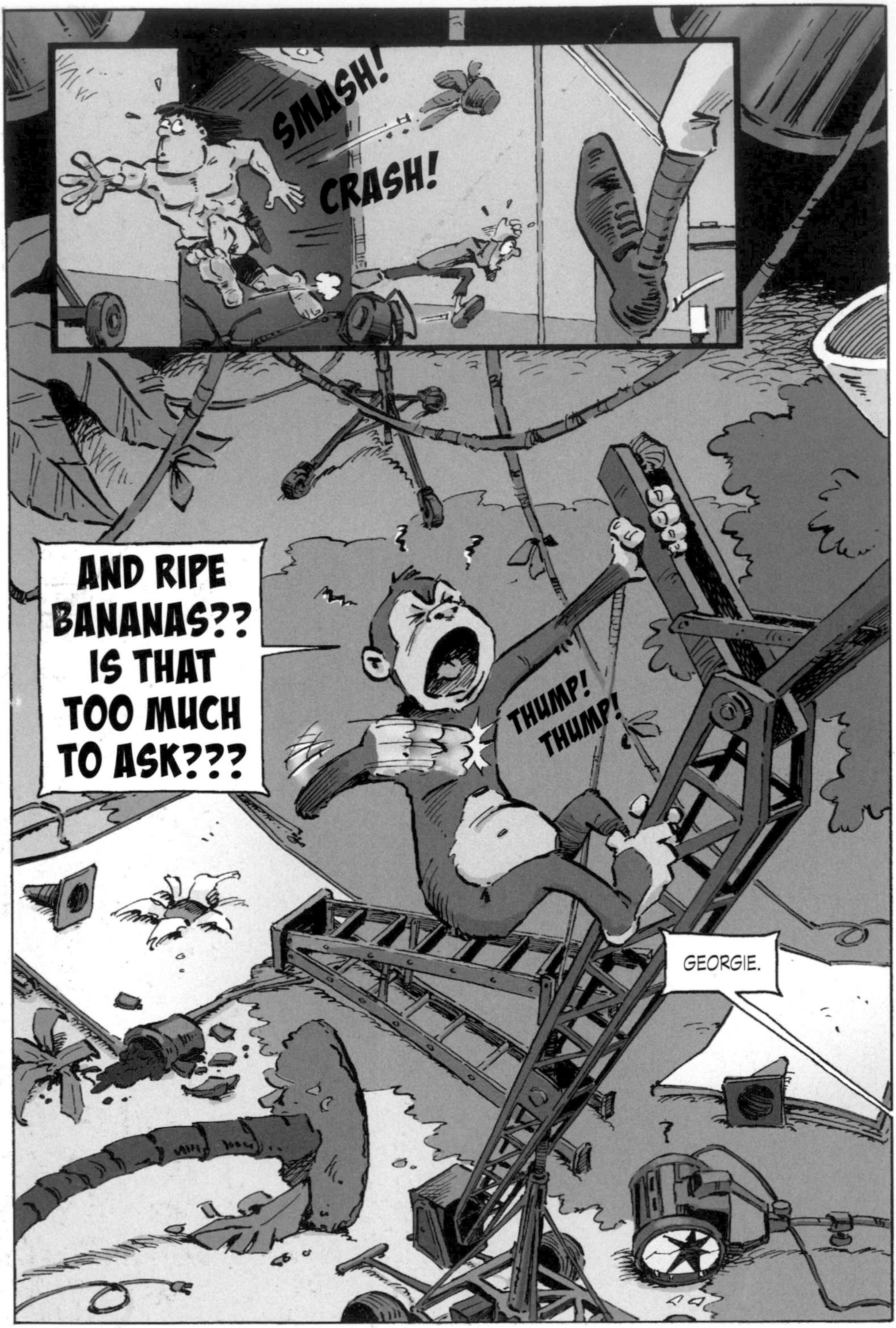
SMASH!
CRASH!
AND RIPE BANANAS?? IS THAT TOO MUCH TO ASK???
THUMP! THUMP!
GEORGIE.

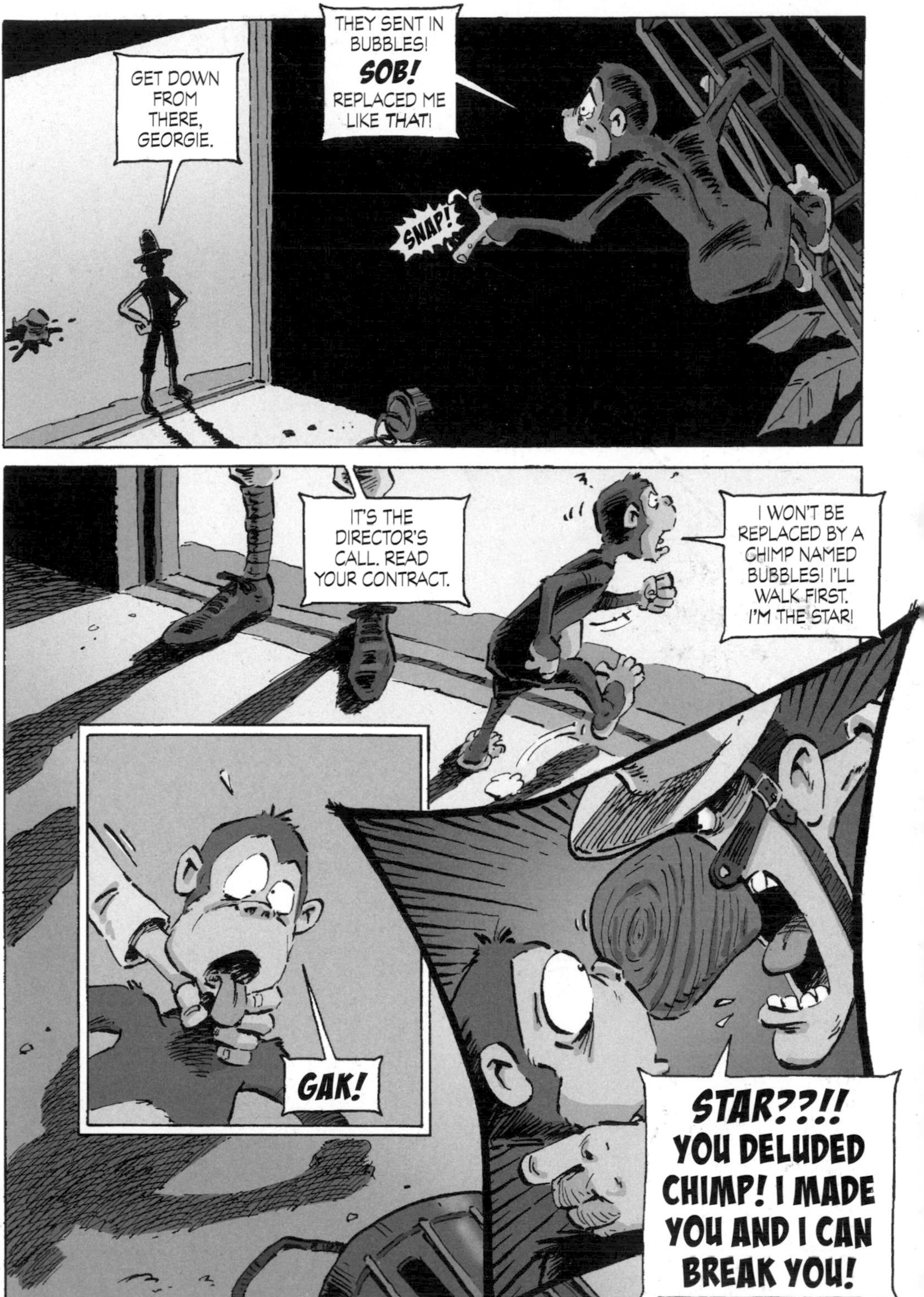
GET DOWN FROM THERE, GEORGIE.
THEY SENT IN BUBBLES! SOB! REPLACED ME LIKE THAT!
SNAP!
IT'S THE DIRECTOR'S CALL. READ YOUR CONTRACT.
I WON'T BE REPLACED BY A CHIMP NAMED BUBBLES! I'LL WALK FIRST. I'M THE STAR!
GAK!
STAR??!! YOU DELUDED CHIMP! I MADE YOU AND I CAN BREAK YOU!

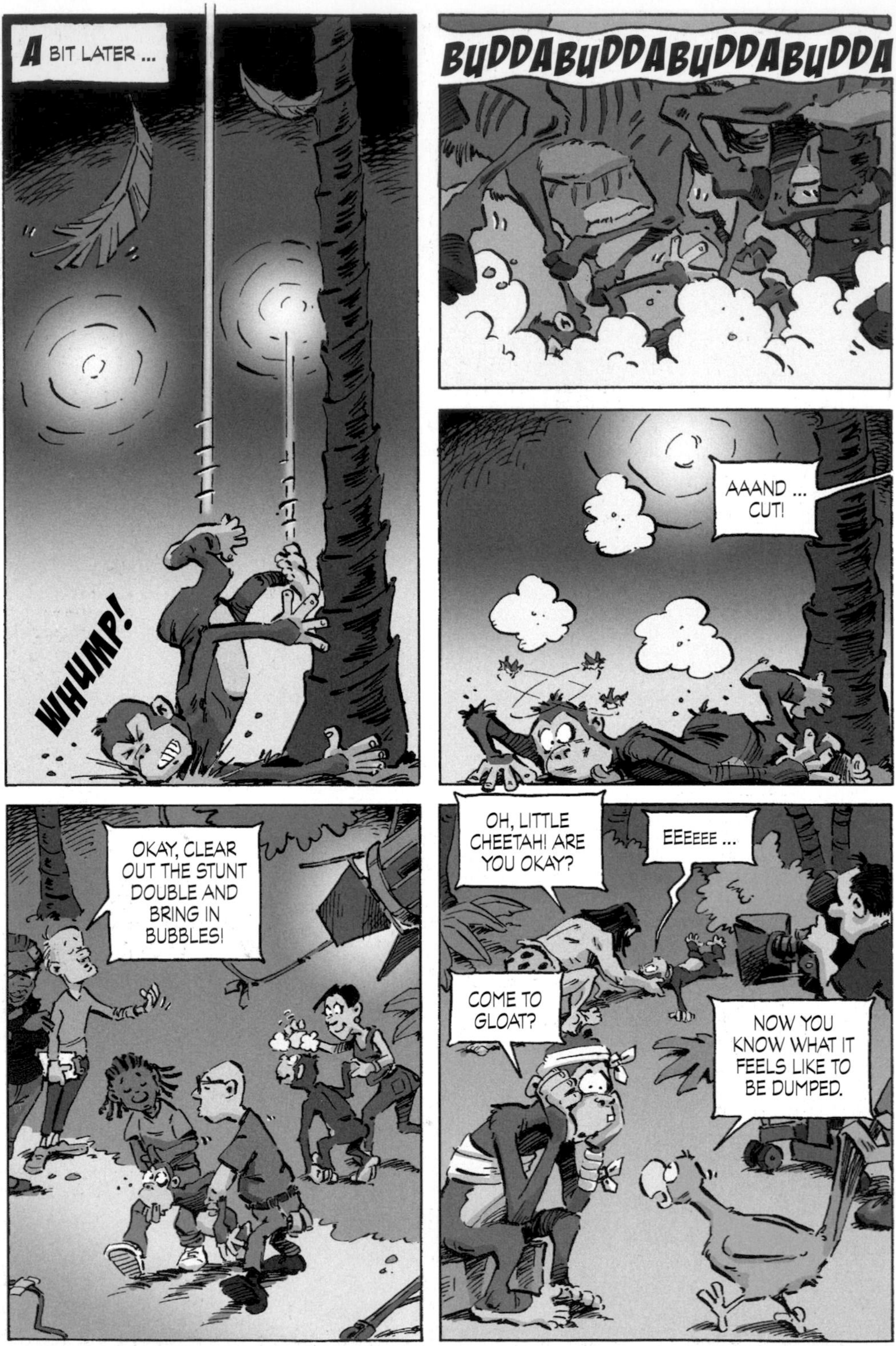
A BIT LATER ...
WHUMP!
BUDDABUDDABUDDABUDDA
AAAND ... CUT!
OKAY, CLEAR OUT THE STUNT DOUBLE AND BRING IN BUBBLES!
OH, LITTLE CHEETAH! ARE YOU OKAY?
EEEEEE ...
COME TO GLOAT?
NOW YOU KNOW WHAT IT FEELS LIKE TO BE DUMPED.

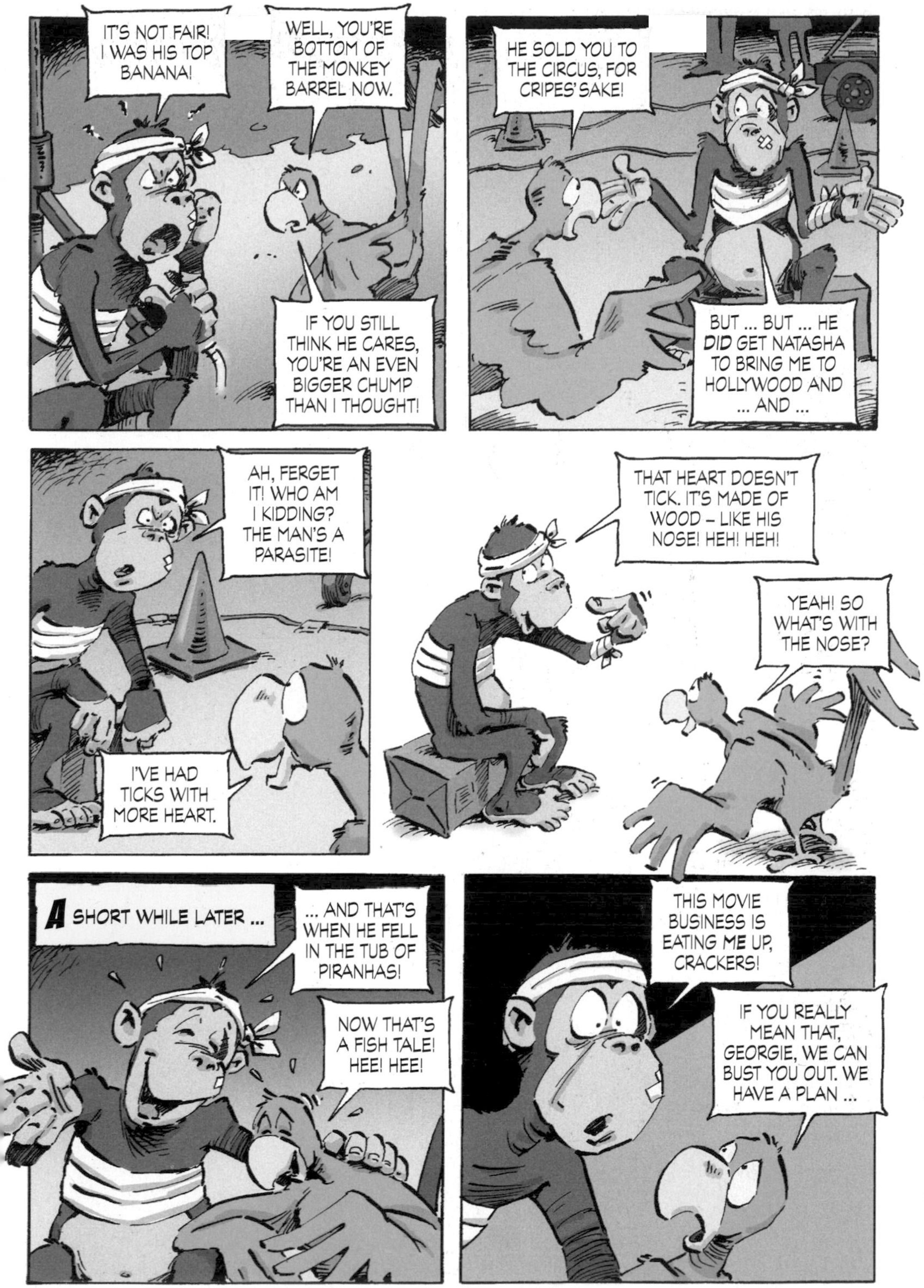
IT'S NOT FAIR! I WAS HIS TOP BANANA!
WELL, YOU'RE BOTTOM OF THE MONKEY BARREL NOW.
IF YOU STILL THINK HE CARES, YOU'RE AN EVEN BIGGER CHUMP THAN I THOUGHT!
HE SOLD YOU TO THE CIRCUS, FOR CRIPES' SAKE!
BUT ... BUT ... HE DID GET NATASHA TO BRING ME TO HOLLYWOOD AND ... AND ...
AH, FERGET IT! WHO AM I KIDDING? THE MAN'S A PARASITE!
I'VE HAD TICKS WITH MORE HEART.
THAT HEART DOESN'T TICK. IT'S MADE OF WOOD – LIKE HIS NOSE! HEH! HEH!
YEAH! SO WHAT'S WITH THE NOSE?
A SHORT WHILE LATER ...
... AND THAT'S WHEN HE FELL IN THE TUB OF PIRANHAS!
NOW THAT'S A FISH TALE! HEE! HEE!
THIS MOVIE BUSINESS IS EATING ME UP, CRACKERS!
IF YOU REALLY MEAN THAT, GEORGIE, WE CAN BUST YOU OUT. WE HAVE A PLAN ...

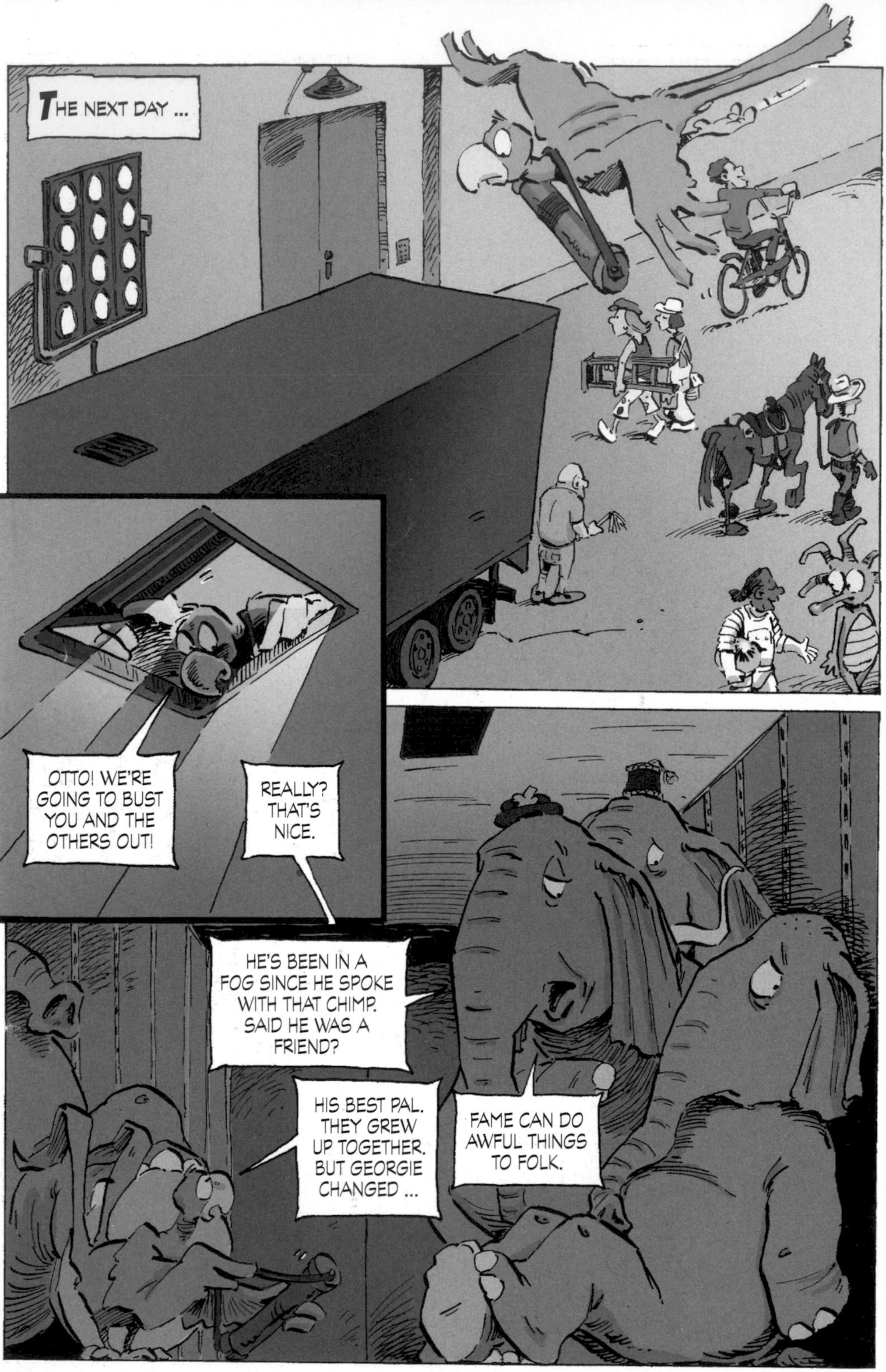
THE NEXT DAY ...
OTTO! WE'RE GOING TO BUST YOU AND THE OTHERS OUT!
REALLY? THAT'S NICE.
HE'S BEEN IN A FOG SINCE HE SPOKE WITH THAT CHIMP. SAID HE WAS A FRIEND?
HIS BEST PAL. THEY GREW UP TOGETHER. BUT GEORGIE CHANGED ...
FAME CAN DO AWFUL THINGS TO FOLK.

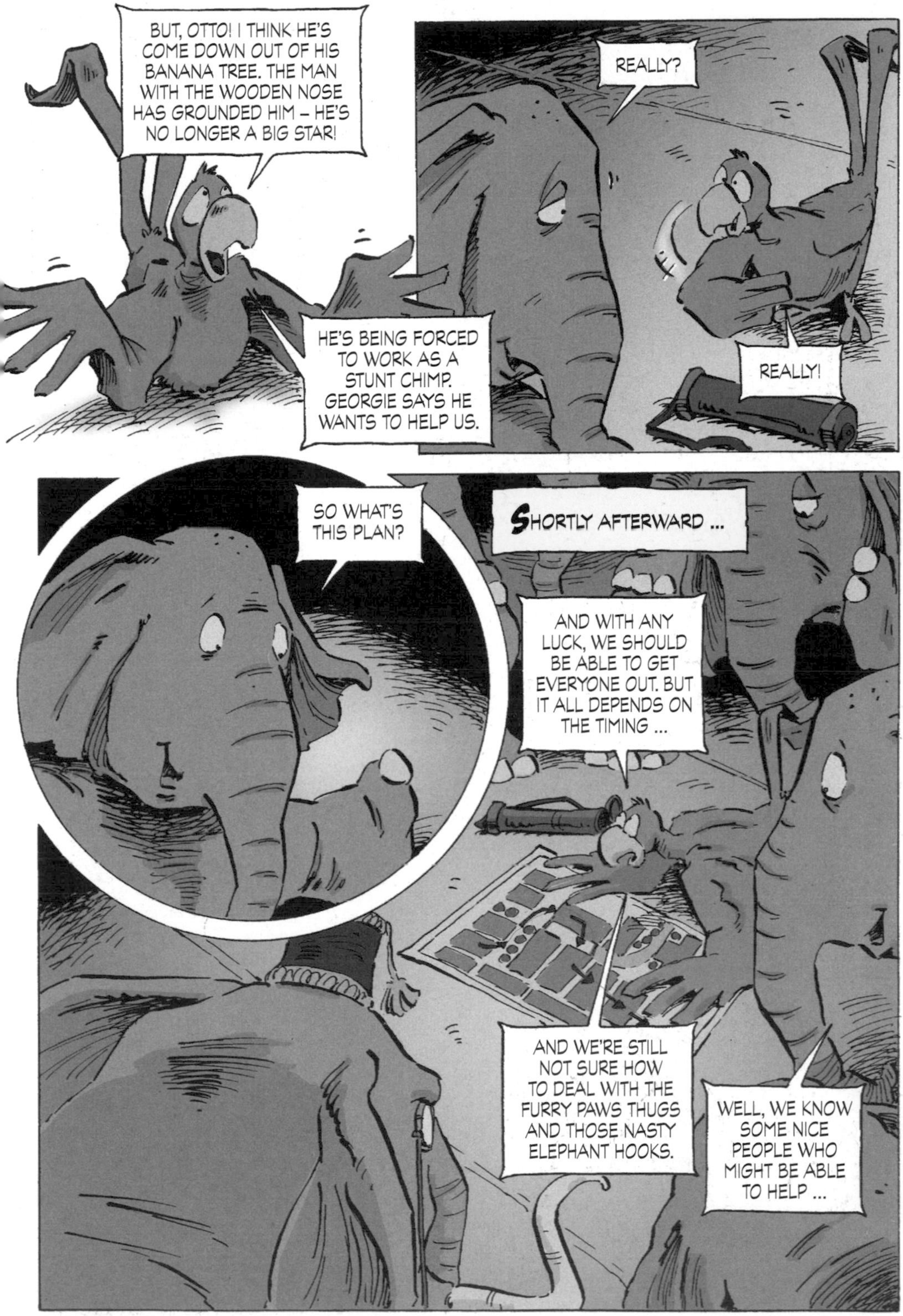
BUT, OTTO! I THINK HE'S COME DOWN OUT OF HIS BANANA TREE. THE MAN WITH THE WOODEN NOSE HAS GROUNDED HIM – HE'S NO LONGER A BIG STAR!
HE'S BEING FORCED TO WORK AS A STUNT CHIMP. GEORGIE SAYS HE WANTS TO HELP US.
REALLY?
REALLY!
SO WHAT'S THIS PLAN?
SHORTLY AFTERWARD ...
AND WITH ANY LUCK, WE SHOULD BE ABLE TO GET EVERYONE OUT. BUT IT ALL DEPENDS ON THE TIMING ...
AND WE'RE STILL NOT SURE HOW TO DEAL WITH THE FURRY PAWS THUGS AND THOSE NASTY ELEPHANT HOOKS.
WELL, WE KNOW SOME NICE PEOPLE WHO MIGHT BE ABLE TO HELP ...

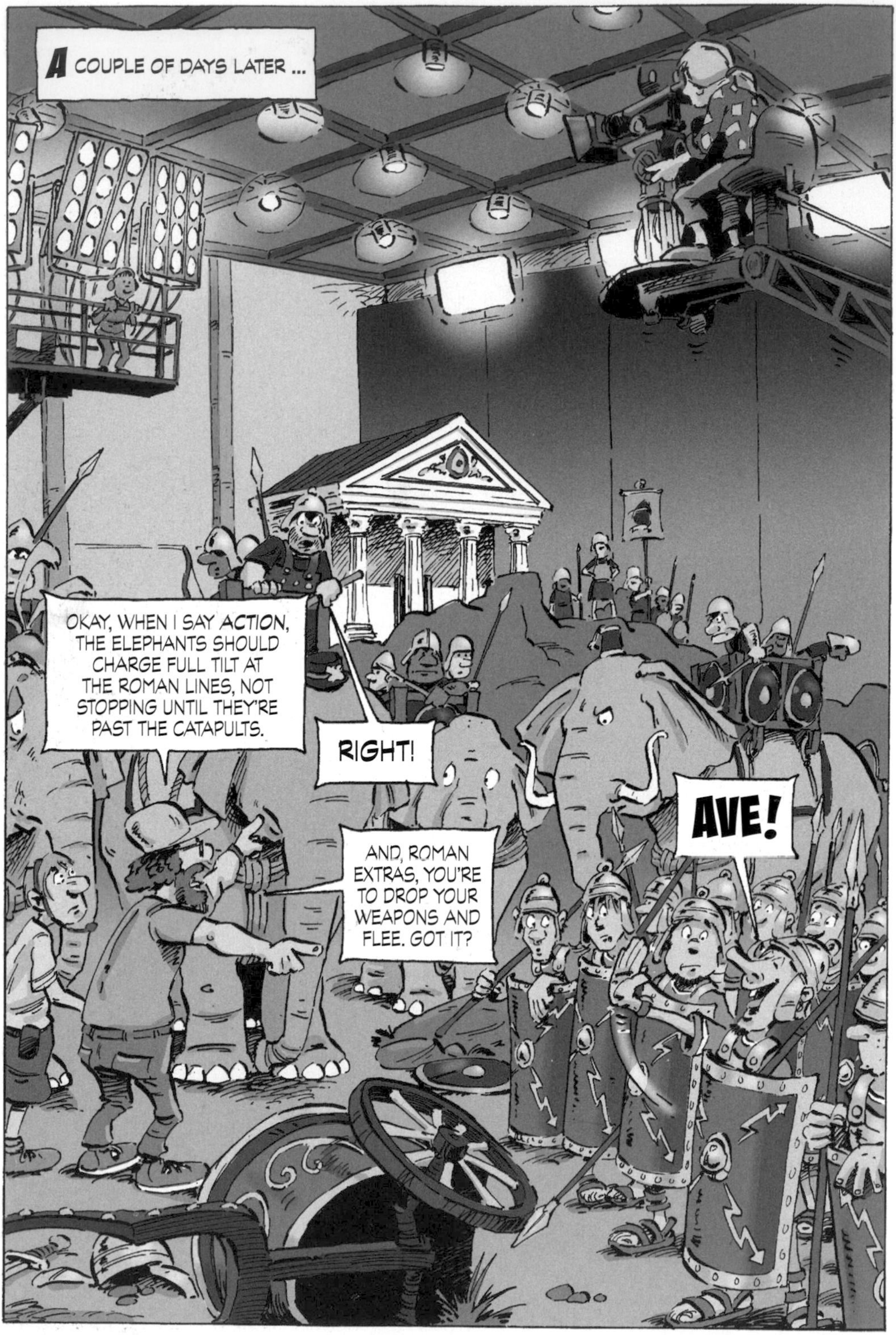
A COUPLE OF DAYS LATER ...
OKAY, WHEN I SAY ACTION, THE ELEPHANTS SHOULD CHARGE FULL TILT AT THE ROMAN LINES, NOT STOPPING UNTIL THEY'RE PAST THE CATAPULTS.
RIGHT!
AND, ROMAN EXTRAS, YOU'RE TO DROP YOUR WEAPONS AND FLEE. GOT IT?
AVE!

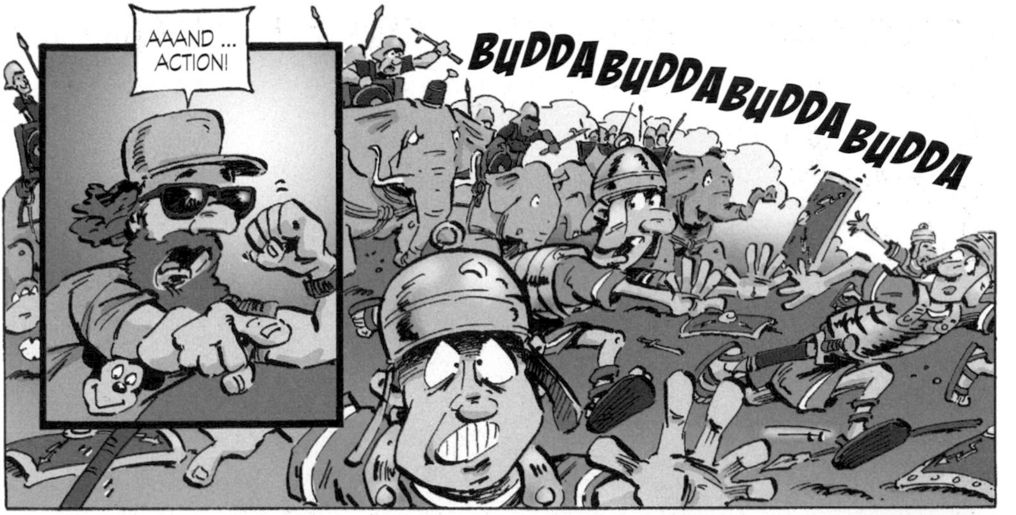
AAAND ...
ACTION!
BUDDA BUDDA BUDDA BUDDA

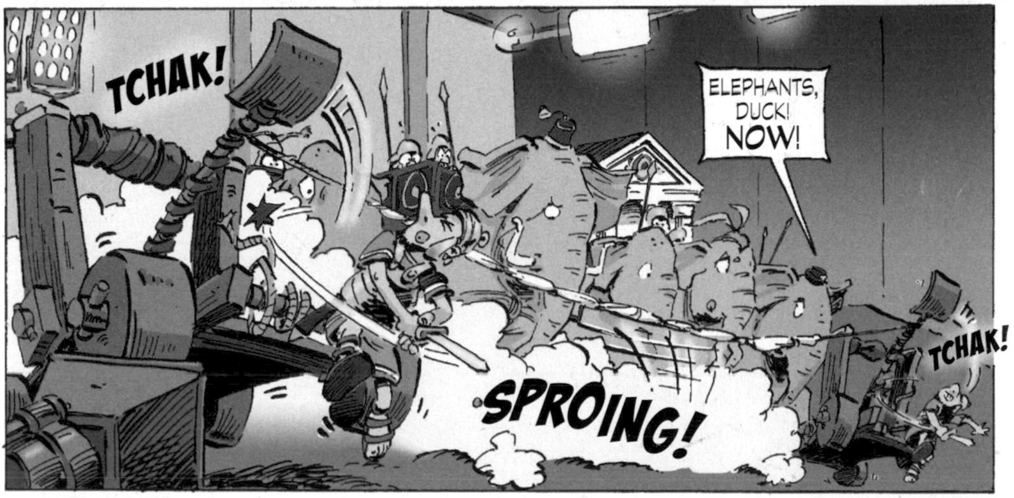
TCHAK!
ELEPHANTS, DUCK! NOW!
SPROING!
TCHAK!

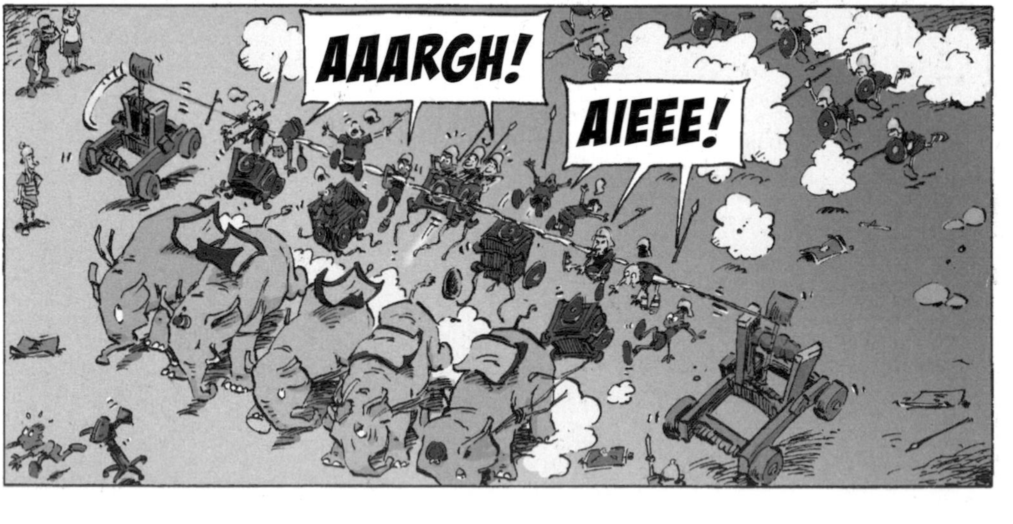
AAARGH!
AIEEE!

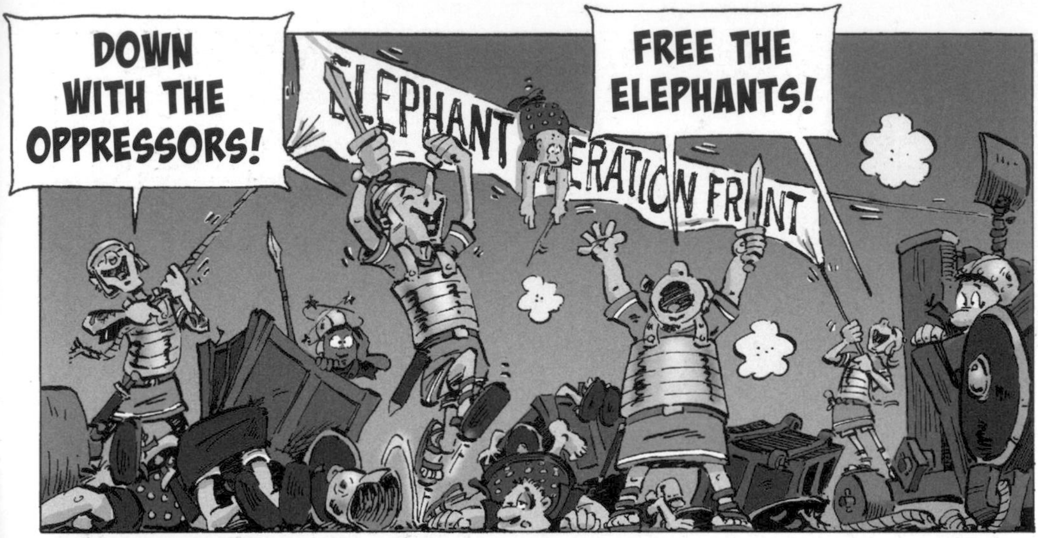
DOWN WITH THE OPPRESSORS!
ELEPHANT
FREE THE ELEPHANTS!

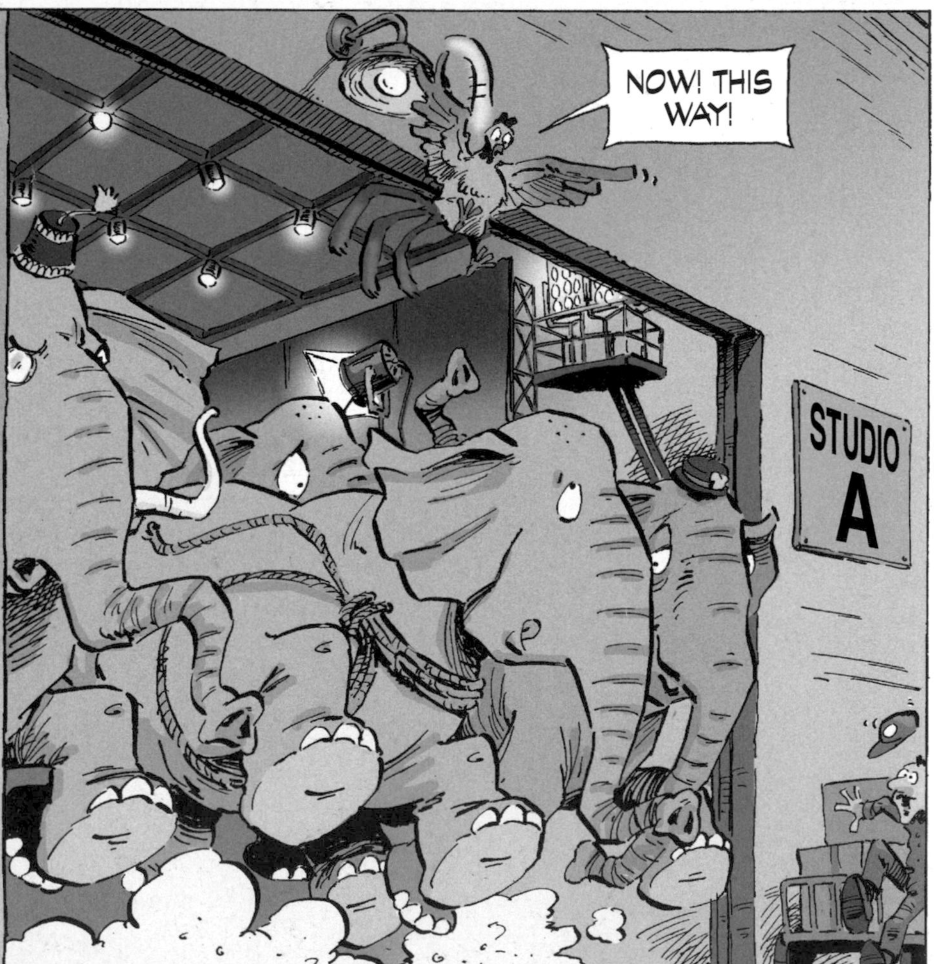
NOW! THIS WAY!
STUDIO A

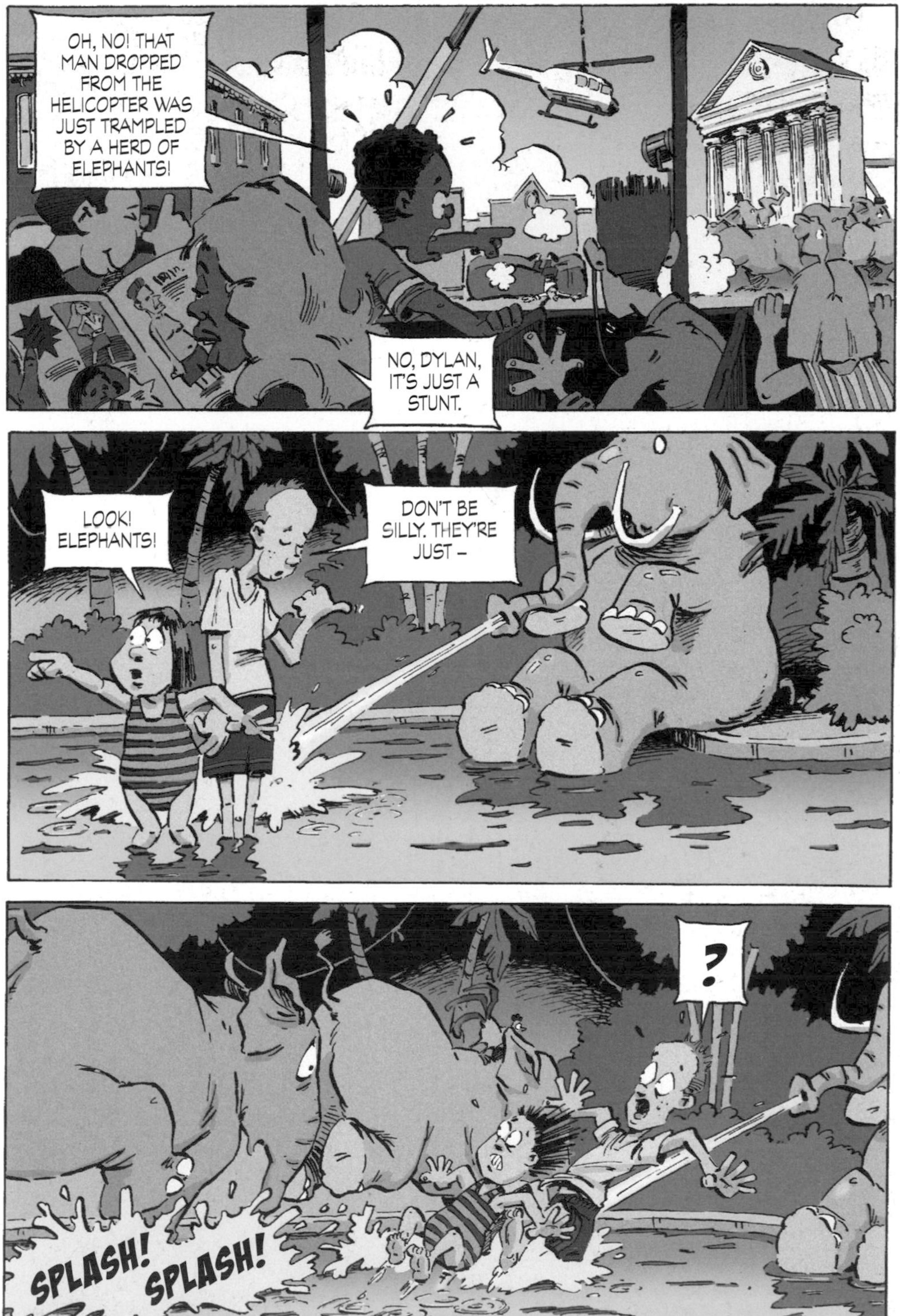
OH, NO! THAT MAN DROPPED FROM THE HELICOPTER WAS JUST TRAMPLED BY A HERD OF ELEPHANTS!
NO, DYLAN, IT'S JUST A STUNT.
LOOK! ELEPHANTS!
DON'T BE SILLY. THEY'RE JUST –
?
SPLASH! SPLASH!

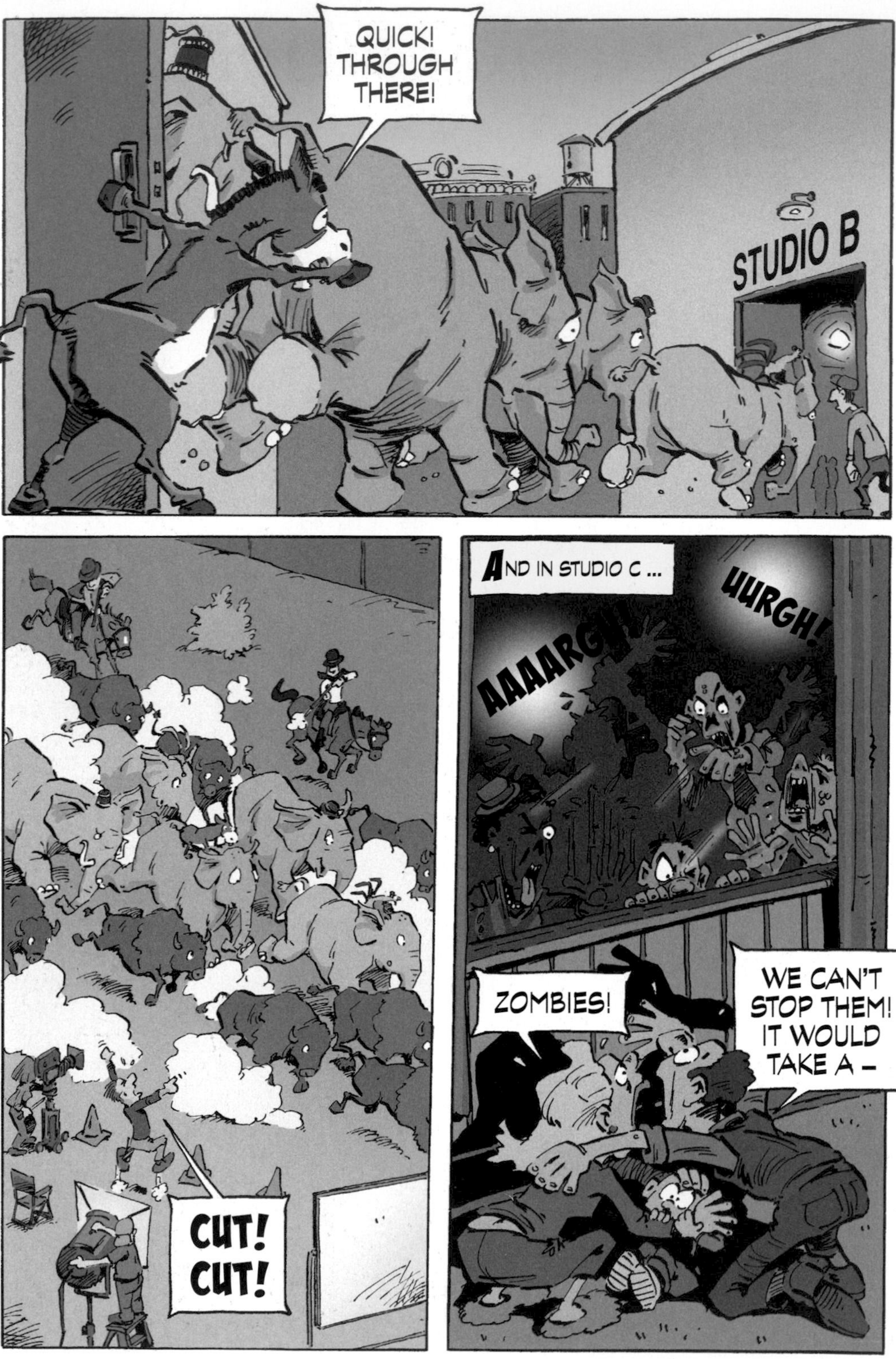

QUICK! THROUGH THERE!
STUDIO B
CUT! CUT!
AND IN STUDIO C ...
AAAARGH!
UURGH!
ZOMBIES!
WE CAN'T STOP THEM! IT WOULD TAKE A –

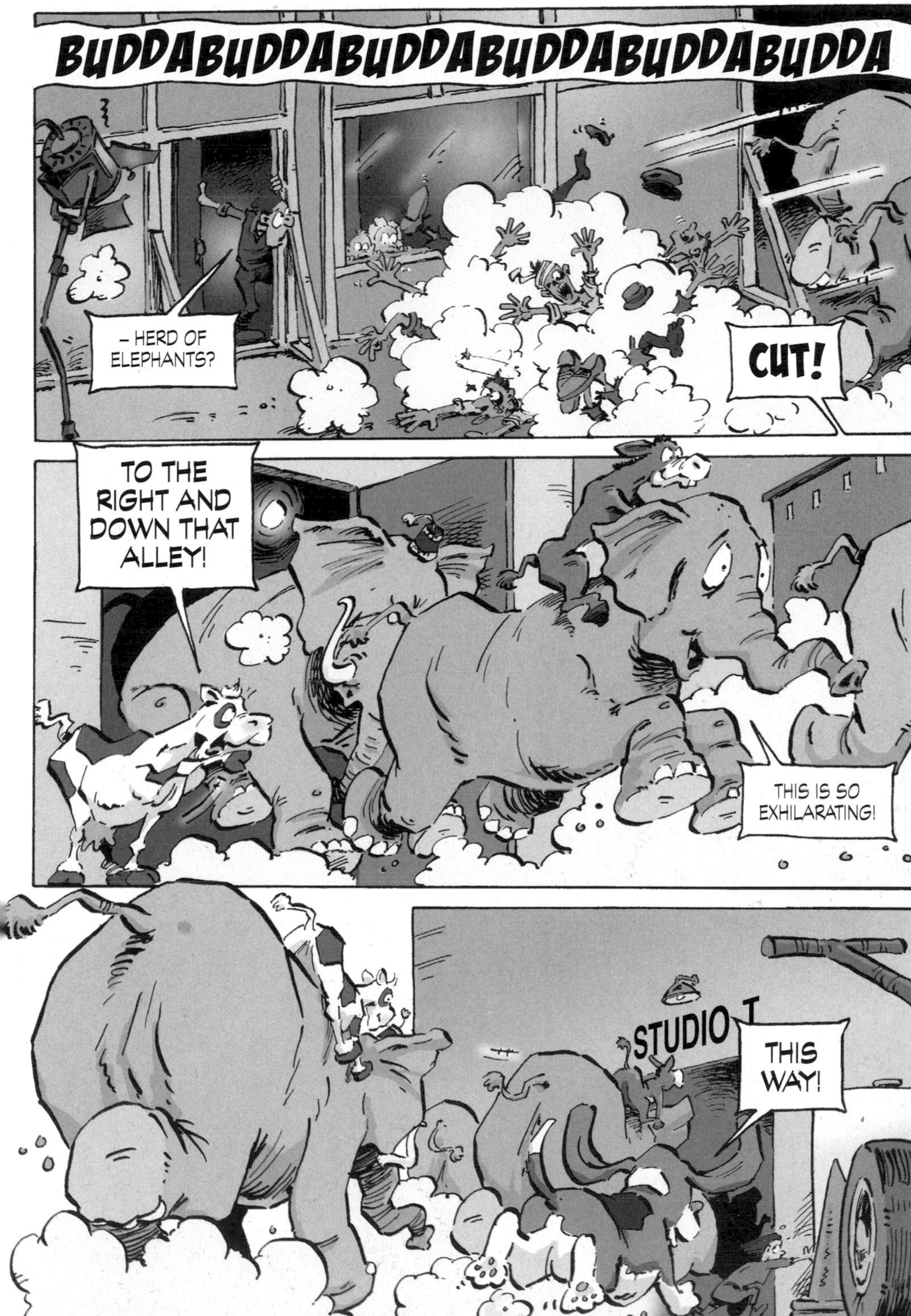

BUDDABUDDABUDDABUDDABUDDABUDDA
– HERD OF ELEPHANTS?
CUT!
TO THE RIGHT AND DOWN THAT ALLEY!
THIS IS SO EXHILARATING!
STUDIO
THIS WAY!

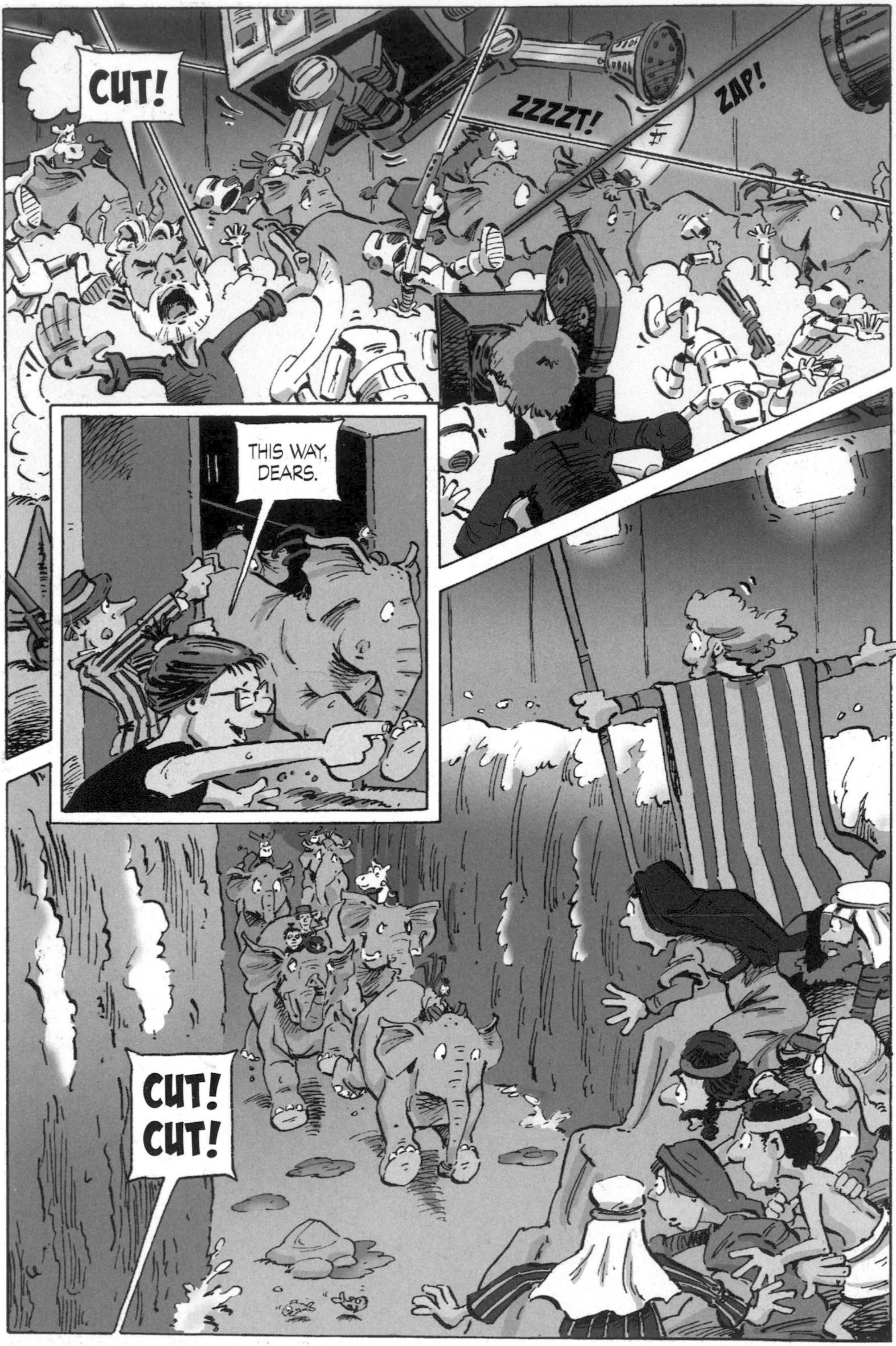
CUT!
ZZZZT!
ZAP!
THIS WAY, DEARS.
CUT! CUT!

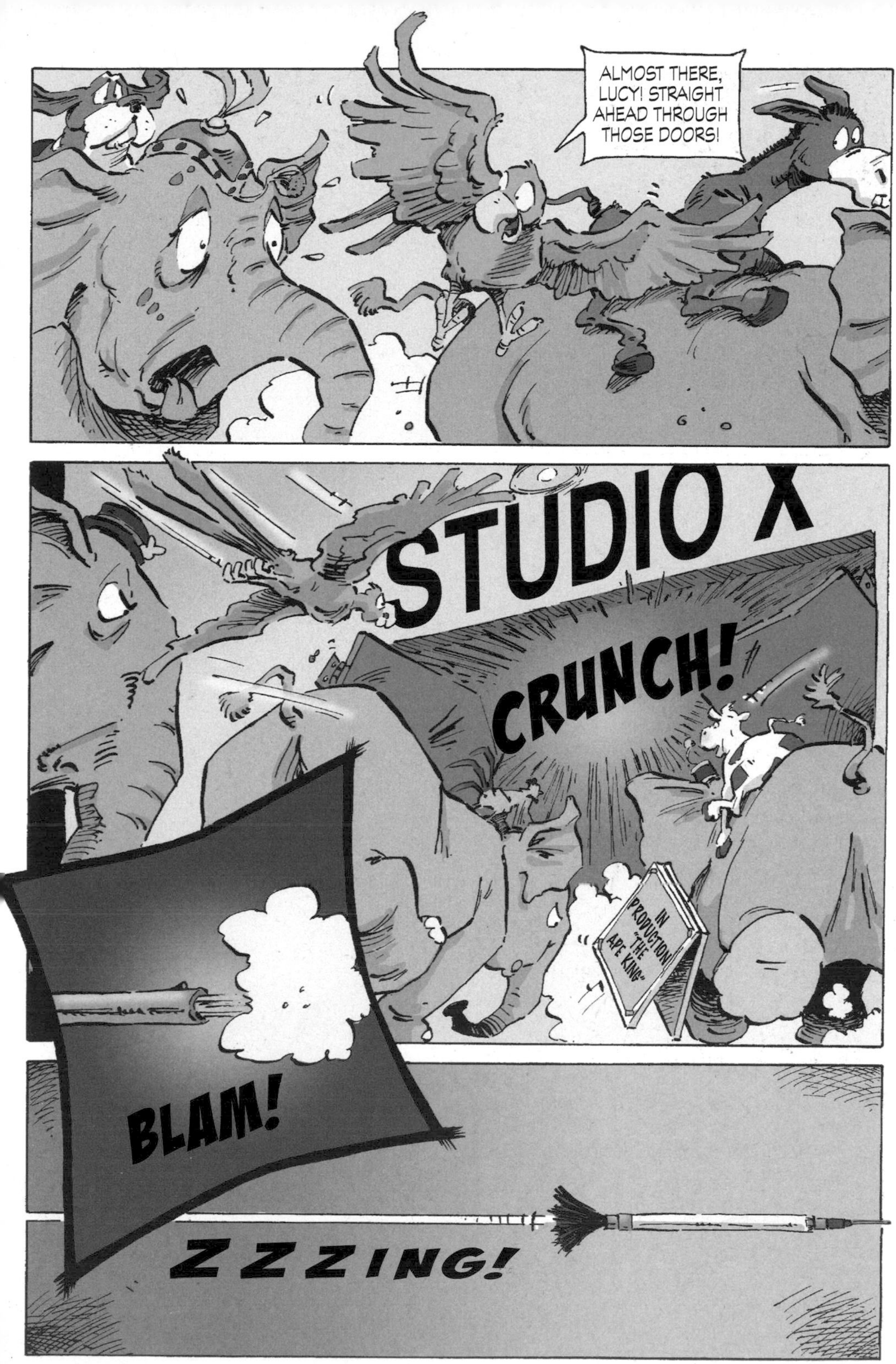
ALMOST THERE, LUCY! STRAIGHT AHEAD THROUGH THOSE DOORS!
STUDIO X
CRUNCH!
IN PRODUCTION "THE APE KING"
BLAM!
ZZZING!

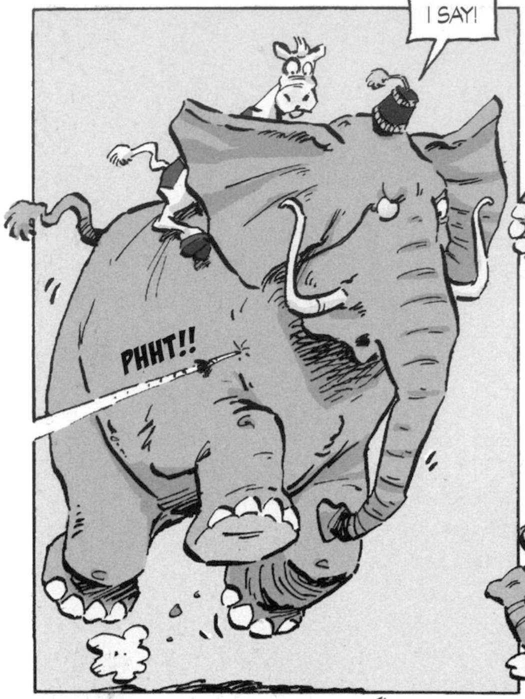
I SAY!
PHHT!!

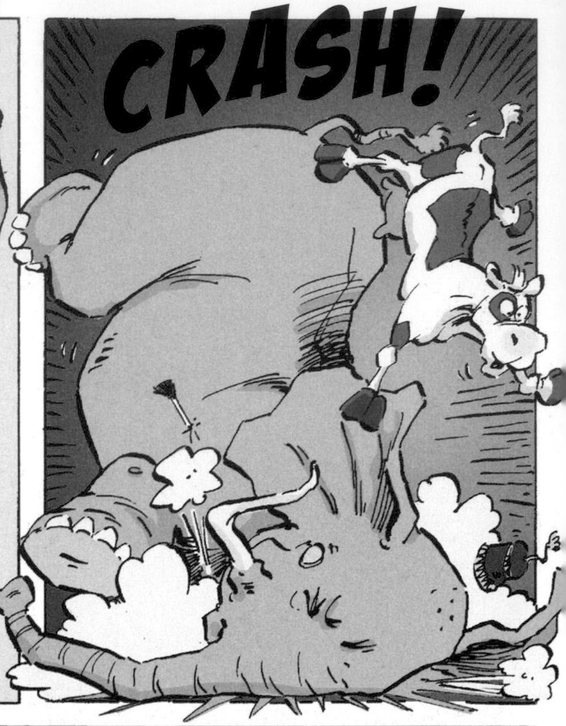
CRASH!

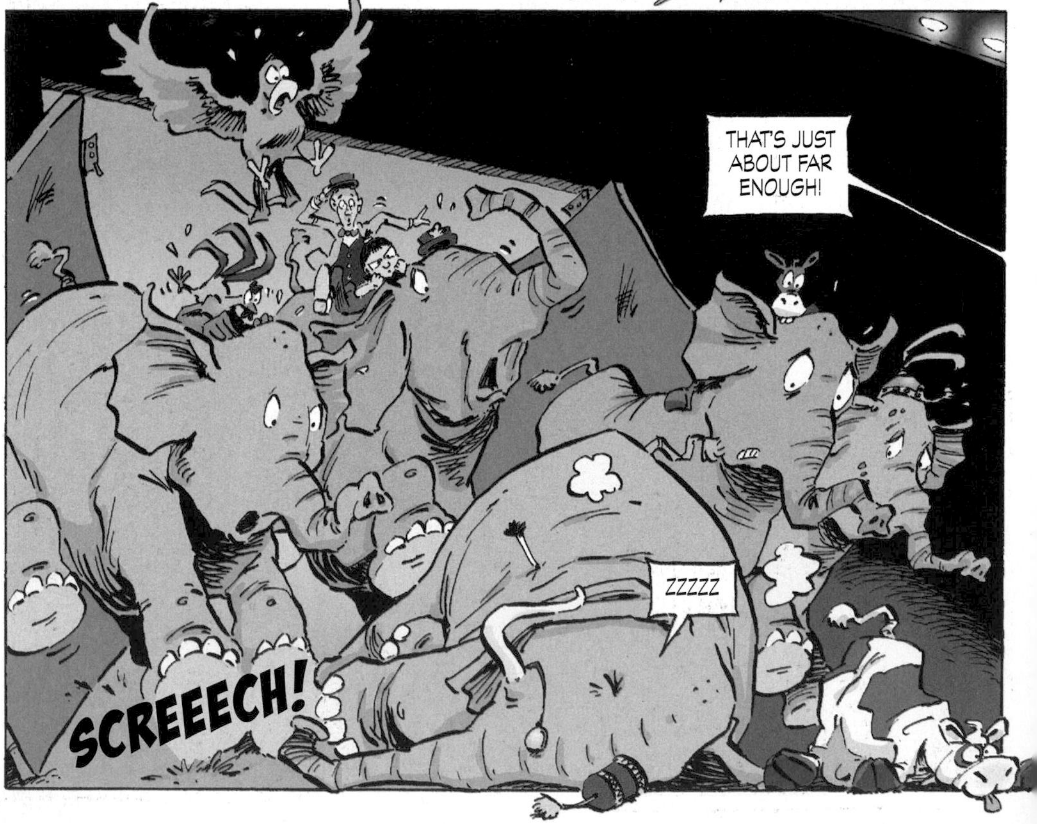
THAT'S JUST ABOUT FAR ENOUGH!
ZZZZZ
SCREEECH!

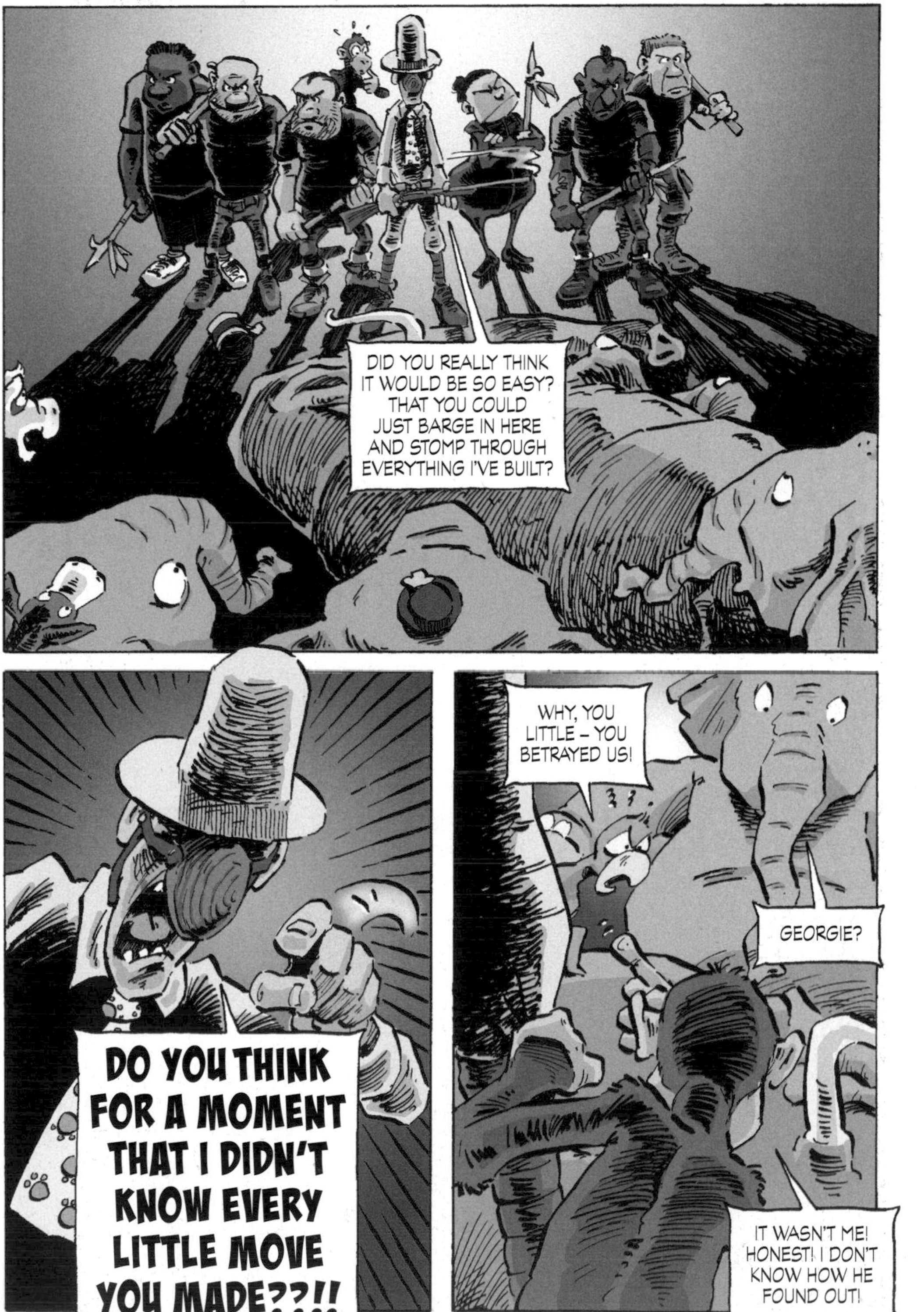
DID YOU REALLY THINK IT WOULD BE SO EASY? THAT YOU COULD JUST BARGE IN HERE AND STOMP THROUGH EVERYTHING I'VE BUILT?
DO YOU THINK FOR A MOMENT THAT I DIDN'T KNOW EVERY LITTLE MOVE YOU MADE??!!
WHY, YOU LITTLE – YOU BETRAYED US!
GEORGIE?
IT WASN'T ME! HONEST! I DON'T KNOW HOW HE FOUND OUT!

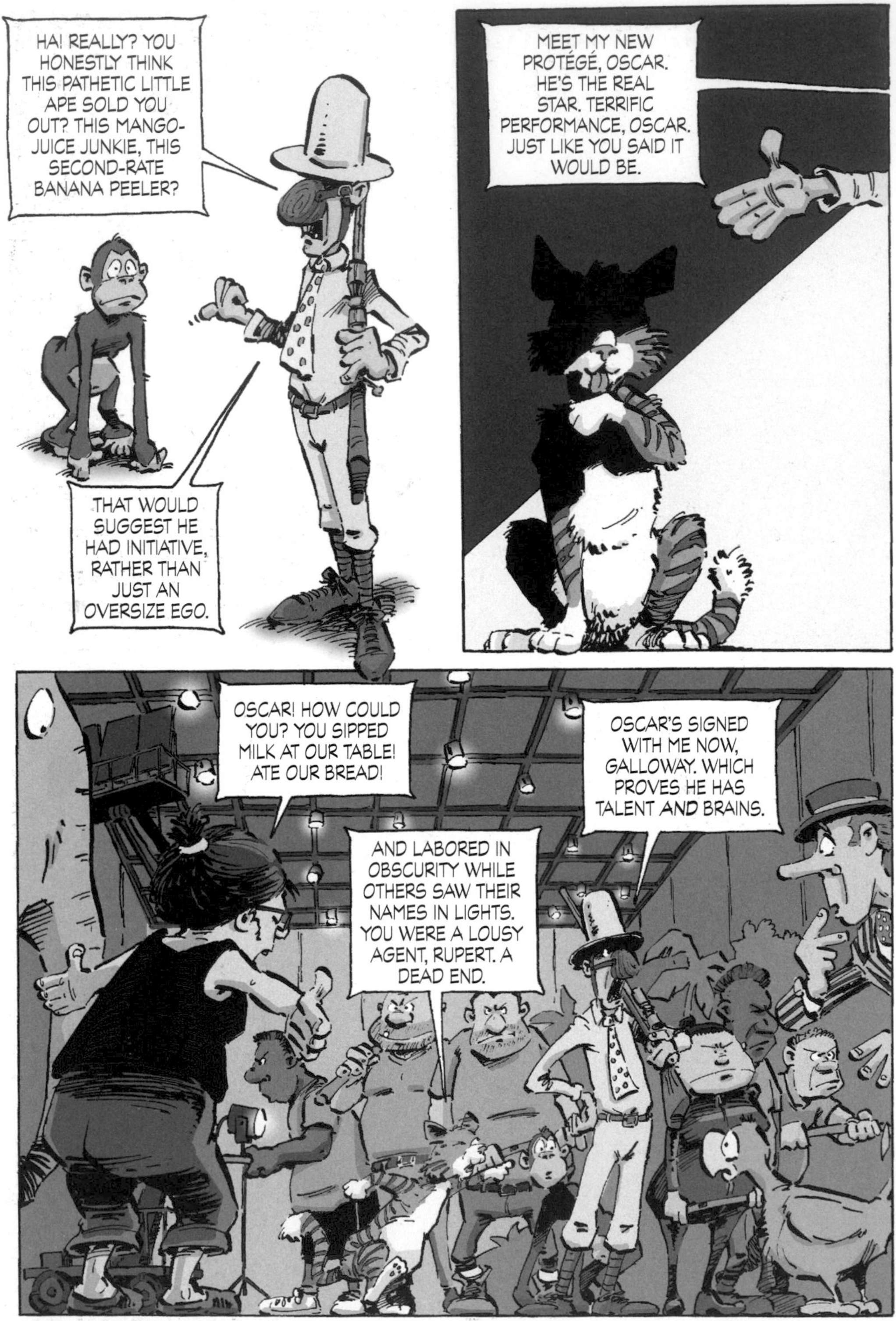
HA! REALLY? YOU HONESTLY THINK THIS PATHETIC LITTLE APE SOLD YOU OUT? THIS MANGO-JUICE JUNKIE, THIS SECOND-RATE BANANA PEELER?
THAT WOULD SUGGEST HE HAD INITIATIVE, RATHER THAN JUST AN OVERSIZE EGO.
MEET MY NEW PROTÉGÉ, OSCAR. HE'S THE REAL STAR. TERRIFIC PERFORMANCE, OSCAR. JUST LIKE YOU SAID IT WOULD BE.
OSCAR! HOW COULD YOU? YOU SIPPED MILK AT OUR TABLE! ATE OUR BREAD!
AND LABORED IN OBSCURITY WHILE OTHERS SAW THEIR NAMES IN LIGHTS. YOU WERE A LOUSY AGENT, RUPERT. A DEAD END.
OSCAR'S SIGNED WITH ME NOW, GALLOWAY. WHICH PROVES HE HAS TALENT AND BRAINS.

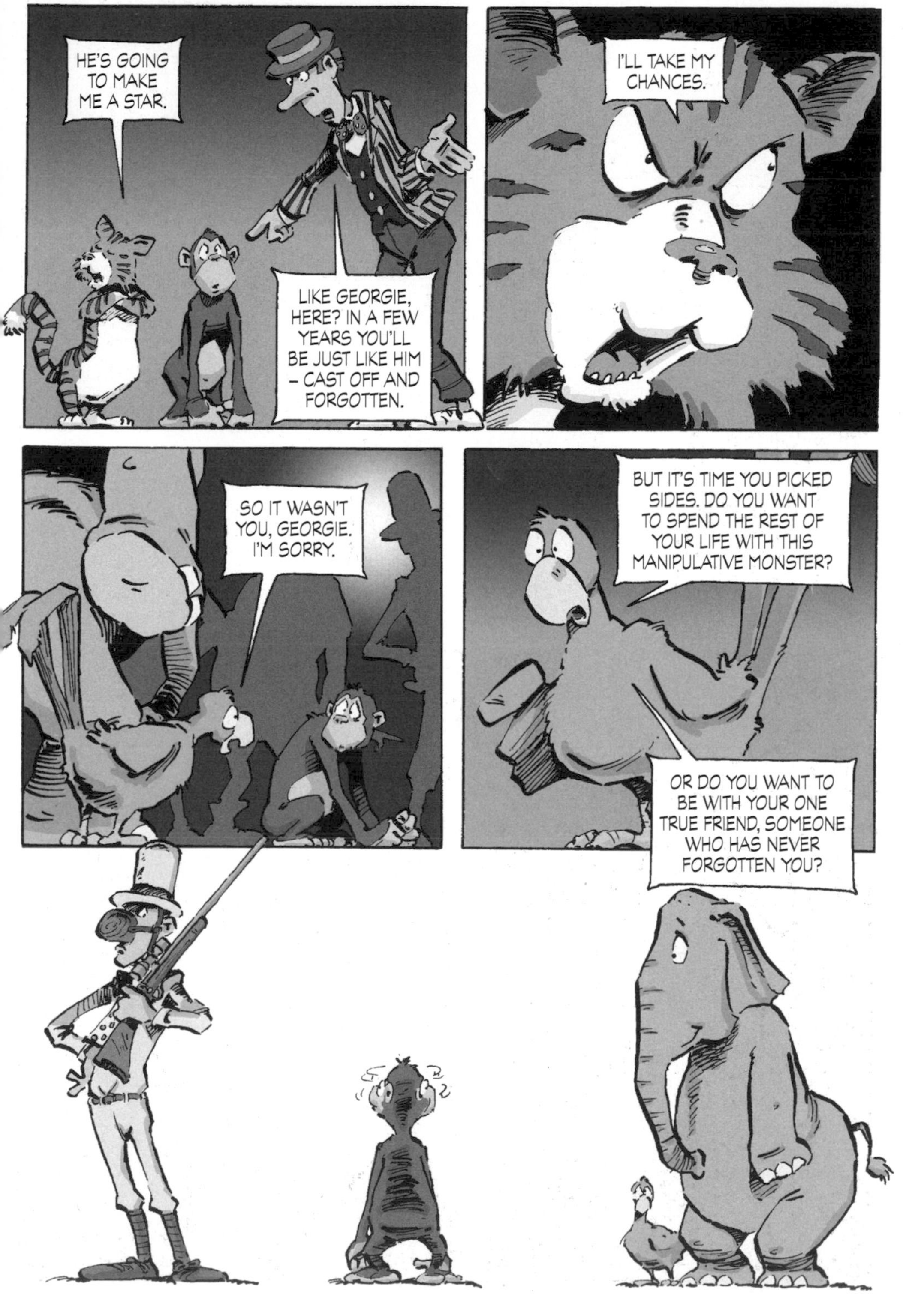
HE'S GOING TO MAKE ME A STAR.
LIKE GEORGIE, HERE? IN A FEW YEARS YOU'LL BE JUST LIKE HIM – CAST OFF AND FORGOTTEN.
I'LL TAKE MY CHANCES.
SO IT WASN'T YOU, GEORGIE. I'M SORRY.
BUT IT'S TIME YOU PICKED SIDES. DO YOU WANT TO SPEND THE REST OF YOUR LIFE WITH THIS MANIPULATIVE MONSTER?
OR DO YOU WANT TO BE WITH YOUR ONE TRUE FRIEND, SOMEONE WHO HAS NEVER FORGOTTEN YOU?

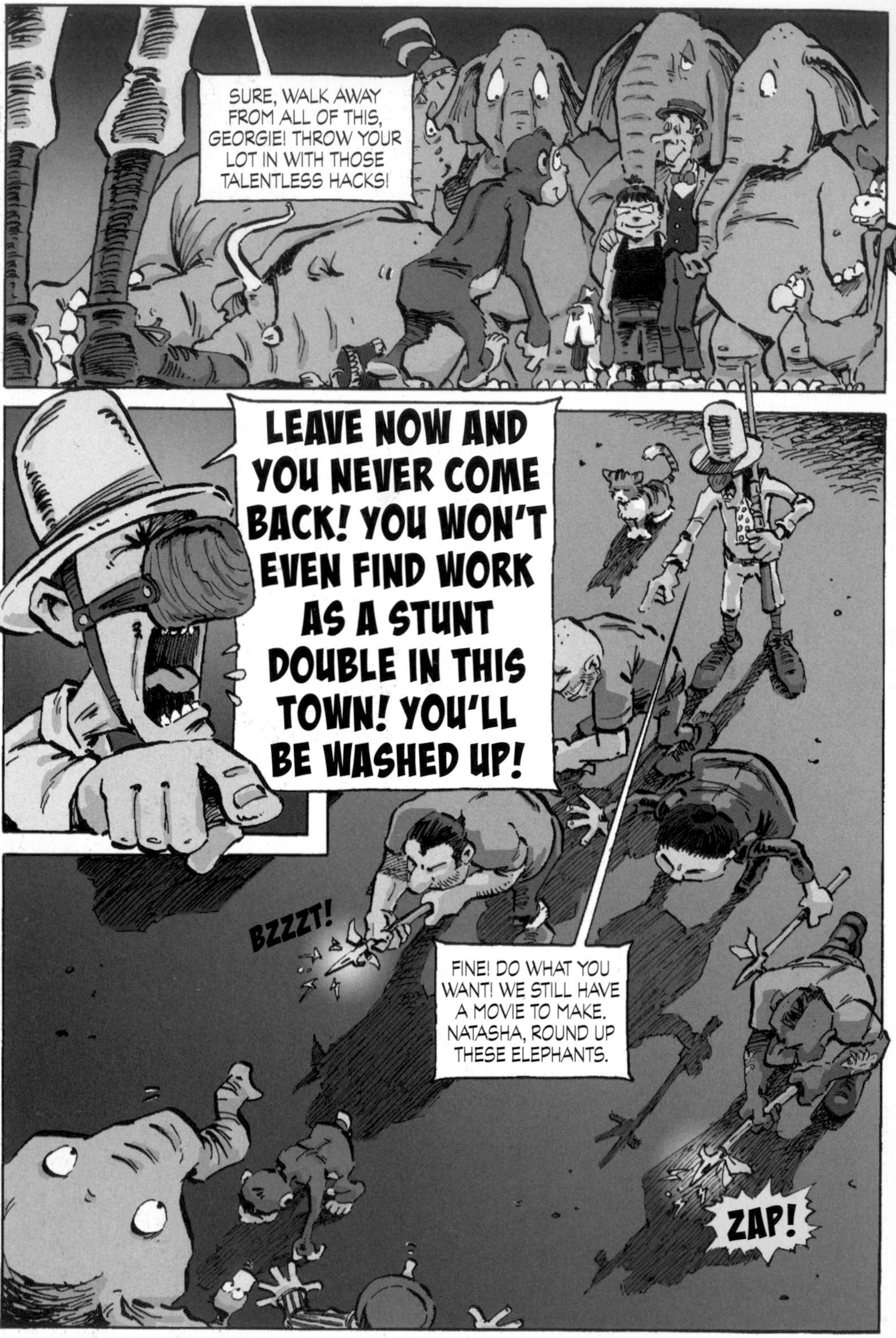
SURE, WALK AWAY FROM ALL OF THIS, GEORGIE! THROW YOUR LOT IN WITH THOSE TALENTLESS HACKS!
LEAVE NOW AND YOU NEVER COME BACK! YOU WON'T EVEN FIND WORK AS A STUNT DOUBLE IN THIS TOWN! YOU'LL BE WASHED UP!
BZZZT!
FINE! DO WHAT YOU WANT! WE STILL HAVE A MOVIE TO MAKE. NATASHA, ROUND UP THESE ELEPHANTS.
ZAP!

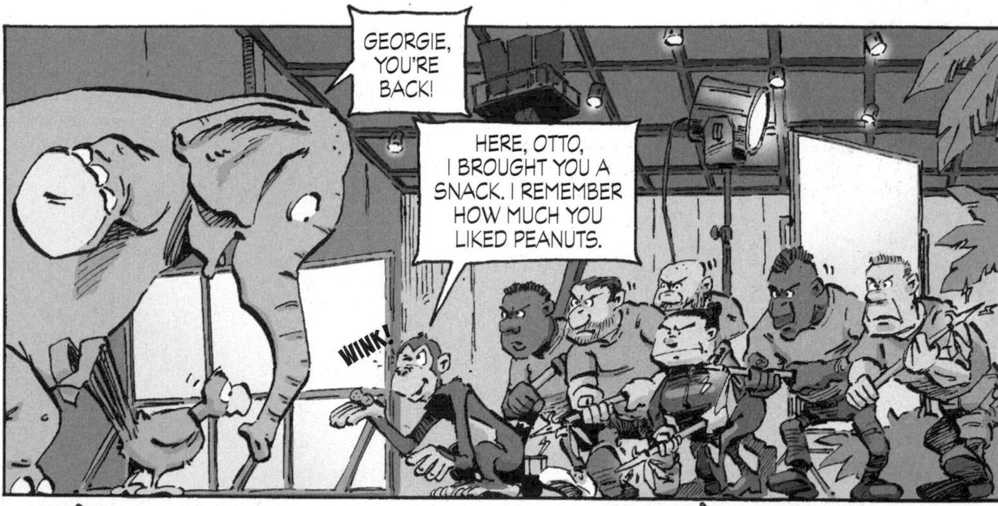
GEORGIE, YOU'RE BACK!
HERE, OTTO, I BROUGHT YOU A SNACK. I REMEMBER HOW MUCH YOU LIKED PEANUTS.
WINK!

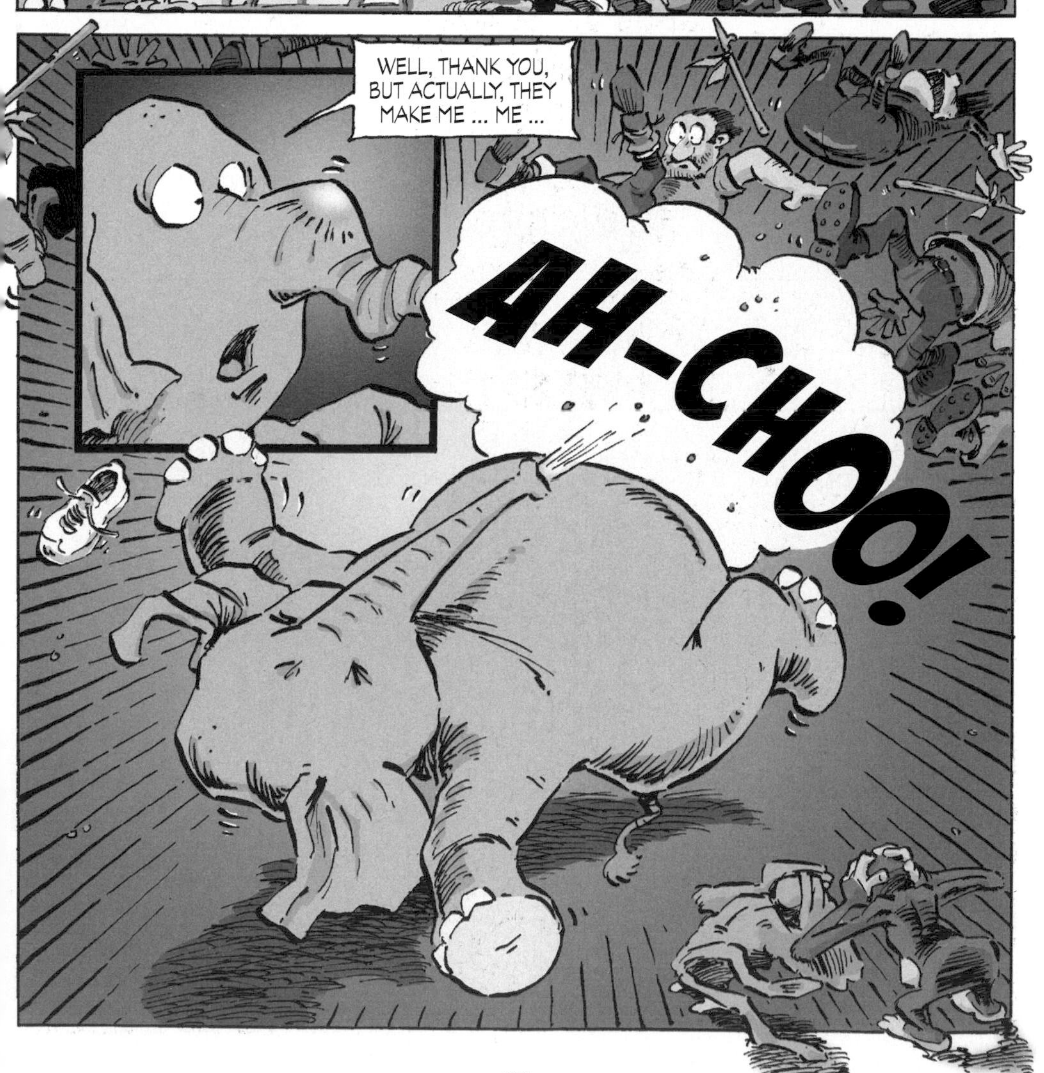
WELL, THANK YOU, BUT ACTUALLY, THEY MAKE ME ... ME ...
AH-CHOO!

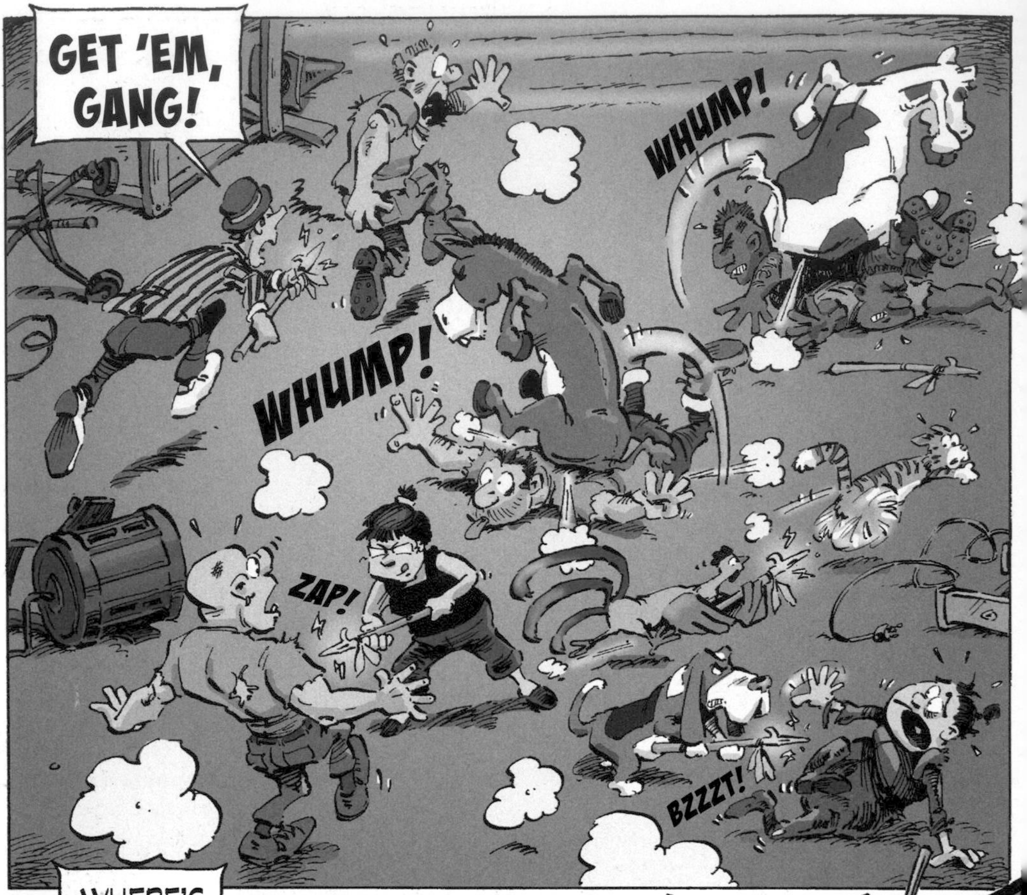
GET 'EM, GANG!
WHUMP!
WHUMP!
ZAP!
BZZZT!

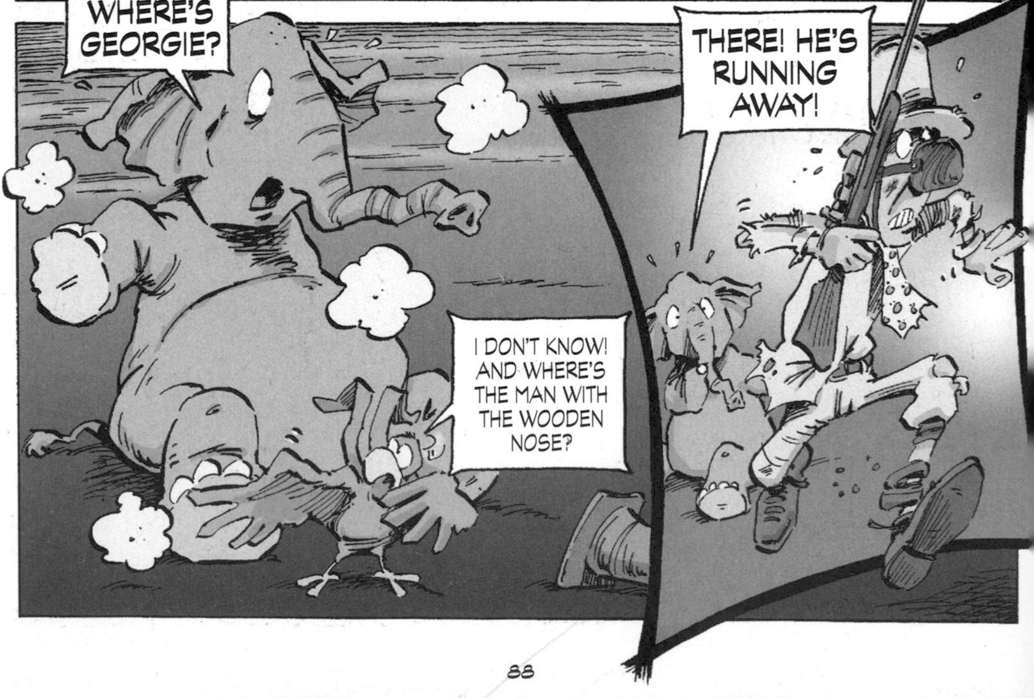
WHERE'S GEORGIE?
I DON'T KNOW! AND WHERE'S THE MAN WITH THE WOODEN NOSE?
THERE! HE'S RUNNING AWAY!

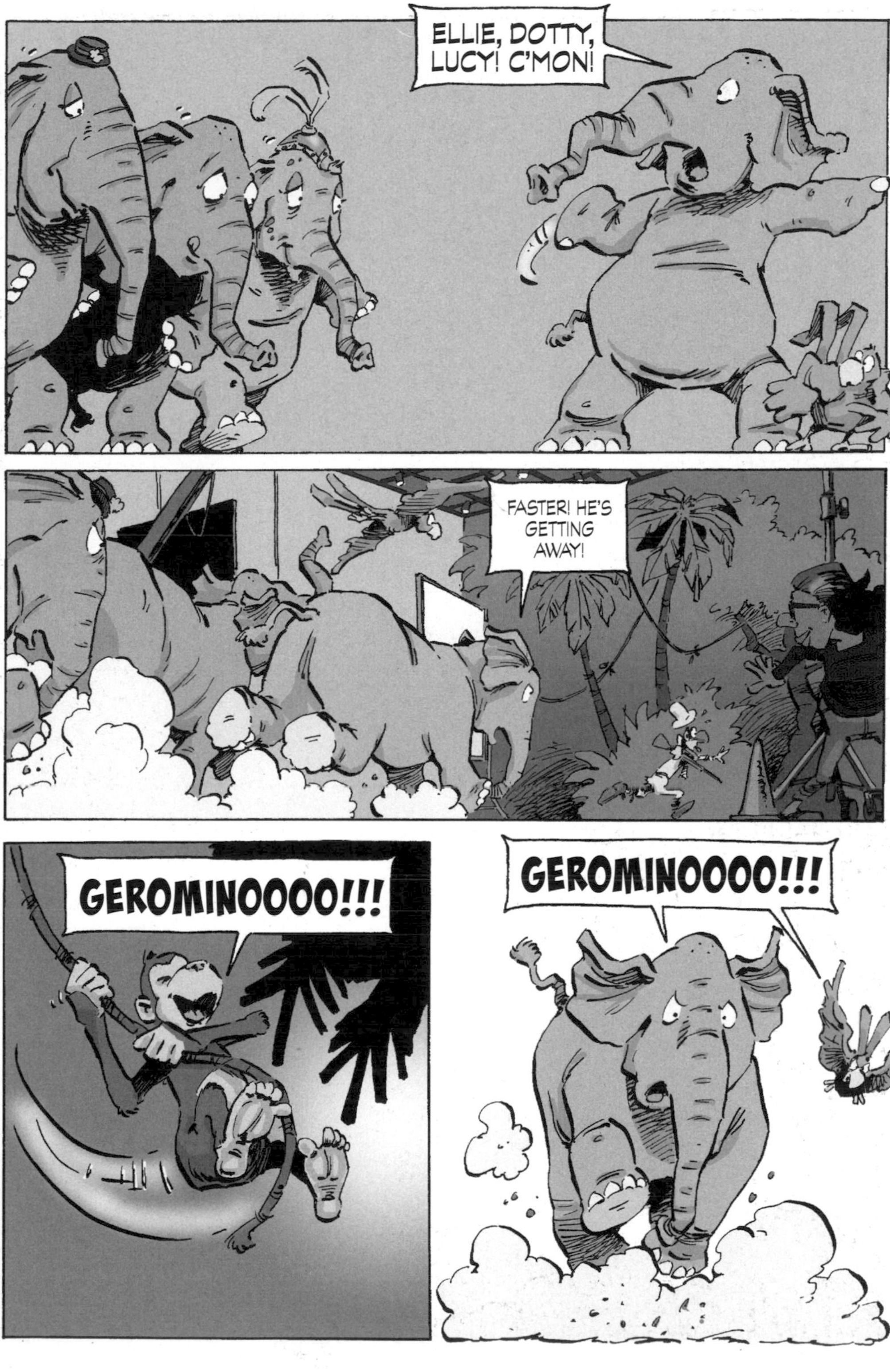
ELLIE, DOTTY, LUCY! C'MON!
FASTER! HE'S GETTING AWAY!
GEROMINOOOO!!!
GEROMINOOOO!!!

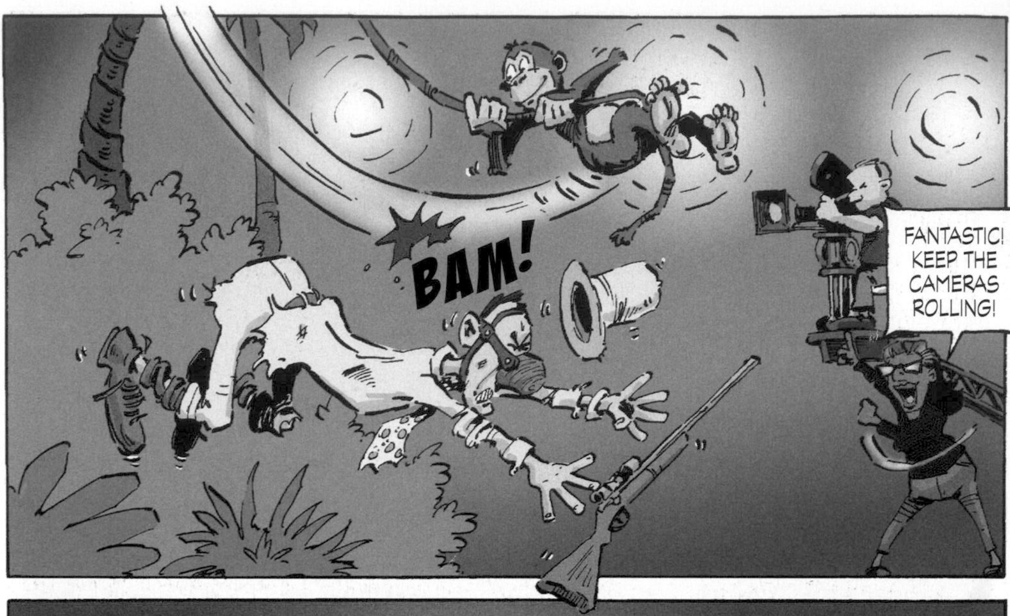
BAM!
FANTASTIC! KEEP THE CAMERAS ROLLING!

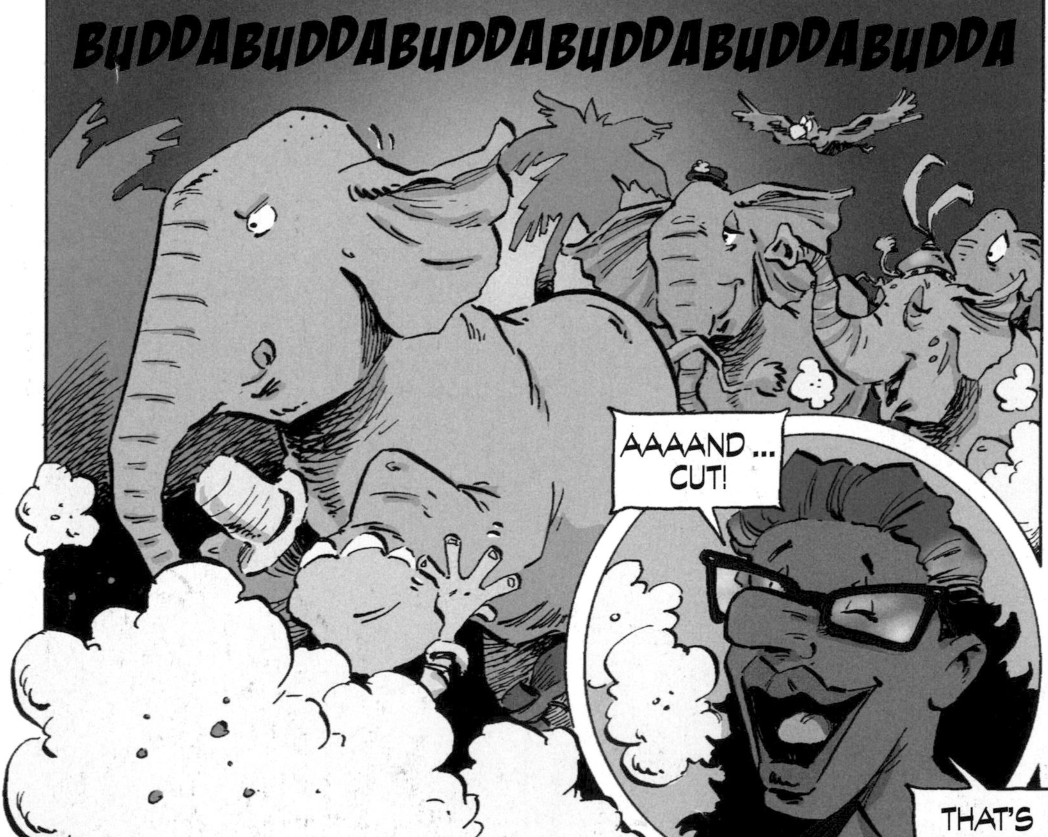
BUDDABUDDABUDDABUDDABUDDABUDDA
AAAAND ... CUT!
THAT'S A WRAP!

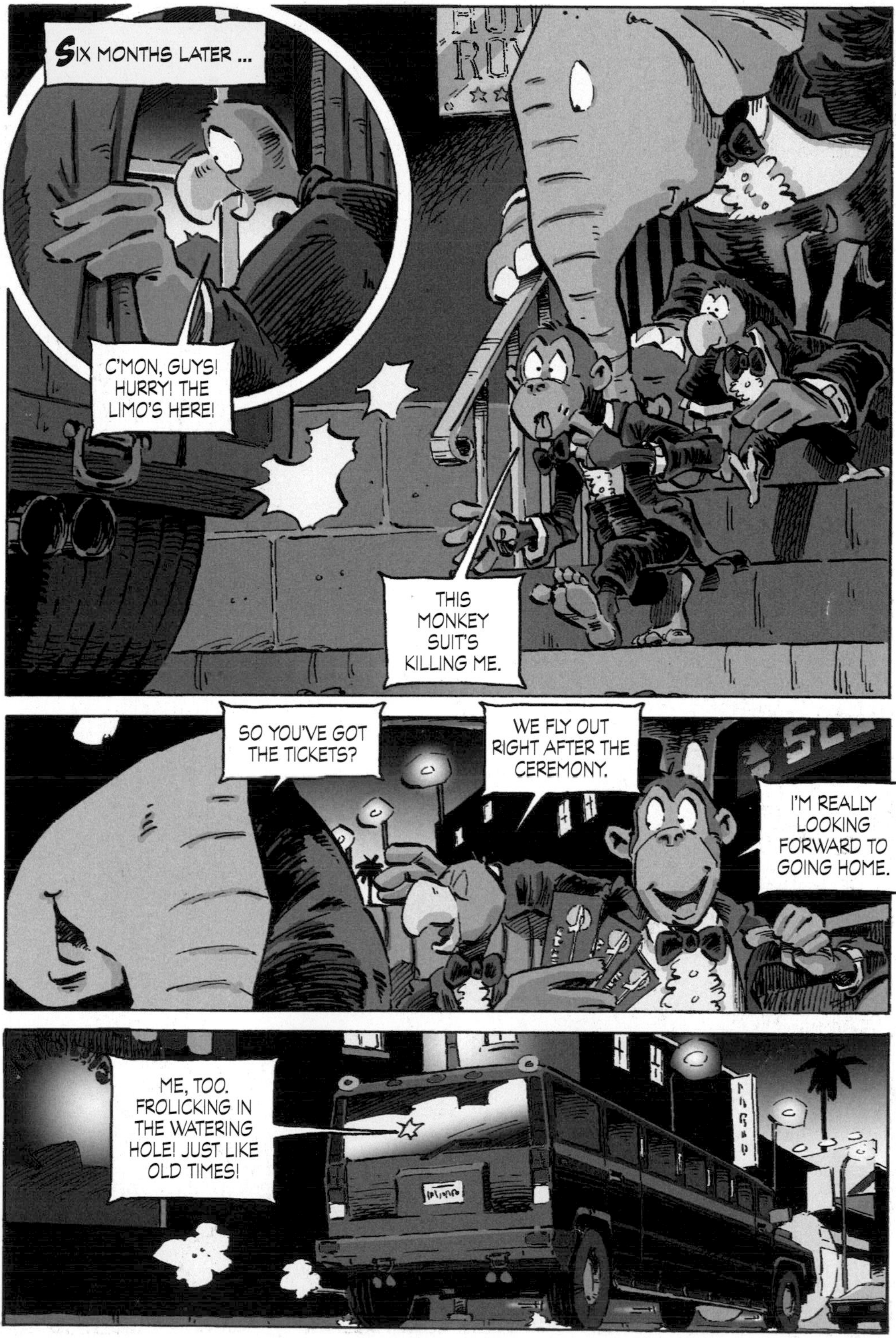
SIX MONTHS LATER ...
C'MON, GUYS! HURRY! THE LIMO'S HERE!
THIS MONKEY SUIT'S KILLING ME.
SO YOU'VE GOT THE TICKETS?
WE FLY OUT RIGHT AFTER THE CEREMONY.
I'M REALLY LOOKING FORWARD TO GOING HOME.
ME, TOO. FROLICKING IN THE WATERING HOLE! JUST LIKE OLD TIMES!

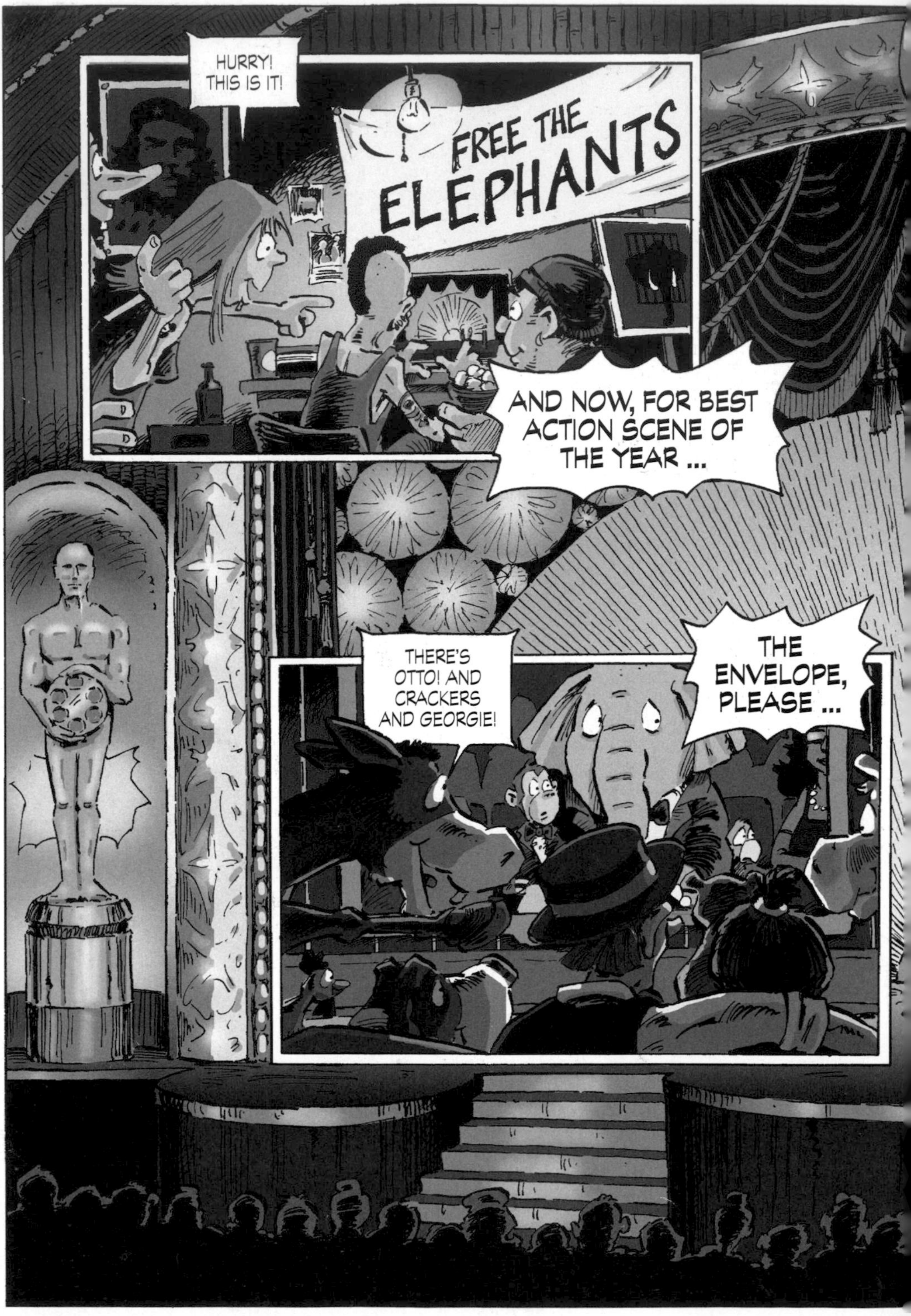
HURRY! THIS IS IT!
FREE THE ELEPHANTS
AND NOW, FOR BEST ACTION SCENE OF THE YEAR ...
THERE'S OTTO! AND CRACKERS AND GEORGIE!
THE ENVELOPE, PLEASE ...

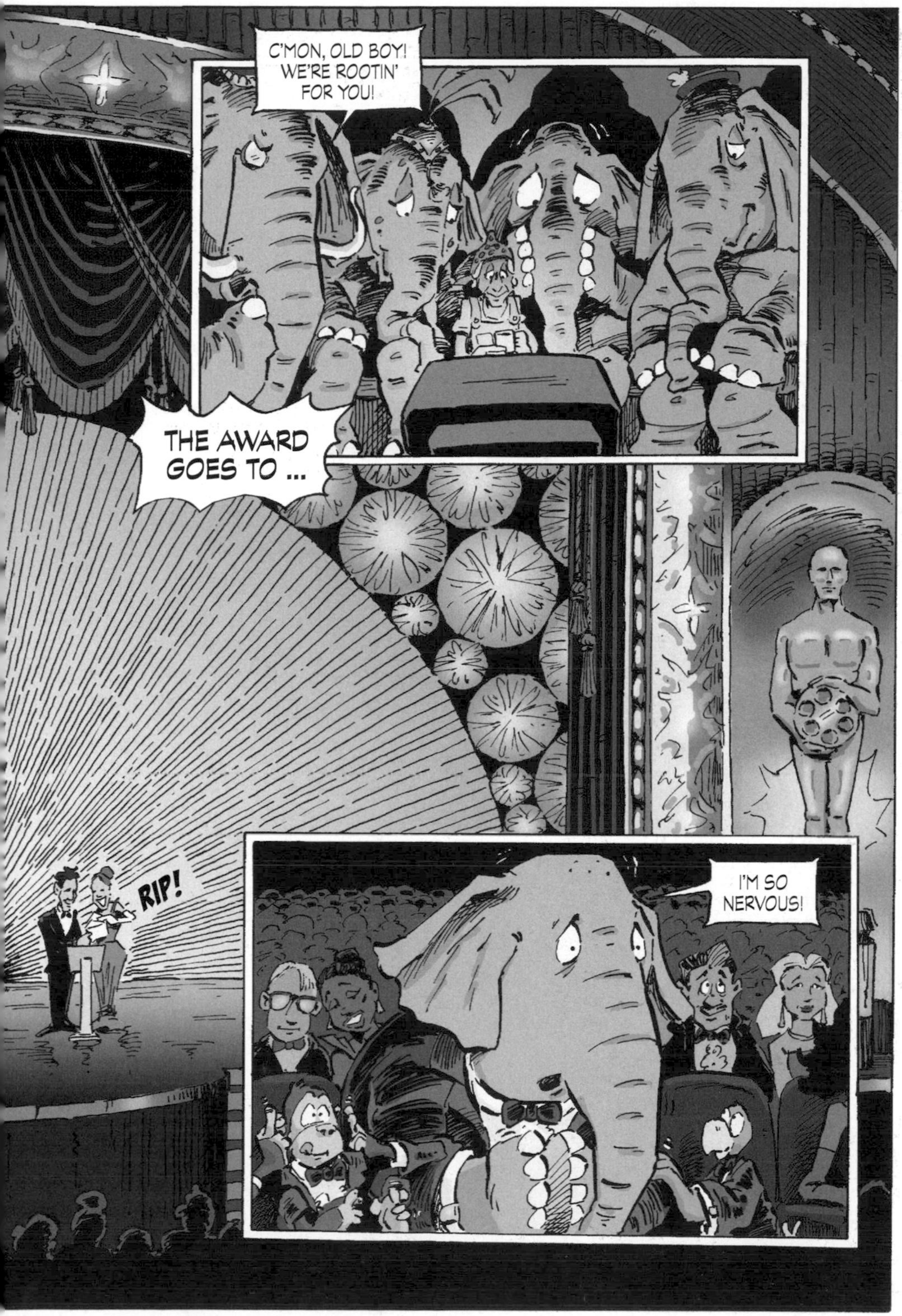
C'MON, OLD BOY! WE'RE ROOTIN' FOR YOU!
THE AWARD GOES TO ...
RIP!
I'M SO NERVOUS!

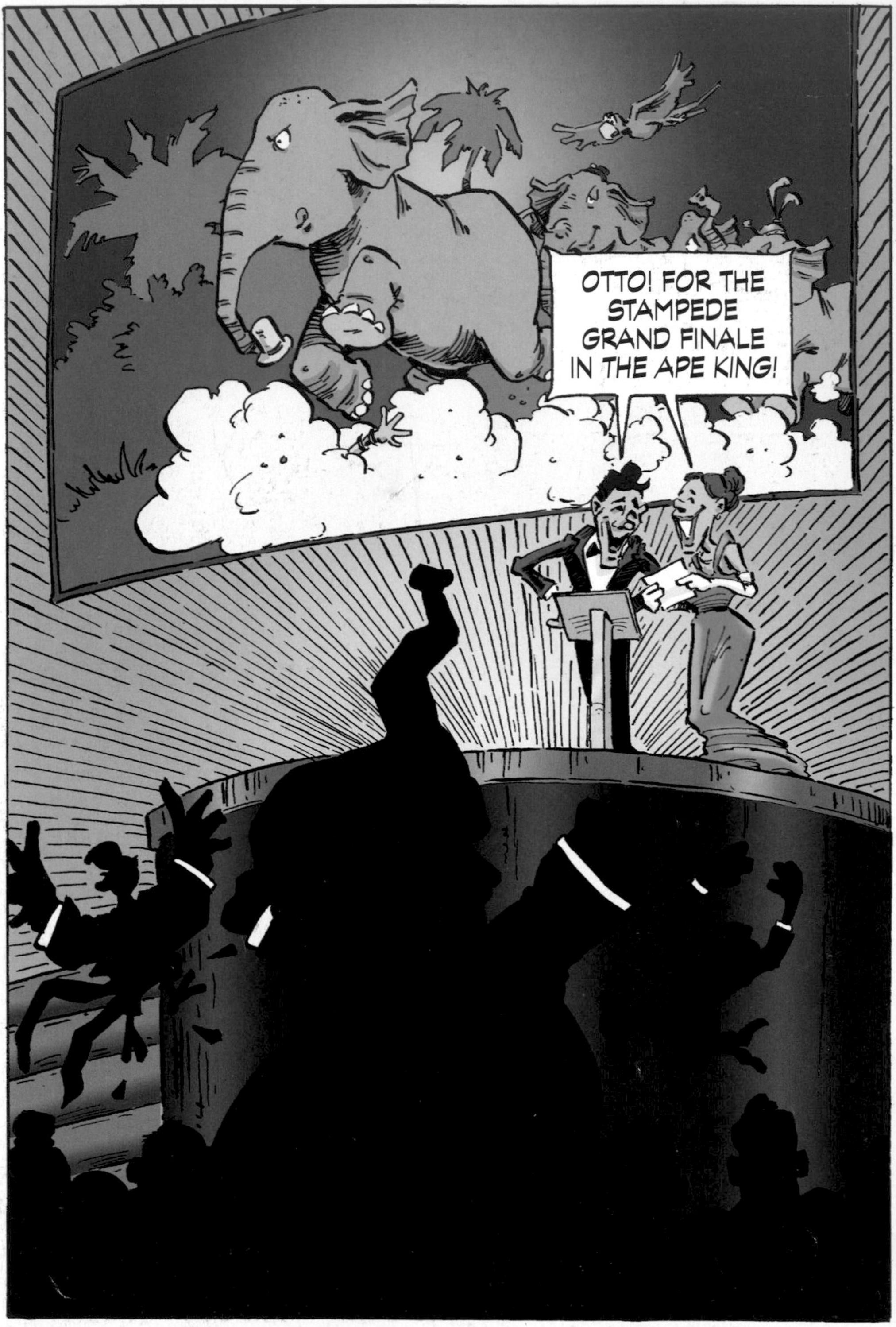
OTTO! FOR THE STAMPEDE GRAND FINALE IN THE APE KING!

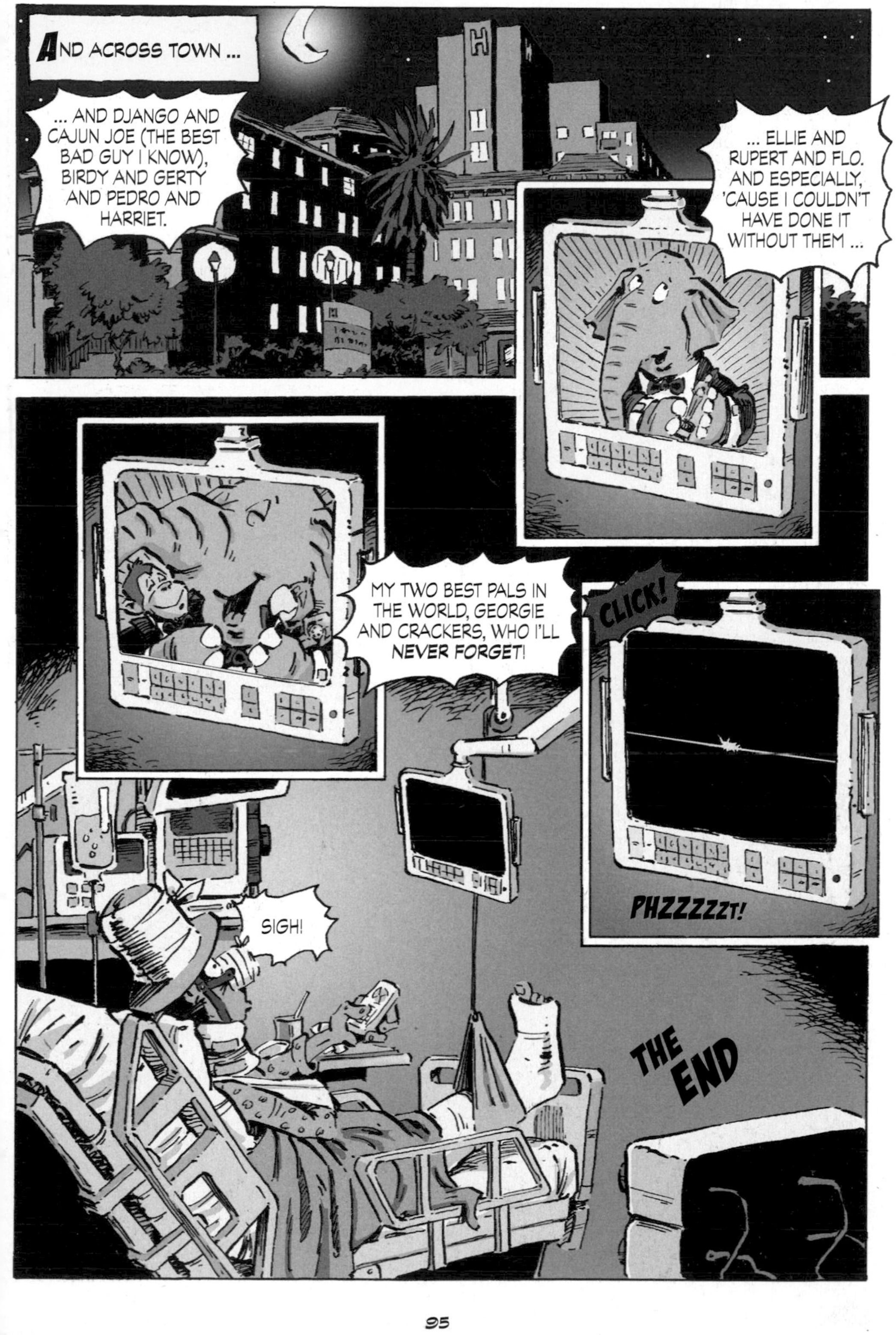
AND ACROSS TOWN ...
... AND DJANGO AND CAJUN JOE (THE BEST BAD GUY I KNOW), BIRDY AND GERTY AND PEDRO AND HARRIET.
... ELLIE AND RUPERT AND FLO. AND ESPECIALLY, 'CAUSE I COULDN'T HAVE DONE IT WITHOUT THEM ...
MY TWO BEST PALS IN THE WORLD, GEORGIE AND CRACKERS, WHO I'LL NEVER FORGET!
CLICK!
PHZZZZZT!
SIGH!
THE END

FOR ALBERTO UDERZO, WHO TAUGHT ME EVERYTHING I KNOW

Kids Can Press acknowledges the financial support of the Government of Ontario,
through the Ontario Media Development Corporation's Ontario Book Initiative;
the Ontario Arts Council; the Canada Council for the Arts; and the Government of
Canada, through the CBF, for our publishing activity.

Published in Canada by   Published in the U.S. by
Kids Can Press Ltd.   Kids Can Press Ltd.
25 Dockside Drive   2250 Military Road
Toronto, ON M5A 0B5   Tonawanda, NY 14150

www.kidscanpress.com

The artwork in this book was rendered in pen and ink line and colored in Photoshop.
The text is set in Graphite Std Narrow and BadaBoom Pro BB.

Edited by Stacey Roderick
Designed by Bill Slavin and Marie Bartholomew

The hardcover edition of this book is smyth sewn casebound.
The paperback edition of this book is limp sewn with a drawn-on cover.
Manufactured in Buji, Shenzhen, China, in 8/2014 by WKT Company

CM 15 0 9 8 7 6 5 4 3 2 1
CM PA 15 0 9 8 7 6 5 4 3 2 1

Library and Archives Canada Cataloguing in Publication

Slavin, Bill, author, illustrator
      Big star Otto / written by Bill Slavin with Esperança Melo;
art by Bill Slavin.

(Elephants never forget ; 3)
ISBN 978-1-894786-96-6 (bound)   ISBN 978-1-894786-97-3 (pbk.)

      1. Graphic novels I. Melo, Esperança, author II. Title.
III. Series: Slavin, Bill. Elephants never forget ; 3.

PN6733.S55B527 2014   j741.5'971   C2014-903327-3

Kids Can Press is a *corus*™ Entertainment company